Someone made sure C
dead ending. Now an
out who pushed the Sw

MW01709542

Boston heiress Cecilia Swann had everything—looks, brains, and money galore. Her love of life was legendary, as was her rampant fear of heights. Leaping off a building was the last thing she would ever do. So when she dies that way, Eja Kane, her best friend since childhood, vows to prove it was murder. Eja isn't gorgeous, blue-blooded, or glamorous; she's a wisecracking failed novelist who's battling a few extra pounds and a set of lowered expectations about life in general and men in particular. But when it comes to loyalty and courage she's as tough as a junkyard dog and twice as likely to bite.

Can she resist taking a chunk out of her arrogant partner during the search for CeCe's killer? CeCe's handsome fraternal twin, Deming Swann, has taunted Eja since childhood. His film star looks and sense of entitlement drive her crazy. Now, however, the rules between them change as they put aside their differences in order to avenge CeCe. Before long, Eja and Deming must battle their own passions as they unravel the trail of a ruthless killer.

"Dive in! What starts out as a murder investigation quickly becomes a lush and lavish dance for the hero and heroine of Swann Dive. Arlene Kay is a versatile author and she has another winner."
—Lane Stone, Author, the TIARA INVESTIGATIONS MYSTERIES

"Join mystery writer Eja Kane as she becomes embroiled in a real-life mystery when her best friend is murdered. This book is highly entertaining, filled with wit, charm, and romance. I can't wait for the next book in the series!"
—Jaye Roycraft, Author, RAINSCAPE

"Swann Dive is a sexy and suspenseful ride through Boston that kept me up well past my bedtime! Arlene Kay had me guessing until the end."
—Kate George, Author, the BREE MACGOWAN MYSTERY SERIES

The Boston Uncommons Mysteries

Swann Dive

Mantrap

Gilt Trip

Swann Dive

Book 1: The Boston Uncommons Mystery Series

by

Arlene Kay

ImaJinn Books

IMAJINN

ImaJinn Books
PO BOX 300921
Memphis, TN 38130
Print ISBN: 978-1-61194-419-8

ImaJinn Books is an Imprint of BelleBooks, Inc.

Printed and bound in the United States of America.

ImaJinn Books was founded by Linda Kichline.

We at ImaJinn Books enjoy hearing from readers. Visit our websites
ImaJinnBooks.com
BelleBooks.com
BellBridgeBooks.com

10 9 8 7 6 5 4 3 2 1

Cover design: Debra Dixon
Interior design: Hank Smith
Photo/Art credits:
Man (manipulated) © George Mayer | Dreamstime.com

:Ldsz:01:

One

I TRY TO AVOID Sunday brunch. For a recovering chowhound like me it's a straight shot into Dante's third circle with all the other gluttons. On this particular morning, I was lured to Mistral, one of Boston's swankiest spots, to celebrate another career triumph by Cecilia Swann, my best friend since pre-school. Resistance was futile, as it had been since kindergarten, when she'd commandeered my crayons. I vowed to make the most of a free meal and try to be a good sport.

My lackluster literary career had been a conscious choice, not the anonymity of course, just the dream. An MFA from Brown would never enrich me until I wrote the elusive bestseller. That dream was still a work in progress.

As I walked through the restaurant's elegant doors, I mouthed my mantra. Patience, Eja Kane. Your turn will come.

I was ten minutes early—I'm always early. It's a character flaw that has dogged me all my life. Sometimes, particularly when dealing with my best friend, it comes in handy. I claimed our table and browsed the menu. CeCe was always fashionably late. That girl loved to make an entrance, and, with her looks, she drew the eyes of every man in her path. I lacked the elegance gene that was hardwired into her DNA, but today, garbed in crimson with my exuberant curls tamed by gel, I felt like a contender.

Everything on the menu looked phenomenal, including the prices. I blanched at twenty-dollar omelets, but CeCe could easily afford them. Besides being a rising legal star, she was a bona fide heiress, the much-beloved daughter of mega-rich Bolin Swann. That simplified things for me. As her faithful retainer and head cheerleader, I accepted occasional treats without a scintilla of guilt.

While weighing the merits and calorie count of salmon egg-white frittata versus huevos rancheros, I pondered the many edicts of the nanny state. Why compel restaurants to torture diners with information they already knew or suspected? Calorie counts are the very antithesis of lavish Sunday brunches, a conspiracy by sadistic ectomorphs to ruin things for the rest of us.

By eleven twenty, I got antsy. The waiter was hovering, and CeCe Swann was nowhere to be seen. Mistral is a popular place, with a line of patrons that stretches out the door. I tried to brazen it out but caved after ten minutes. An egg-white dish with a tempting breadbasket calmed my nerves as I plotted revenge against my faithless friend. I'd taken a lot of guff from CeCe over the years, but this really fried the frittata. She'd actually stood me up after dragooning me into coming! My fingers ached from the increasingly terse text messages I sent. *She'd better have a good excuse. Scratch that. She'd better have a damn good excuse that didn't involve some man.*

At noon, I slipped the waiter my one viable credit card and prepared to leave. When my phone rang, I reached for it without much enthusiasm. Caller ID confirmed my suspicions: CeCe Swann on the line. I didn't answer right away. Who needs a battle royal after ingesting a scandalous number of carbs? I decided to let her stew until I'd exited the restaurant and was standing on Columbus Avenue. Even she acknowledged that you never abandon your friend for a cretinous male unfit to shine your stilettos. Whatever happened to female solidarity?

I answered on the eighth ring. A woman whose stern, headmistressy voice I didn't recognize greeted me.

"Who's this?" I asked. "Where's Cecilia Swann?"

"Lieutenant Euphemia Bates, Boston Police. To whom am I speaking?"

If my throat hadn't closed, I would have applauded her good grammar. So few people observe proper syntax these days. A sudden chill unrelated to the weather curled my toes. Something was very wrong.

"I'm . . . I'm Eja Kane. CeCe's friend. Where is she? Please tell me."

She grunted. "Oh. You're the one who left all these texts."

"You have her phone. Why? Is she okay?"

Maybe someone robbed her, stole her phone. That would explain everything. Her business and professional life was encapsulated in that smartphone. Some of Boston's grand poohbahs were available for immediate speed dial at the stab of her manicured finger. CeCe must have freaked out, demanded special treatment, and pissed off the cops.

That was just like her. She'd been raised to expect that.

"Let me speak with Ms. Swann, Lieutenant. I'm sure we can resolve things."

Euphemia Bates cleared her throat. "I can't do that, Ms. Kane. Do you know where your friend is right now?"

I was weary of cop games and irritated with CeCe. "She's somewhere in transit. My text messages should tell you that."

Euphemia Bates seemed impervious to snubs and slights. Her voice never wavered as she plowed right through our conversation.

"Maybe you can help us. We haven't found any other identification except this phone."

I relaxed. Now at least I could breathe. Just as I suspected, CeCe's phone had been lost or stolen, and somehow the cops got hold of it. Puzzling, but not that unusual when the Swann family was involved. They carried serious weight in the Hub.

Lieutenant Bates pressed her advantage. "I'll send a car over for you. You're at Mistral, right?"

"But I . . ."

She spit out a command before my muddled synapses could fire. "Stay there."

I SPENT THE NEXT ten minutes fruitlessly dialing every contact I could think of. CeCe's home number didn't answer. The law firm of Sevier, Miles and Swann referred all inquiries to their answering service. Calls to her parents and famously arrogant twin brother Deming went straight to voicemail. Since her former fiancé Jem Russell and I were sworn enemies, I didn't have his number. For the first time ever I wished that I did. Things were desperate enough to warrant a call, even though I loathed the duplicitous creature. I mouthed a silent prayer to Sir Thomas More, patron saint of Boston lawyers. CeCe and I both admired him for his sense of humor and vast intellect. He'd understand if one of his tribe had gone temporarily AWOL over an unworthy man.

"Ms. Kane? Ms. Eja Kane?" The patrolman stood before me, hands lightly touching his gun-belt. He was a tall, gangly redhead, probably a rookie. His nameplate read Jennings.

"Lieutenant Bates sent me, ma'am." He gestured toward the cruiser hugging the curb. "This way, please."

My gait was stiff and awkward as I climbed into the back seat.

Something, some harbinger of doom, had incapacitated me. Passersby gawked, wondering no doubt, what sordid crime I was guilty of. When Jennings flipped on the siren, heads turned, and several pedestrians craned their neck to peer in at me.

The final insult. CeCe owed me big-time for this one.

"What's this all about, Officer? Where's my friend?"

His smooth countenance gave new meaning to the term *poker face*.

"I'll let the lieutenant fill you in. We're almost there." With that, he took a sharp left, pulling into a side street in the financial district abutting a thirty-story building that I'd never noticed before. The whole area was a sterile maze of glass and steel trying way too hard to be Manhattan. It was largely a mystery to me.

Most Sundays these streets would be deserted. Not today. Police cars, news vans, and an ambulance ringed the perimeter of the high-rise. The front entrance was sealed off by yards of yellow police scene tape.

That eerie feeling swept through me again. To my knowledge, CeCe had no reason to be here, especially on a beautiful autumn Sunday when we'd scheduled brunch. A cold sweat trickled down my neck, and for a moment I felt light-headed. Jennings swung open my door and offered his arm.

"You okay, ma'am? You're kind of pale."

In times of stress, good manners fly out the window. I forgot that Jennings was a rookie—early twenties by the look of him—trying hard to be tough.

"I most certainly am not okay, Officer, and until I find my friend, I won't be."

He gaped at me, as though I were an alien. A sprinkling of ginger-colored freckles surfaced on the bridge of his nose, like a grown up Opie from the land of Mayberry. His befuddled look suggested that he'd skipped the chapter on female rage in the police manual.

Before things deteriorated, the cavalry arrived. A steely-eyed African-American woman edging comfortably into middle age drew close and extended her hand, a police badge swinging from the lanyard around her neck.

"I'll take it from here, Jennings. I'm Euphemia Bates, Ms. Kane. Thank you for coming. Please follow me."

Two

EUPHEMIA BATES was a study in contrasts. Despite her brusque manner, she allowed a spark of compassion to strike her large brown eyes. That frightened me. Anger, arrogance, or indifference were preferable because that meant CeCe was okay. A cop's compassion didn't augur well for my friend's welfare.

She herded me through the lobby toward an elegantly appointed conference room. Euphemia. That name was solid and strong, something my grandma's peers might have used. I vaguely recalled that St. Euphemia was an early Christian martyr who died horrifically. That didn't mean much. Death was no picnic for anyone with martyr attached to her name.

"Let's sit down in here and talk, shall we?" Lieutenant Bates wedged her chair into a corner and leaned back against the wall. She was tall, somewhere north of six feet and slender enough to be a model. Her sculpted features, now molded into a cop's mask, reminded me of an Etruscan princess. I was woolgathering, trying to dull my senses by trivial observations. It didn't work.

"Any problem if I record our conversation?" She made it into a throwaway line, as if it were the most natural thing in the world to do.

I was tired, weary of playing the pawn in this elaborate chess game. "I won't say another word until you tell me about my friend. What's happened to Cecilia Swann? Where is she?"

Euphemia pressed her lips into a thin, firm line. "I'm sorry, Ms. Kane. Your friend is dead. We weren't sure of her identity until quite recently." She sighed. "You see, her purse is missing. We had only her phone, and it's in a sad state."

Nothing prepares you for death, no matter how they soften the blow. My stomach clenched, but I didn't faint. Numbness spread through me instead, short-circuiting my pain receptors. I was hollow, the hollow woman. All of a sudden I chuckled. My chuckles turned to laughter, great braying peals of laughter. CeCe loved T.S. Eliot, especially "The Hollow Men." Had her world ended with a whimper or a bang?

"Ms. Kane, do you hear me?" Lieutenant Bates nodded to a corpulent man who had slipped into the room. "Get her some coffee. Now."

She slithered around the table as gracefully as a garden snake and grasped my shoulder. I fully expected her to slap my face the way they do in the movies.

"Calm down. I know this is a shock, but I need your help."

I raised my head and caught her eye. "What happened? Please tell me."

She clenched her jaw and spit out the words. "We think—this is very preliminary, remember—the evidence suggests that Ms. Swann committed suicide."

"No. Absolutely not. CeCe was the last person to harm herself. She loved life, believe you me." I trotted out every cliché in the book. Not very imaginative for a writer. I could see that Euphemia Bates had gone into neutral. She'd probably heard those words a hundred times before from angst-ridden survivors.

I clutched the edge of the table in a death grip. "She was at the zenith of her career, a federal judgeship. That's why we were celebrating at Mistral." I nodded as if that were the deal-breaker. *As if any sane woman would kill herself before brunch.* I summoned every ounce of courage in my possession and pressed forward. This was truth-telling time, and I had to know.

"Was it pills? She never took much medication. Considered it a sign of weakness."

A deep sigh from Mia. I'd decided to call her that. Euphemia was just too formal and awkward for women discussing death. *Mia* was a friendlier, more approachable name. She retrieved a printout from her briefcase and started reading.

"At 8:45 a.m. Ms. Swann walked into the lobby of this building and boarded the elevator. Security tapes confirm that as well as the testimony of another resident who'd just finished walking her dog."

I leaned forward, trying to make sense of it. "Why this building? She didn't live here. Was she meeting a client or something?"

Another neutral look from Mia. "We don't know. We may never know. I understand that Ms. Swann lived approximately a mile away in Back Bay."

"Beacon Hill, actually. Right on Beacon Street."

I adored CeCe's place. Three bedrooms, three baths overlooking the Common and the State House. It was the ultimate insider's pad in a venerable building where vacancies seldom occurred. Her parents presented it to her when CeCe graduated from law school.

"She lived alone?"

"Mostly. Unless you count Cato."

Mia raised exquisitely shaped brows. "Cato?"

"Her odious Springer Spaniel. Believe me, CeCe would never abandon him."

Cato was a rescue, an ill-tempered cur that no sane person would ever take.

"Okay. Let's get through this, Ms. Kane. I know it's tough." More fumbling through a sheaf of papers. "Ms. Swann asked how to access the roof garden. It's on the thirty-second floor." She put special emphasis on the words *roof garden.* "Two hours later, a resident on the twelfth floor found your friend's body in an interior courtyard. It broke her fall."

"No. That's not possible!" I rose slowly, steadying myself again. "CeCe would never jump. She was terrified of heights. Saw a shrink about it even. That's why she lived on the second floor."

"I'm sorry, Eja." She patted my arm, as if to quell the tremors coursing through my body.

I felt a sudden rush of adrenaline. Fight-or-flight impulse they call it. I chose to run, not fight. This was all nonsense. Some stranger had appropriated CeCe's cell phone. It had to be. I grabbed my purse and surged toward the door in time to collide with Deming Swann.

HE'D NEVER APPROVED of me. Even in grade school Deming cast malevolent glances my way whenever we met. That didn't bother me since I'd always considered my best friend's brother a Grade A prick. Maybe it was his smugness and air of casual superiority. He didn't even have a nickname. How weird is that? CeCe used his middle name, calling him Brother Bjorn just to taunt him. I called him names that were unprintable.

Deming Swann looked like a model crossed with a film star. Blonde Swedish mama and hot Eurasian dad—do the math. He'd spent his whole life hearing that from gaping, drooling females, and it showed. Even I appreciated his thick black hair and sculpted features, but male beauty aside, what little personality he had was unpleasant. He epitomized the strong silent type: a gym rat who was brusque to the point of rudeness. For CeCe's sake we minimized hostilities and avoided each other, retreating behind a thin wall of civility. She'd always teased me about it, quoting a mangled version of Shakespeare. Believe me, if this lady protested too much, attraction had nothing to do with it. I'd spent the better part of thirty years loathing her brother.

Things were different today. I flung myself into his arms and sobbed all over his Kiton suit. To his credit, Deming did the manly thing by producing a beautifully starched handkerchief and gently dabbing my tears.

"It's not true," I babbled. "You know how she was, Deming. She wouldn't even climb a stepladder. It must be a mistake."

He gazed down at me, grasping my arms. "It's true, Eja. I just saw her body." His voice broke. "My sister's body. Go home and rest. I'll handle everything."

It was tempting. So easy to bury my head in the covers and will away this nightmare. I raised my eyes to his and stopped in my tracks. Those eyes. He had her hazel eyes. Of course he did. They were siblings, fraternal twins, after all. Deming Bjorn Swann was the evil dark twin to her blond beauty. Seventy-four inches of pure menace. CeCe and Deming looked and acted nothing alike, except for those eyes. That was enough for me.

I clung to him as he beckoned to Mia Bates. "Lieutenant, my parents asked me to act on behalf of our family. I'd like to see the security tapes and everything else connected with Cecilia's death. Tomorrow, if possible."

Euphemia Bates wasn't happy, but she bowed to higher powers: money and influence. That currency bought the same special treatment in Boston that it did in the rest of the world. She gave Deming a curt nod and checked her BlackBerry. "Ten a.m.?"

"Thank you." He turned, steering me toward the door. "Come on. I'll drive you home."

I waited to speak until we'd cleared the lobby. "Where are you going, Deming? You're up to something. I know that look."

He'd always been arrogant. Deming Swann dusted off his impossibly fine suit coat and dismissed me. "Go home, Eja. This is a family matter."

My stubborn streak transcended my grief. He had eight inches and fifty pounds on me, but I had determination. I planted myself in his path, refusing to budge. "You're right. I'm part of her family whether you like it or not. Deal with it, Deming."

He winced, and for once, I felt a twinge of compassion. He'd lost his sister after all. We should be consoling each other, not picking scabs.

Deming eyed the doorman, who immediately sent a parking attendant scurrying for his Porsche. Employees anticipate the needs of people like the Swanns without ever hearing a word. They had something special, a look or gesture that communicated authority and privilege. CeCe wore it like a crown. That part of Swann magic had always eluded me, but it was alive and well in her brother.

He opened the car door and spooned me into the soft leather seat. Deming was rife with contradictions, gentle or profoundly curt as the mood struck him.

"I'm going with you," I repeated, snapping my seat belt in place. "Don't even think of stopping me. I know where you're headed. If you dump me, I'll tell Lieutenant Bates you destroyed evidence."

Deming wrenched the steering wheel to the right and edged into traffic. Emergency vehicles ringed the perimeter like metal sentries. All except one. The coroner's van had vanished, along with the earthly remains of my friend.

"You're hysterical," he growled. "I'm going directly home after I drop you off."

His face was impassive, harder to crack than Boolean logic.

"No, you're not." I was calm now, almost tranquil. "You're going to search CeCe's flat. Wouldn't want the cops to find anything embarrassing there, huh? I know all your moves. Let me help."

He stomped on the brake with such force that I strained against my shoulder harness. His frown joined the wrath of Ares with the pride of Narcissus. CeCe always joked that her goal in life was to separate Deming from his mirror.

"You know nothing," he hissed. "Stay out of this."

Horns blared as the Porsche remained splayed across the boulevard, blocking traffic. Deming mumbled several expletives before changing course. "Okay. Have it your way. We'll both go there, though what you're up to mystifies me."

I folded my hands in my lap like a perfect lady. "CeCe didn't commit suicide. We both know that. She was buoyant, on top of the world. She'd always wanted to be a judge, even in grade school. Remember that little gavel she used to clobber you with?"

Deming held out his right arm, traffic-cop style. "Hold on. What's this judge stuff?"

I could tell by his expression that he was serious. He really didn't know. Had CeCe excluded her twin brother from the biggest coup of her career? I gingerly edged into the danger zone, hoping to soften the blow.

"She just found out yesterday. Prescott Lewis . . ."

"Lewis! What's that scumbag up to?" Deming curled his lip in a particularly vile scowl that still looked rather sexy. "I told him to leave her alone."

I stared straight ahead, terrified of making a misstep. Prescott Lewis a scumbag? I doubted that the man even knew the term. He was the most white-bread guy imaginable; wouldn't say excrement if he spread it on toast. The Lewis family was as close to Boston royalty as one could get short of disinterring a Cabot or a Lodge.

"I'm waiting, Eja." He swung the Porsche into a fire zone and turned off the engine.

"Don't threaten me. Apparently you and CeCe didn't share everything, did you? She'd been nominated for the bench. Federal. At least, they planned to nominate her. What's more, CeCe was in love. Seriously in love. She said so."

Deming's smooth golden skin paled. "No. She would have told me." He toyed with his car keys. "Truth is, we weren't on the best of terms lately. If Prescott Lewis was involved that explains everything. We quarreled about him. Bitterly."

My curiosity was at the boiling point, but I buttoned my lip. Maybe he'd explain later, when the shock wore off. Deming unleashed the horses in that monster motor and veered into the fast lane. His eyes looked vacant, unfocused, as if he were on autopilot. By violating every traffic ordinance in Boston, he got us to Beacon Street in five minutes flat. Naturally, a toady with a specious smile appeared the moment we reached CeCe's building.

"Watch this for me, will you, Brendan?" Deming slipped the attendant a bill and hauled me out of the Porsche.

Boston has plenty of august buildings, and the Tudor was right up there with the best of them. Just looking at it always inspired awe in me. Everything I lusted for and aspired to in a sanctuary was there: beautiful moldings, high ceilings, and location, location, location. CeCe loved it. Told me I'd have to kill her to get it. My eyes filled as I saw the French writing desk silhouetted in her second-story window, the bronze lamp switched on to illuminate its fruitwood curves. Mrs. Grey, her housekeeper, would have come and gone by now, oblivious to the tragedy.

"I'll find the concierge and get a key," Deming said, nodding to the doorman.

"No need." I dug into my bag and found CeCe's key ring. Like everything she owned, it was elegant, an elaborate hunk of sterling with her initials entwined.

"How'd you get that?" Deming asked. "She never gave me a key. Didn't trust her twin brother." His lips twisted in a bitter smile. "She said you were closer to her than any sister. I guess that proves it."

"Sounds more like typical sibling stuff. You were always protective of her, Deming. It's a wonder she ever had a boyfriend with you glowering at any guy who gave her a second look."

He brushed back a wing of black hair and sighed. "I tried, especially after that fortune hunter conned her into eloping. Looks like I failed, doesn't it?" He hustled me through the lobby into the mirrored elevator and stabbed the button. "My sister had horrible luck with men, but she kept hoping. Too bad she never found Prince Charming."

I'd forgotten CeCe's ill-fated marriage. It didn't last long—just long enough to break her heart. He was a charming cad who boasted an excellent game of tennis and enough blarney to co-opt the Eastern Seaboard. Young Cecilia Swann was mesmerized, swept up in the fantasy of love. Before anyone realized the danger, my friend said, "I do" in a sleazy Las Vegas wedding chapel staffed by Elvis impersonators. Fortunately, when confronted by the full force of the Swann legal team, her erstwhile spouse caved quickly. CeCe was only seventeen; he was thirty-seven with two ex-wives and a trio of children for whom he owed child support. A quiet annulment ended the escapade, and CeCe never mentioned him again—even to me.

We sped down quiet corridors redolent with fifty years of glitz and glory. Each floor in the Tudor contained only two apartments, or residences, as they were termed. Sixteen lucky owners kept the surroundings pristine and private. Most of the other tenants were older, retirees or well-established married couples who shared but one common factor—enormous wealth.

My hands shook as I inserted the key. *Damn Medeco locks! Keep out everyone, including the owners!*

"May I? These things are tricky." Deming opened the door with one deft twist.

Immediately, a flood of memories assailed me: the French room scent, the art deco sculpture in her foyer, and the unearthly shriek emanating from Cato. Without warning, the irascible spaniel bared his teeth, charged, and attacked Deming's shin.

"Fuck! Cut it out, you little bastard!" Deming shook Cato off and grabbed him by the collar. "He's always hated me. My sister thought it was hilarious."

"You're not alone," I said. "Cato hates everyone. Except CeCe, of course." I'd learned from experience that bribes were the only way to Cato's heart. I reached into a Chinese ginger jar, found a biscuit, and pitched it down the hallway. "Here. Go enjoy yourself."

Deming inspected his cuffs and shrugged. "That mutt is S.O.L. now. Back to the pound for him."

"What?"

"He's toast. No one with any sense will have him. I'll take him over to the shelter myself tomorrow, bright and early. That's one trip I'll actually enjoy."

Reality hit me like a sledgehammer. She wasn't coming back. Ever. My best friend since childhood was gone, and I'd never see her again. "I'll take him," I said without thinking. "CeCe would want that. For some reason, she loved Cato. Said he was the only man she could count on."

To my horror, I started sobbing and couldn't stop. Deming looked about helplessly then headed straight for the wet bar. I glanced up to find a tumbler of Hennessy Ellipse coming my way.

"Here. Drink this. I'll join you." He swirled the golden liquid in his glass. "I'm the one who started her on cognac, you know. Our dad's a champagne man. Nothing but Krug for him. Mom's even worse, almost a teetotaler."

I took long, slow sips of my drink. Anything to quell my tears and stave off the inevitable hiccups. The taste of cognac had never appealed to me, but I loved the deep, rich color. It was warm and comforting, two qualities I badly needed now.

"Funny," Deming said. "Your eyes are the color of this cognac. Caramel. *Hmmph.* Never noticed it before." He seemed astounded that I even had eyes. After taking a vigorous sip, he shook off sentiment like Cato shed fleas. "Let's drink a toast to my sister, shall we?" He waved an album my way that was stuffed with photos. "This was her memory book. That's what she called it. Most of her photos are in here. The ones she cared about anyway. I think it's appropriate to see them, reminisce a bit. Cecilia was sentimental. She'd like that. Then we'll get down to business."

Three

"LET'S GET ON with it," Deming said. "Maybe we'll see this mystery man you mentioned." He turned away from me before I could protest.

"Wait a damn minute!" I wedged myself next to him on the couch. "Haven't you ever heard of sharing? Two heads are better than one, you know."

"*Humph.* Depends on whose head you're talking about. Anyway, Swanns don't share."

I caught a ghost of a smile on that handsome face. He'd always enjoyed a good joke at my expense, but no matter. His opinion of me was irrelevant. I was only there for CeCe.

"What if the cops show up?" I asked. "They'll confiscate everything that's even remotely suspicious."

Deming shrugged. "Unlikely. That lieutenant"—he checked her card—"Bates, Euphemia Bates. Anyway, she's convinced that Cecilia killed herself. They don't waste resources searching the home of a suicide."

"CeCe's a Swann, not some anonymous statistic. That name means something, buddy boy, and from what I saw, Mia Bates is nobody's fool. She'll cover all the bases."

Deming paused, looking uncertain, curiously vulnerable and almost mortal.

"We can take things over to my place," I offered. "That way they'll be safe."

"I suppose that's okay. After we meet with her tomorrow I can always come back and finish up. Gather up the photos and anything you see on her desk while I find a bag. She must have something we can use."

"Try her closet," I said, as he stood frozen in place. "Never mind, I'll do it."

CeCe was a connoisseur of every upscale tote, handbag, and luggage brand in existence. I found two large Bottega Veneta satchels in her closet and began stuffing them with loot.

"A little help," I snapped at Deming. Cognac had made me feisty and left him lethargic. He resembled a cold, bloodless sculpture straight from the Louvre.

We filled both bags with photos, correspondence, and anything portable. I shrugged off any misgivings I might have had about invasion of privacy by using the greater good theory. We might find something, some clue only we could decipher that would lead to CeCe's murderer. She'd understand. Hell, she would lead the charge if she could. Better us than some brash policeman who neither knew CeCe nor cared. We loved her and always would.

Deming lugged the totes to the elevator while I corralled Cato. His lead and potty bags were neatly arrayed in the utility closet along with toys and kibble. Seeing them made me ache even more for my friend and the void in my life. She inhabited this space so fully that I could almost touch her. If only that were possible.

I trussed Cato up in his harness, tiptoed out the door, and joined Deming at the elevator.

"What if Jaime sees us taking this stuff?" I asked him. "The cops always ask the concierge about anything suspicious."

Deming snorted. "That guy will only see the hundred bucks I hand him, believe you me. He knows which side his bread is buttered on." He pressed the button and moved out of range of Cato's teeth.

Sure enough, Jaime was so busy bowing and scraping to imperious Mr. Swann that he was oblivious to everything else.

After we stowed the bags I lifted Cato into the back seat.

"That mutt better behave if he knows what's good for him," Deming growled. "One tooth mark on that seat, and he's history."

We sped through Back Bay, the nation's most elegant landfill, aided by a temporary lull in traffic. My condo building lay in the shadow of the soaring Prudential Tower bracketed by other anonymous, featureless structures of similar design.

"Where's your garage opener?" Deming asked.

"Nowhere. I don't have a car, remember? No need to pay for a space." I pointed upward. "You'll have to park in the Prudential garage. That's safe enough. Pricy, though."

He dropped off Cato and me and zoomed away in a cloud of dust. My shoebox condo was only 800 square feet—closet size for a Swann but a cozy nest to me. It was the one tangible relict of my marriage complete with a whopping mortgage. By using CeCe's decorating tips, I'd managed to transform a mundane space into a chic *pied-a-terre*. I was proud of it.

I watched Deming closely while he surveyed the place, looking for even a hint of condescension. To my surprise he nodded briskly.

"Not bad. Small, but serviceable. It suits you."

"Thanks. I'm afraid I don't have anything to drink but Pellegrino."

He reached into a satchel and produced his answer. "Don't worry. I brought the Hennessy with me. Just in case."

"I guess we might as well get started." I unpacked the first satchel and spread the photos in CeCe's memory book on my coffee table.

"Do you believe this?" Deming fumed. "She had a regular rogues' gallery here." He shuffled and dealt photos as if they were playing cards. The first face I saw was my least favorite person, Jem Russell, in quite a memorable shot. He sported a thick mustache, toothy grin, and a barely-there pair of bulging Speedos.

"Ugh! Gross! CeCe destroyed all his pictures," I said. "We even had a special ceremony. I watched her burn them."

"Apparently not." Deming gritted his teeth as he turned over the photo. "This thing is dated last month. They must have reconnected."

I thought about CeCe's threat to bring Jem to brunch. She was teasing. Had to be. On the other hand, that Speedo bulge was rather impressive, especially on cold, lonely nights when the urge struck.

Jem Russell was her Achilles' heel, a handsome former fiancé with some very bad habits. He'd left her at the altar—literally—by eloping with a waitress from the Pancake House. Two days later when he'd sobered up, Jem came crawling back begging for forgiveness. Only a full-scale intervention by her family and yours truly had pried them apart. Meanwhile, Jem returned to whatever rock he'd crawled out of while CeCe soldiered on.

"Maybe she was using him as a boy toy. You know. Friends with benefits." I liked that idea. It was so CeCe.

A spot of color appeared on each of Deming's cheeks. "Impossible!" He ducked his head and turned over another photo.

"Maybe she was on a nostalgia kick. You know, CeCe's greatest hits." I grinned at the thought.

"More like her greatest misses. Those creeps almost destroyed my sister." Deming nodded toward the cognac. "Another round?"

"Sure." I seldom drink, but tonight I yearned for oblivion. Maybe alcohol could deaden my senses and cleanse me of pain, at least for a while. It was worth a try.

I reached into the pile and grabbed more photos. These were

older, somewhat grainy mementos of her distant past and ours as well. Our prep school presentation of *Othello.* Predictably, CeCe was Desdemona; I was her understudy. Life imitating art. We'd thought it was kinky when Deming was cast as Othello, but in the end, the joke was on me. CeCe got laryngitis, and I had to endure the faux love scenes and grisly violence with her brother looming overhead. Deming was an excellent actor. You'd almost believe he enjoyed brushing his lips across my hand and embracing me. Desdemona's murder was another matter. Deming actively relished the chance to throttle me even though it was only make-believe.

"Hey! Look at this one." His voice grew husky as he thrust a faded photo my way. It was an artifact more precious to me than gold: a wrinkled portrait of three little kids pulling a sled. CeCe looked ecstatic, golden curls spilling out of a beret as she gestured wildly. Despite the snow, I wore only one glove. Typical. That kind of carelessness drove my mother nuts. I was grinning, a wide toothless grin as Deming yanked my long dark ponytail. We'd been so close in those days, The Three Musketeers: CeCe, me, and her tall, dark twin. He'd trailed after us, serving as our bodyguard and chief tormentor.

I wanted to bawl my eyes out. Maybe I was woozy from the cognac; perhaps it was the collective weight of too many memories. More than anything I wanted to will away reality and see my friend again. I yelped as the brandy snifter slipped from my hand and decorated my lap.

"Excuse me," I said, as I lurched toward my bedroom. Deming seemed oblivious, as if he were in another world. Maybe he was. A world where childish pranks, games of tag, and hide-and-seek consumed each day. We'd felt safe in those innocent times, insulated from the darkness of the outside world.

I stumbled into the bathroom, stripped off my clothes, and turned on the shower. No one could hear my howls with water coursing over my body. I soothed myself, using shampoo and honey gel, crying for CeCe and our youthful dreams. Afterwards, I wrapped myself in a thick Turkish bath sheet and carefully blotted my hair. The ache had temporarily subsided, and at least the sticky sweet brandy smell had vanished.

A sudden sound made me whirl around. I saw Deming standing in the doorway with clenched fists and trembling lips that spelled pain and vulnerability. He was staring at me. One glance at his lower parts said that he was also aroused. I fumbled for my towel, gasping as it fluttered to the floor.

He took two long strides, reached out, and carried me to the bed.

THEY SAY THAT death makes you celebrate life. I can't say for sure. All I recall of that frenzied, febrile night was the gentle touch of his lips brushing my skin and the haunting sound of him moaning my name. We both unleashed desire so primitive that it both terrified and enthralled me. Our naked bodies clung to each other, hungering for more, using tongues and teeth and nails to scale the heights and plumb the depths.

I usually hide my body, using voluminous clothing to conceal me from scrutiny. CeCe was a sylph, but my breasts and curves felt ponderous next to her sleek silhouette. That night was different. I felt beautiful, a voluptuous siren consumed by passion and hungry for sex. Beautiful? Me? Instead of seeing my flaws in face and form, I was emboldened. Every doubt, evasion and inhibition was erased by his touch. When he tore off the top sheet I welcomed the scrutiny. No more shy, retiring Eja. I didn't hide a thing.

The heat of Deming's golden skin warmed my heart, feeding my greed for even more. I was ravenous, insatiable, out of control. We caressed each other slowly then desperately, melding into one until release claimed us. It was a dream, so removed from reality that I felt no fear. Shame would come later, suffusing every pore with the ache of remembrance. How CeCe would have laughed! She'd wanted this for so long, and now she'd gotten her wish.

I AWAKENED EARLY the next morning, sprawled over my bed with Cato curled up next to me. No trace of Deming or the normal debris of lovemaking, just Cato's raucous snores assaulting the air. My cheeks burned as I wondered whether or not it had really happened. I'm no stranger to fantasy. Like most women, I've had the occasional crush. But making whoopee with my best friend's twin on the night she died? No way. I'd known Deming Swann since preschool, and in all that time he'd taken pains to snub, taunt, and torture me. Deming dated girls with glacial beauty and wealthy papas, members of the social elite. I'd never once surfaced on his radar screen, and that was fine with me.

My phantom lover had plied me with compliments and soft kisses that consumed my soul—proof positive that it wasn't Deming. He was the most detached man I'd ever met, a cold fish who thrived on cynicism. There was a simple explanation for everything—temporary insanity and terminal horniness fueled by alcohol.

Both Deming and I had made too many toasts and ingested too much cognac for our own good last night. My aching head testified to that. When grief finally subdued us, we'd each staggered off for a date with Morpheus. Alone. End of story. That must be the truth. I patted Cato, and the spaniel leapt up, dancing around the door in an urgent pantomime.

"Okay, okay. I hear you." I rummaged through the closet until I found some running gear. CeCe was a svelte size six, and I am not. Fortunately, garments containing Lycra are forgiving enough to excuse that. Shoes were no problem. I stepped into the worn Sauconys she'd left in my closet last week, ran a comb through my hair, and brushed my teeth. Makeup could wait. I looked ravaged, more victim than avenger, but the right concealer could work miracles. CeCe had more pots and potions than Sephora. I might borrow a few this afternoon.

After last night, I hoped to avoid Deming Swann. Maybe forever. The dangerous brew of alcohol and nostalgia had made me shed my inhibitions. How else to explain that salacious dream of mine? I wasn't responsible. My subconscious absorbed every trace of guilt. Better to stay the course and ignore any carnal stirrings. Mustn't lose my edge around a shark like Deming who could ace any screen test for the lead in *Jaws*.

As the elevator doors closed, a muscular arm wrenched them apart.

"Running away? Guilty conscience?"

He looked disgustingly chipper. I discounted the sarcasm and averted my eyes from Deming's form-hugging tracksuit. All things considered, he'd weathered the night's excesses far better than I had. Probably a triumph of superior Swann genes over my peasant roots. He seemed perfectly normal: smug and supercilious with no trace of sentiment. Just the way I liked him. This Deming Swann was a known commodity, a distant echo from our childhood. We were bound together in a daunting quest to vindicate CeCe. After that there'd be no need to see him ever again.

"I'm attending to Cato. A dog has needs, after all." I kept my manner sprightly despite the urge to smack the sneer off his face.

"Besides, how did you get past my concierge?"

Deming tossed his head back and grinned. "It's not magic. As long as you look the part, most of those guys won't bother to stop you. I blend in."

Without CeCe around I refused to tolerate her brother's nonsense. There was that frown again. Fair is fair—I had to admit he looked Byronic. Any woman with eyes would acknowledge that Deming Swann was handsome bordering on gorgeous. Anyone who didn't know him, that is. In my lustful fantasy, I'd discovered how perfect his body was, every part of it. Daylight hadn't changed that, but his real-time personality was far removed from the tender man who'd stirred my dreams last night.

He curled his lip and slicked back a thick strand of hair. Normally, I'm a fool for men with great hair, but there are exceptions. With hands on hips he glowered.

"I'm leaving for the police station promptly at nine thirty. Be ready, if you plan to see that security tape."

I checked my watch. "It's barely seven. No problem."

"I already jogged before breakfast. Grab your things, and we can drop Cato at CeCe's place and change. We'll leave from there." He issued an edict rather than a request.

I ground my teeth despite the danger it posed to dental health. "I suppose so." I stuffed some clothes in one of the Bottega totes and handed it to Deming. "Here. Keep this while I walk my poor dog."

Cato's needs were satisfied by a short promenade around the block. When we returned, Deming Swann was parked aggressively across the driveway, blocking the entrance. Was he trying to annoy me, or was it an attempt to dispel lingering doubts about last night?

I lifted Cato into the Porsche and hopped in myself before Deming had time to open the door. Courtesy, my foot! I decided to minimize as much personal contact as possible.

When we reached the lobby of CeCe's building, the concierge approached Deming with a look of horror mixed with panic.

"Mr. Swann! A reporter from the *Globe* was just here. He said . . ." Tears flooded the man's eyes. "Miss Swann . . ."

For once Deming did the right thing. He patted the doorman on the back and nodded. "I'm afraid it's true, Jaime. Miss Swann had an accident yesterday."

I saw the puzzled look in the man's eyes. "That reporter said horrible things. He said Miss Swann . . . that it wasn't an accident."

Deming's icy stare was enough to freeze Jaime and everyone in the lobby. "That's untrue. As a friend of my sister's, I know you'll discourage hurtful rumors about her."

"No, no sir," Jaime stammered. "Miss Cecilia was the nicest lady in this building. I told that reporter to leave, or I'd call the police."

"Excellent." Deming grabbed Cato's lead and thrust it at the doorman. "Watch him for me, will you? Ms. Kane and I have matters to discuss."

I sputtered like a dying engine. "But . . . but."

Deming's solemn features were pure stone. Jerusalem gold limestone, beautiful but cold and unyielding.

"No time. We need to finish searching that flat before the cops trample over everything. You got me worried about it last night." He raised a thick black brow. "Unless you're not up to it."

Last night's good will evaporated. I'd been dreaming. Same old, same old. Deming Swann hadn't changed one bit from his bullyboy days in prep school when he'd put ants in my purse. I gave him a tight-lipped smile and dangled CeCe's keys in his face.

"Let's go. I'm the one with the keys, remember?"

We whisked up to the second floor in strained silence. "Let me take that," Deming growled, snatching the key chain. I was too worn to fight him for it, especially since I couldn't manage that damn Medeco lock. He flicked open the door and swept inside without waiting for me.

"What are we looking for? Do we have any idea?" I'd decided to let him take the lead for now. Later on, I'd formulate my own plan.

Deming folded his arms and shot me a look of disdain. "I plan to confiscate anything that might embarrass Cecilia or my family. Naturally, as a partner in our firm, I'll also take custody of any client files."

"Oh, yeah? Isn't that called evidence tampering? You're an officer of the court."

"You forget. I'm also her twin." His eyes had a suspicious sheen to them. He turned away so quickly I couldn't be sure.

"Do what you have to do. I've got something else in mind." I sprinted for CeCe's bedroom and her antique French box. She loved that thing. Stashed all her mementos in it.

I wasn't sure what I'd find—love letters, press clippings, jewelry? No matter. I knew what wouldn't be there—a suicide note. My friend did not kill herself. Euphemia Bates was way off track to even suggest it. Cecilia Swann, that pampered daughter, beloved sister, and loyal friend would never hurt us that way. Like most cops, Mia would probably take the easy way out to avoid stepping on some big Boston toes. My task was to provide her with an alternative.

I knelt down and reached under the bed, looking for the box. It had to be there. Only last week I'd seen her open it. She used a tiny key that she kept on a gold chain.

"Find anything interesting?" He loomed over me with his hand out. "Give it here."

I reached into the armoire and found something to distract him. Despite her angelic face, CeCe was a mistress of erotic arts. She owned all manner of sex toys and knew how to use them. I nodded toward the cabinet and watched Deming blush.

"Good Lord! What the hell is this?" He dangled a particularly vulgar appliance in the air as if I were the culprit.

"Oh. That's part of CeCe's pleasure chest. Guess you'll be confiscating those things. No need for the cops to snicker about her."

Deming Swann, man of the world, turned pink.

"You're not shocked, are you? Grow up, for God's sake. CeCe was almost thirty-four years old. She liked men and they liked her. I thought you'd grown beyond that."

Deming sat down, holding his head in his hands. "No. I mean, yes, of course, I'm familiar with erotica. It's just that . . ." His voice trailed off. "I never thought about my sister using stuff like that. It's different for you. You've already had one husband."

I sped over to the walk-in closet and renewed my search.

"Yes, I did. Thanks so much for opening old wounds."

Typical! In one fell swoop, he'd revived the lowest point of my life. My self-confidence had never been high. That's why I'd trailed happily in CeCe's wake, avoiding mirrors, grateful to skip the limelight. Poor self-image, she'd called it. Oh, I was smart. There were objective measurements to gauge intellect. I'd spent my academic career being smart, studious Eja, while CeCe scooped every social prize in sight.

Then I met Gabriel Mann. It was miraculous, a fantasy straight out of Edith Wharton. We'd both joined the Mensa chapter at Brown, and by some incredible twist of fate, this blond Norse god chose me to love. When we married, I blossomed like a parched desert flower after irrigation. All my dreams culminated in that walk down the aisle. We sailed through graduate school convinced that literary stardom was only months away. When reality hit, we adjusted. Both of us took freelance jobs and spent our spare time writing. Gabriel was a genius, the next Hemmingway. Everyone said so. I squandered my talent by writing popular fiction. Romantic suspense, no less! We laughed about it, commiserated, and buoyed each other's spirits. My third novel became a moderate success, and I sensed the change before I could prove it. Fewer laughs, less time spent together. Before I knew it, he'd slipped away. Six months later, Gabriel made it official. He'd found someone, a nubile coed who thought he was F. Scott and Nicholas Sparks rolled into one sexy package.

I'd smothered him, stifled his creative impulses: He didn't love me anymore. Our divorce was swift and relatively painless, a sad coda to a song that had already ended. He got his muse; I kept the heavily mortgaged condo and our aged cat.

I didn't date much after that.

"You're crying." Deming looked perplexed. "Did I hurt your feelings? You were way too good for that slug anyway. I heard he's had two other wives and three kids since you."

"Forget it. That's ancient history." I hid my face in a mound of CeCe's clothes as Gabriel's "no-kids" rant rang in my ears. He'd gone ballistic every time the subject arose.

"No kids. No way." Since when had he become Daddy Dearest?

"Funny that you've never married," I said. "I'm sure there's a long line of candidates."

If last night's fantasy meant anything, Deming Swann was unadulterated catnip to sentient females. Fictional heroes usually are.

He shrugged. "Never found the right woman, I guess. Lord knows I've tried hard enough."

His escapades with women were the stuff of legend. In his checkered past, Deming dated half the debutantes on the Eastern seaboard and broke some hearts, lots of them. In the process he'd dodged several lawsuits and at least one paternity test.

"What are you looking for?" Deming bent down as I groped blindly for the prize.

CeCe's safe was cleverly concealed in the wall of her closet next to the built-in drawers. I'd always lusted after that closet with its beautiful wood and modular units. Like everything Swann, it was top quality, far beyond the means of the hoi polloi.

"Her safe. I can't find that French box, but there's still her safe. It's in here somewhere. Grab a flashlight, will you?"

"Safe!" Deming tugged a lock of shiny black hair, squawking like an affronted hawk. "She never mentioned that. Why would she need a home safe? We have one at the firm."

"Stop whining and help me. Shine that light on the panel." I pressed the push-button lock, inputting the only code CeCe ever used, Cato #1. Hardly original, but it did the job. The door swung open, disgorging a mound of jewelry, several folders, and one very scary gun.

GUNS MAKE ME nervous. The second amendment aside, they do more harm than good. Not everyone agreed with me, especially CeCe. She was a fierce proponent of gun ownership whose first legal triumph involved the appeal of a local handgun ordinance. It made her famous; Boston's Annie Oakley they'd called her. As I stared at that hunk of metal death, Deming muscled in and took charge of the weapon.

"For heaven's sake, Eja. It won't bite you. Act your age."

"I don't like them. My family never owned guns."

He frowned as he examined the damn thing. "Well, mine did. Cecilia and I were both marksmen. Won competitions even." He held the thing closer to his face. "Hmm. We always used Glocks. Wonder where she got this thing."

I hate gaping, but that hunk of steel mesmerized me. "Be careful, for God's sake. What kind of gun is it?"

He heaved an exasperated sigh and backed out of the closet. "It's not loaded. That's the first thing I checked. This, my girl, is a Walther PPK, a semi-automatic handgun of some repute. Ian Fleming was particularly fond of them."

"Big whoop. Put it away, Mr. Bond, while we check out these papers. We're on a tight schedule, remember?"

I carried everything into the dining room and dumped it on the table. CeCe loved that table. Imported it from Italy and polished it daily. Actually, Mrs. Grey, her cleaning lady, polished it, but the result was the same: a mirror-bright finish.

"Wonder where she kept her luggage?" Deming said. "She had enough of it. We could use it to bag this stuff."

"Downstairs. CeCe has a storage locker. Every resident does." I tossed him her canvas grocery bag. "Here. Use this until we have more time."

We scooped the mess into the bag, changed our clothes, and headed for the elevator in strained silence. Jaime was prowling the lobby, nursing his shin and dangling Cato's lead. Deming negotiated some sort of custody agreement with him that temporarily spared us from the spaniel's sharp teeth. From the way Deming reached for his wallet, I suspected it was a cash transaction.

"Come on. Get in the car." He opened the passenger's side door and tucked me into the Porsche. "Are you up to this, Eja?"

"What do you mean?"

Deming shrugged. "Just don't go all girly on me when we see the tape. It won't be easy, you know."

I fumbled with my purse to avoid facing him. Staring into those hazel eyes was more than I could bear. They were her eyes, bright, sparkling, and full of life. In my dream, he'd trained them on me and whispered such sweet things. Now they were glacial pools awash with icy shards.

"Right. No problem." I bit my lip and did deep-breathing exercises. This wasn't about me. It was my final gift to CeCe, a duty I'd never shirk. There might be clues on that security footage. If there were, I'd find them or die trying.

I'D NEVER TOURED police headquarters, although I'd fantasized about it. My novels tended to gloss over unpleasant details like perp walks, institutional smells, and florescent lighting. They were character-based, relatively antiseptic studies of mayhem. Now I faced the real thing, and it wasn't pretty.

Deming fed a parking meter on Tremont Street and hustled me up the stairs to the only entrance. To my surprise, the building was far less intimidating than most official structures. I expected a rough granite outcropping that mirrored the stony face of a big city police officer. Boston's cop shop was different. Its four-story facade was modern; no gothic spires here. My tension dissipated as we approached the desk sergeant.

"I'll handle this," Deming muttered. He passed Mia's card to the sergeant and waited, perfectly poised, for things to happen. He didn't wait long. Euphemia Bates appeared almost magically and swept us into the visitors' elevator. I marveled at her composure as she matched Deming's imperious look with one of her own.

"This way." Mia herded us into a fourth-floor conference room. "They've got everything set up for us." She touched my arm. "Ready for this, Ms. Kane? It won't take long."

We sat around the no-frills table, staring at the large flat-screen television mounted on the wall. My palms were sweaty, and my heart rate soared. That made sense. Deming, on the other hand, sat motionless, another take on an elegant marble sculpture straight from the Gardner.

"It starts when your sister enters with the other tenant." Mia shook her head. "So much for controlled access buildings. If you look the part, no one questions anything."

Deming threw a supercilious look my way that clearly said, "Aha!"

Three cheers for technology; the image was clear and unambiguous. At exactly 8:15 a.m., Cecilia Swann swept into the building to start her final journey.

Thirty minutes later she was dead.

Four

I GULPED WHEN I saw her. My pal Cecilia, beautiful as ever, held the door for the dog walker and calmly followed her through the lobby toward the elevator. They exchanged smiles and chatted as she patted the woman's shepherd. CeCe loved all animals—dogs, cats, and brutish males. Every fortnight we volunteered at the no-kill shelter, doing all manner of pro-bono tasks. She was their attorney; I wrote and published the newsletter.

I bit my lip and focused on the screen. The sound quality and clarity were amazing. I heard my friend's laughter, saw her point upward as she asked about the roof. The roof! Cecilia Swann was acrophobic, terrified of the slightest incline. She'd never vault up thirty-two floors with a smile on her face, unless she had a damn good reason. For CeCe that meant one of two things: love or money.

They stepped inside the car, and that was it. Mia explained the absence of security cameras in the elevators. There'd been no need, and residents valued their privacy. To my horror, I saw that I was clutching Deming's hand like a lifeline. His vacant stare told me that he hadn't noticed.

"I'm sorry there isn't more, but I think the tape raises some very serious issues. Ms. Swann went voluntarily to that rooftop. We know that." Mia sounded firm but regretful. There was that compassion again. "The autopsy and test results may take a few days though. Takes a while for analysis, no matter what those television shows say."

"Wait a minute," I said. "Run the tape once more. Please."

She sighed, caught Deming's eye, and pressed the replay button. This time I scrutinized every detail, hastily scribbling notes in my leather agenda. When it ended I had more questions than answers. I also had renewed certainty that CeCe didn't kill herself. Not on her life.

"Okay, Eja, what's going on?" Deming's voice lacked vitality, as if watching his twin had sapped all his strength. It was a side of him I'd never seen before.

I swallowed, pretending it was an academic exercise or a public forum. This was my one chance to help CeCe. Analysis laced with a strong side of logic was called for. Bureaucrats of all stripes discount emotional displays and those who make them. They'd seen and heard it all too many times. If I played the aggrieved friend, my window of opportunity would slam shut.

"I'm glad we saw this, Lieutenant. The tape confirms my belief."

Deming did a double take. Mia's eyes widened, but she stayed calm and forced a smile. "Care to explain?"

"I studied two things: CeCe's mannerisms and her clothes. Remember, she was scheduled to meet me for an 11:00 a.m. brunch at Mistral, a very exclusive restaurant. She's dressed for that. Just look at her—Akris cashmere coat, Hermes purse, and, the kicker, to-die-for Chanel boots."

Deming blanched at my unfortunate choice of words, but Mia looked intrigued.

"Go on," she said. "I'm with you."

"CeCe loved those boots. They were so expensive even she thought twice about buying them. And that purse, straight from Hermes. They call it Garden Party."

"My mother gave it to her." Deming's voice broke as he said it. "She loved that thing."

I nodded. "She just got it. Probably hadn't even been used before."

"Okay, she looked like a million bucks. What does that really prove?" No more guest appearances by Mia. She'd morphed into Lieutenant Euphemia Bates. "Consider this," she said. "Maybe Ms. Swann wanted to look her best at the end."

"Where was her purse? Did you ever find it?"

She shrugged. "Not yet. It may have fallen to the street and been picked up. It happens. We'll find out when someone uses her credit cards."

I gulped a lungful of air and forged on. "Consider her manner, then. CeCe was a cucumber. No stuttering, shaking, or tears. She chatted up that woman right away. Trust me, if she were contemplating suicide, she'd be more withdrawn. After all, she was brought up Catholic. Right, Deming?"

He almost smiled. "Very. It's a mortal sin for Catholics. You take the express elevator straight to Hell for committing suicide. My sister wasn't particularly religious, but some things stick with you."

"I think she was meeting someone. Business or pleasure, I can't really say, but she had her briefcase with her. What happened to it?" I gave Euphemia Bates my fiercest stare.

She'd handled tougher customers than me, but Deming was another matter. The Swanns were a force to be reckoned with in Boston.

"We didn't find her briefcase either, I'm afraid. I noted the same things when I previewed the tape. Our detectives are doing some checking. I'll get back with you in a few days." Her eye contact said she was speaking to Deming, not me.

He nodded. "One more thing, Lieutenant. My sister chose that building for a reason. Have you canvassed the residents to see if anyone was expecting her? Maybe she was meeting one of them on that roof."

Mia absorbed his comments without changing her expression. She'd probably aced Inscrutability 101 at cop school. Top-flight lawyers and cardsharps perfect that same look.

"Point taken, Mr. Swann. We're working with the management of that building where your sister died. They demanded a court order before relinquishing their tenant list, but we've got that under control. Her accident happened only twenty-four hours ago. I think you'd agree that under the circumstances . . ." Mia spread her palms upright.

He didn't answer. Deming stayed motionless, favoring Mia with a look of expectation. In his world, people leapt to anticipate his needs.

I'd grown up on a different planet where assertiveness was my watchword. It avoided mixed signals and needless complications.

"You probably know this already," I said. "But what's their policy on that roof garden? Most high-rises restrict access for the very reasons we're discussing. I'll bet you need a key or something to get in."

Deming flashed me a look that bordered on admiration.

Mia wasn't as pleased. She glanced down at her notes. "Hmm. Another good point, Ms. Kane. Believe it or not, we already thought of that. My guys are meeting with the manager this afternoon." Her lips were set in a grim, unyielding line. An easy, predictable case now had some twists to it, and Euphemia Bates was not pleased. "I understand your feelings, but know this. My people are experienced detectives, and they're very good at their job. If someone hurt your sister, we'll find him—or her."

"Thanks for your time, Lieutenant." Deming rose gracefully and took my arm. "Come on, Eja. We have things to do."

"YOU MADE SOME good points in there," Deming said. "You were almost . . . lawyerly."

"Thanks."

Normally I would have said something snarky, but today I let it pass. After all, what did he expect? I was always the smart, studious one. Since we both had the right to be off our game, I cut him some slack.

Neither of us spoke as we climbed into his Porsche and headed back to Beacon Hill. Searching CeCe's place was even more crucial now that the cops were back in the mix. Lieutenant Bates was smart and industrious. She had already dispatched her minions throughout the city to gather information. Searching CeCe's place would be next as soon as she had probable cause. With any luck, we'd beat her to it.

"Bring that bag up, will you?" I pointed to the tote with the contents of CeCe's safe. My fingers tingled at the thought of sifting through it. She must have kept something important in there. Otherwise, why have a safe?

"You take it. I'll go down and look for that luggage," Deming said. "Don't worry. Jaime will take me there."

I smiled bravely, despite visions of tussling with that stupid Medeco lock. As it turned out, I didn't have to worry. The door swung open without any hesitation, disgorging Cato. The little darling didn't nip my ankles this time. Quite the opposite. He brushed my legs and gave a pathetic whimper.

"What's wrong, little guy?" I stooped down, patting his silky head. Cato was shivering as if something had really spooked him. Maybe it was the loneliness. Maybe it was something worse. I slammed the door and fastened the bolt. Deming would have to knock when he came back.

There was nothing out of order, but it felt strange. CeCe's French room scent had been displaced by something else, a woodsy masculine fragrance that I couldn't identify. It wasn't Deming's. He used only Creed. Of course. I was being stupid. Jaime probably stepped inside when he delivered Cato. The guy had better taste than I thought.

"Forgive me, CeCe," I said, dumping the carryall on her marble table. Defiling that shiny slab of rock was a necessary sacrilege. Exigent circumstances and all. I divided the contents into three piles: jewelry, documents, and miscellaneous. Jewelry was simple: her Rolex, Patek Philippe and Bulgari watches, assorted gold and diamond necklaces, earrings, bracelets, and chains. There was also one surprise: something that looked suspiciously like an engagement ring. It was a jaw-dropping diamond that had to be five karats—five beautiful, flawless karats. I'd never seen it before, and God knows, I'd remember a sparkler that big. Any woman would.

CeCe stored her good jewelry in the bank, a constant joke to those who would have treasured her lesser gems. I racked my brain, but nothing explained that ring. She'd said she was in love, but this was something more. Much more.

I squinted, checking out the band. There it was, a beautifully inscribed clue that meant nothing to me. "CLS from Raven." Raven, who the hell was that? I'd never once heard her call anyone, male or female, by that name. Was this birdman the reason for the cheeky grin and soaring spirits she'd displayed lately? No way. She would have told me. No woman could keep quiet about an engagement, especially a magpie like CeCe. I'd shrugged when she'd announced that she was in love. That happened at least twice a month.

I pushed the documents away until Deming arrived. Lawyers were persnickety about anything that smacked of disclosure, and I wasn't up for a custody battle with Attorney Swann. Speaking of which—I checked my watch. Where the hell was he? Deming was hardly the type to hang out in the lobby fraternizing with the help. That made me restless. If I panicked, sounded the alarm, he'd freeze me out right away. Swanns hated "unseemly attention," as CeCe once advised me. Her dad employed a publicist to keep their name *out* of the tabloids. That guy had his work cut out for him now. I hadn't scanned the *Globe* this morning, didn't have the heart for it. The demise of a prominent citizen like Cecilia Swann wouldn't go unnoticed.

For once, Cato came to the rescue. Dog walking was the perfect excuse to loiter and chat with anybody and everybody. I fastened his harness, grabbed my keys, and led him to the elevator.

JAIME WAS bustling about the lobby attending to his constituency. Doormen in buildings like this make a tidy sum. With the right attitude, every smile or nod translates into cold hard cash. I edged toward him, taking care to steer Cato away from the heels and calves of the innocent.

"Jaime, have you seen Mr. Swann?" I channeled my ultra-cool, unharried persona, topping it with a warm smile.

His puzzled look pushed every alarm button in my head.

"I'm sorry, Ms. Kane, but I took Mr. Swann down to her locker right before noon. Is something wrong?"

"No, no. No problem. He's probably sorting through his sister's things. Don't worry. I'll find him." I started strolling toward the elevator when Jaime called out.

"People have no respect, you know. That's what I told that man today."

I whirled around, forsaking every bit of cool. "Man?"

Jaime nodded. "He came around asking about Ms. Swann's apartment. Wanting to buy it. I told him to get lost."

"Probably just a friend of Ms. Swann's." I baited my trap carefully, waiting for Jaime's response.

"Oh no, Ms. Kane. I knew all her regulars. This man was a stranger."

I should have asked for a description, but every nerve in my body was crying foul. Deming was in trouble. I knew it with a certainty that floored me.

"Let me just check on Mr. Swann. The lights work, I suppose?"

A wide grin split Jaime's pleasant face. "Lights on, security camera too. We're careful at the Tudor, Ms. Kane."

I pressed the basement button. "Good to know."

Cato's guard hairs stood straight up the moment we stepped into the basement. Despite Jaime's assurances, the place was dark and creepy with only emergency lighting switched on. My faith in the Tudor's security system suffered a sudden, fatal blow.

Even under the best of conditions, I'm a klutz. In semidarkness, managing high heels and a frantic dog, I'm hopeless. Fortunately, I'd accompanied CeCe to her locker on many occasions. That was some comfort. I knew enough to hook a sharp right and inch my way down the dimly lit corridor. The place was tomb silent, an unfortunate metaphor if ever there was one. Cato complicated the situation by lunging forward, snarling like a hound from hell.

"Easy boy," I said with false cheer. "No need to panic."

As we neared CeCe's locker, I heard a noise. Nothing loud, more like a mewing cat. Cato's ears stood straight up as he dragged me toward it. I had no weapon, not even my purse, but I laced the house keys through my fingers and prepared to defend myself. The tension was unbearable. My heartbeat was so erratic I expected to keel over at any minute. Fortunately, that wasn't necessary.

"At last," Deming grunted. "Glad you finally missed me." He was draped gracefully over the entrance to CeCe's locker, nursing a monster bruise. His thick black mane, matted with globs of gore, gave him the look of a punk vampire.

Blood unnerves me. I fought to remain calm and avoid worsening the situation. Unfortunately, I resorted to the basest of clichés.

"Deming—you're hurt."

He snapped at me like a sea turtle. "What was your first clue? Don't I always groom myself with blood?"

"Let me get help."

"No . . . wait a minute. I can walk if you help me. Let go of that mutt. I'll need your arm around my waist." He slowly rose, leaning heavily against me. The sensation was less unpleasant than I expected. Deming was a wall of hard, toned muscle, just like in my dream.

"What happened to you?" I asked.

"Isn't it obvious? I surprised someone rifling Cecilia's storage area and got clobbered for my trouble. From behind. Otherwise I'd have been fine."

"Man or woman?"

He grunted and said a particularly vile word. "I couldn't tell. I heard a noise and woke up on the floor. Probably a man, but who knows these days. Brutalizing men gives women points with the sisterhood, doesn't it?"

I didn't bother correcting him. CeCe was a black belt in several of the martial arts, but I was more cerebral. Verbal combat was my style.

We limped toward the elevator with Cato trailing behind us. For once, he was too frightened to disobey.

"Now do you believe me?" I asked. "CeCe was murdered. Why else would someone ransack her things and burglarize her apartment?"

He winced as I dragged him over some kind of cable. "What's this about her apartment?"

"It was unlocked when I got there, and her laptop was gone. Lucky thing we took that other stuff with us. So much for those great Medeco locks."

Deming braced himself against the elevator. "Don't you get it? Someone has a key. You don't just pick one of those locks. They're virtually impregnable. I told Cecilia to get a burglar alarm, but she refused. Said the building was secure. Ha!"

I adjusted my arm, bolstering both Deming and Cato as we entered the lobby.

Jaime crossed himself when he saw us. A fit of conscience or the prospect of the unemployment line propelled him across the lobby like a rocket.

"Mr. Swann! You're bleeding! Can I help you, sir?" Anxiety stripped Jaime of his composure. He flapped his arms, hopping from foot to foot in flat-out panic.

"Call the paramedics," I said. "I'll contact the police."

Deming sputtered, "No," and started coughing. "No paramedics. I'll call my family physician." He nodded at Jaime. "If you'll help me up to Ms. Swann's flat, I'll be fine."

Three humans and a dog formed a quiet quartet as we bundled Deming into the elevator. Fortunately, this time the Medeco lock was firmly in place. After Jaime left, Deming sprawled out on CeCe's platinum sofa, holding an ice pack on his head. He closed his eyes as he gingerly dabbed blood with his handkerchief.

"Who's your doctor?" I asked. "Head wounds are tricky. You need to have it looked at."

He shrugged. "They also bleed like the dickens. It's no big deal. Spend time around horses, and you get used to bumps and bruises."

I'd forgotten. Both CeCe and her brother were world-class equestrians. Deming even aced the Olympic tryouts last year. Horses were part of the Swann DNA. Deming's father, grandfather, and uncle had been respected polo players. I loved all animals, including horses, but the thought of swinging mallets and hurdling fences gave me a rash.

"Phone the doctor, or I'll call your mother."

His hazel eyes flashed, raising yet another memory of CeCe. "You always were a nag, Eja. Look on my iPhone. Dr. Harris. Just don't call my mother. She's . . . not been well."

Hard to believe Anika Swann was anything but perfect. I'd always wondered how one woman—somebody's mother, for Christ's sake—could look elegant and self-possessed no matter what the occasion or time of day. Money helped, but she had something more. Chalk it up to those years spent as a runway model, or the three decades in the bosom of the cultural elite. My poor mother with her hair curlers and ruined hose always suffered in comparison.

"Did you hear me?" Deming sounded querulous, almost menacing. "Don't involve my parents. They have enough to deal with now."

I nodded, slipped into the kitchen, and made the call.

Five

TO MY SURPRISE, Dr. Jake Harris arrived in thirty minutes, sporting a medical bag and a warm smile. He was our age, with curly black hair to his collar, smooth brown skin, and a wiry mustache. From their conversation, I could tell that he and Deming knew each other well.

"Thank God you could get away, Dr. Harris. His head is a mess."

Deming glared at me. "Your bedside manner needs work. Florence Nightingale you're not."

Jake Harris gave a good-natured chuckle. "Not to worry. I have what they call a boutique practice, a small number of private patients who keep me on retainer. The Swann family is my favorite."

After he'd probed Deming's scalp and assessed his vital signs, Jake Harris slapped his patient on the back and sighed. "Good thing you're such a hard head. A mere mortal would have cracked like Humpty Dumpty."

"I take it this has happened before," I said.

"Ah yes. Dem's an adrenaline junkie. At Harvard he got smashed on the noggin quite regularly. Tennis and crew, you know." Jake's voice turned somber. "Listen, I just heard about Cecilia this morning." His eyes grew moist, and for a moment I thought he might weep. "I don't know what to say. It's unbelievable, tragic. How can I help?"

Deming pulled himself up on his elbows and grimaced. "Think you could stop by and see my mom? You know her. She'll never admit to needing anything. I spoke with her this morning, and she seemed normal. Way too normal, considering the situation."

"Naturally," Harris said. "You know, CeCe was on my list for Friday, but she never showed. Some sort of mix-up, I expect."

His voice had that kind, compassionate tone that suicides inspire. I couldn't bear it.

"She didn't do it." I stared down the shock in Dr. Jake's face. "And we're going to prove it."

"Eja . . . cut it out." Deming stretched out his arm as if to swat me away. "Don't mind her, Jake-man. They were best friends."

Jake Harris inspected me as if I were a rare virus. "Ah, yes . . . you're the novelist. Eja Kane. Cecilia spoke often about you. You write mysteries, don't you?"

His remark may have been innocent, but it sounded like a challenge.

"So?"

"Nothing. Nothing bad, that is. If it makes any difference, I agree with you. From everything I knew about Cecilia, she was the least likely person to take her own life. She never shrunk from a challenge. Took everything full on."

I ignored Deming's glower and gave the good doctor my sweetest smile. "You probably know how frightened she was of heights."

Jake wiped his face clean of all expression, giving me that neutral look common to doctors, lawyers, and sociopaths. What in the name of doctor-patient confidentiality had I stumbled into?

"CeCe would never, ever jump from that roof," I said. "Knowing her, she'd deal directly with her issues. After all, she kept a gun in her home and knew how to use it. Why make a spectacle of herself?"

Deming hauled himself up to his full height, brushing aside a shock of coal-black hair. "Let it go, Eja. This is not the time."

Invalid or not, Deming Swann annoyed the hell out of me.

"Oh, yeah? Then when *is* the time, Brother Bjorn? When she's in her grave, and everyone's swept it under the rug?" I could feel my voice scaling the octaves and going shrill. To my utter humiliation, I burst into tears. Not quiet, ladylike weeping but big, gusty sobs. Both men seemed horrified by the waterworks, but for me it was therapeutic. I would not—could not—allow my friend to be dismissed. If that offended the Swann sense of propriety, so be it. That went double for the hot doc.

Deming handed me another from his endless supply of linen handkerchiefs. In these days of disposable everything, not many men used them. Despite the source, I applauded the elegant touch.

Jake gave him a questioning look. "I presume you've spoken with the police?"

"Eja's right. The cops want this whole nightmare to quietly disappear. The lieutenant, Euphemia Bates, seems pretty sharp though. I think we've come to an understanding."

"What's that all about?' Jake asked, pointing to his injury. "Somehow I can't believe it's a coincidence."

"Neither can I. Of course, it might be a random burglary. That's always possible, and her purse was missing." Deming shot me a conciliatory look. "But I don't think so. Someone wants something that my sister had, or he thinks she had. I can't for the life of me think what it might be."

I leapt up as my tired synapses suddenly ignited. I'd totally forgotten the three neat piles arrayed on CeCe's dining table.

"Check this out," I said, waving the diamond at them. "Might be worth a little B and E, don't you think?"

"What the hell! That can't be my sister's. She would have told me."

Jake Harris had a tremor in his hand as he reached for the ring. "May I? It's exquisite. My dad was a diamond merchant, so I've seen lots of these."

"Probably belongs to a client," Deming huffed. "That's why she had it in her safe."

"Check out the engraving," I said. "It's hers."

Jake examined the ring and nodded. "She's right, Dem. But I don't understand. Who's this Raven? Her fiancé?"

"Raven? What kind of name is that?" Deming tucked in his shirt and straightened his tie. "Cecilia was not engaged. She would have told me. Come on. I'll freshen up first. Then we'll visit my parents."

THE SWANN FAMILY lived simply—for the monarchs of a small country. When the twins left for college, they'd downsized to a five-floor colonial revival in the heart of Back Bay. The renovation, overseen by Anika, had tastefully preserved the period details, intricate moldings, and soaring ceilings of the home. I'd always loved it.

We descended on them without calling first. Deming waved away my protests, saying this was no time to stand on ceremony. Jake shrugged, climbed into his Jeep, and followed us to Chestnut Street.

"Oh, oh." I pointed to a news van, double-parked in front of the house. Deming aimed his Porsche at it like a death ray, causing the panicked cameraman to flee.

"Serves them right," he said. "Bastards. Vultures preying on the bereaved." He swung the Porsche across the driveway, adjusting his sunglasses against the glare of the light. "Be quick, Eja. Don't gape at them." Deming walked briskly up the walkway and used his key. "We'll wait inside for Jake. Po can take care of him."

Po, the Swann's majordomo, factotum, and family retainer, moved so swiftly I seldom noticed him. He was garbed in black, a tall, slender Chinese man with eyes in the back of his head and the strength of ten. Anyone who bothered the Swanns found that out in a hurry. He had enormous dignity and was respectful but never obsequious to his adopted family. Most called him a treasure, but CeCe considered him a sneak who saw and reported everything to her father.

Deming nudged me toward the beautifully paneled door to the study. "Dr. Harris is right behind us. Show him in, Po."

The study was a triumph of exquisite carving and old-world craftsmanship. CeCe and I used to sneak in there when the coast was clear, gorge on pastries, and solve the problems of the world. Something about the venerable leather sofa and antique Sarouk made this the perfect spot to exchange confidences.

Not today. Today the beautiful room seemed more like a mausoleum than a place of respite. CeCe's parents, Anika and Bolin Swann, sat motionless and hollow-eyed around an untouched tea tray. They were a striking couple straight from central casting. She was a natural blonde with perfect skin and an air of elegance that that drew raves from *Vogue* and *W*. Bolin Swann was simply the most handsome man I'd ever seen. He was closing in on sixty, but looked forty-five, a toned, sexy forty-five with dark, penetrating eyes and major muscles. Deming inherited his long, lean body, golden skin, and abundant black hair from Dad. His hazel eyes were Mama's legacy. No telling where his bad manners came from.

I hung back as Deming embraced his mother and shook his father's hand. Dr. Jake Harris did the same. Comforting the bereaved is tricky, although I'm sure that somewhere, probably in a YouTube video, there are social conventions that govern it. Rules seemed meaningless to me now, in the face of such enormous grief. I chose emotion over logic and led with my heart. I strode forward and squeezed CeCe's mother, letting my arms say what my lips could not.

"I'm glad you're here, Eja. She'd want that." Anika was dry-eyed and statue still. She felt brittle, as if the slightest movement would shatter her into bits. Even her impeccable style seemed slightly off-kilter today.

I didn't hug Bolin Swann. My unrequited crush on him was a guilty secret I'd guard to the grave. It was all theoretical anyway, probably an unacknowledged Electra complex. He'd never encouraged my fantasies by word, gesture, or action. As far as I knew, the Swanns were devoted to each other.

"You were a good friend to Cecilia," Bolin said. "We've always thought of you as a member of our family. Another daughter." He turned to Anika and patted her shoulder. "Go upstairs with Jake, darling. He'll give you something to help you sleep."

She staggered toward the stairway under the watchful eye of her physician. As soon as the door closed, Bolin sharpened his gaze.

"Okay, tell me what you found." He spoke in brisk, no-nonsense sentences, demanding truth not platitudes. This was Bolin Swann the financier, whose holdings dwarfed several medium-size nations. He'd apparently channeled his grief into an aggressive business model that worked for him.

He nodded to Deming. "Tell me about your meeting with the police, son."

Deming's account was masterful, a full but concise summary of our encounter with Euphemia Bates. He left nothing out, including my contributions.

"Fine," Bolin said. "Now explain that contusion on your head."

Deming hesitated. "It could have been a coincidence . . ."

"You don't believe that, do you?" Bolin turned to me. "What's your take on it, Eja?"

I gulped, wondering how to play Switzerland in a shooting war. "CeCe didn't kill herself. Someone lured her to that rooftop and murdered her. I'll go to my own grave knowing that."

He set his jaw. "Well said. We need a contingency plan in case the police drag their feet. Swann Industries has an excellent security division. They can help us."

"Us? Dad, I think you should stay out of this. Mother needs you. Let the cops do their thing first."

"Back off, Deming. This is a joint effort. I owe it to Cecilia and your mother to find the truth. I'll do that with or without your help."

The two of them, mirror images of each other, locked eyes, negotiating an unspoken truce. Suddenly Bolin rang for Po and ordered champagne. When it arrived, he poured each of us a flute of Krug.

"First, a toast to my daughter. Brilliant, beautiful, light of my life. Love you forever, CeCe."

Tears ran down my cheeks as I thought of the color commentary CeCe would have given. She'd always joked about the men in her family, calling them ninja assassins. Tonight they'd bonded in a blood quest to avenge her. I had joined them in it.

Jake Harris slipped silently into the room, poured himself a flute, and raised it. "Whatever you're planning, count me in. I loved her too."

After another toast, we got down to business. I'd been to plenty of self-indulgent brainstorming sessions. They're a staple of academic life and a convenient excuse for inaction. Tonight's exercise orchestrated by Bolin Swann was different. By the time we left the family manse, we'd devised an action plan with real teeth. Deming and I led the discussion, but Bolin and Jake were with us all the way. We zeroed in on four areas: CeCe's presence at the mystery building; the promised federal judgeship; and her personal and professional life.

While the police waited for a warrant, Swann Securities would do a computer run of every resident in the high-rise building and cross-reference for any connection with CeCe. If one surfaced, Bolin would follow up.

Jake got the medical tasks. He'd schmooze with the medical examiner, analyze the autopsy findings, and scour CeCe's charts for any irregularities. They sugarcoated the big *s* word. No one said it, even though it hovered over us like an unacknowledged guest.

"Why bother?" I asked. "She wasn't depressed. Believe me. She was euphoric. Her career was soaring."

Deming turned away before I caught his expression. "Sometimes that's not enough, Eja. Look at it the way Euphemia Bates will see it: My sister was almost thirty-four, she had no husband or children, and that biological clock was ticking away. Maybe she wanted more. All her life she'd gotten everything she wanted."

"True," Bolin said. "Cecilia never had limits—didn't believe in them. She saw obstacles as something to conquer. She knew only one way. Full speed ahead."

I closed my eyes, visualizing her ire whenever I beat her at anything—be it Jeopardy, chess, or final exams. She was a fighter who just wouldn't quit. That's why I knew she'd been murdered, and I intended to prove it.

"But she was happy—in love. I'd never seen her more ebullient."

Deming whirled around, his eyes laser sharp. "What makes you say that? You said you didn't know about this so-called engagement."

"I didn't. Not really. After all, she had quite a social life. CeCe was cagey about it. Never mentioned a name. I intended to grill her at brunch yesterday." I flashed back to that building, all thirty-two floors of it. "What about the shrink she was seeing? He might speak with another doctor about her acrophobia. I know Lieutenant Bates didn't believe me, but that's a big red flag. No way would she have leapt off a building. CeCe got dizzy on a stepladder."

I could tell by the way his eyes darted that Jake was uncomfortable. No doubt about it. Apparently, the stethoscope set had strict rules about discussing patients and their ailments, even dead ones. I knew about the doctor-patient relationship, but I also knew that most men were bigger blabberers than women ever dreamed of being. They cloaked it in different terms—information sharing, analysis, evaluation—but it all added up to the same thing: dishing dirt.

"We'll provide a release, Jake." Bolin nodded at his son. "Dem will draw it up for you." Bolin leaned back in the chair and closed his eyes. "This engagement ring is another complication. I'll check with Anika, but to my knowledge, Cecilia wasn't involved with anyone. Certainly not engaged." He sighed. "I hate prying into her personal life, but . . ."

"Let me help." Three pair of male eyes locked in on me. "I can ask around, say I'm compiling a profile piece on CeCe. A tribute for the family. I am a writer after all."

"Absolutely not! I forbid it." Deming's hazel eyes shot sparks across the room. "It's too dangerous. If my sister actually was murdered, someone will be very nervous. That's all we need, Eja blundering into a murder scheme. We'd end up having to rescue her."

We glared at each other, hackles raised, in a scene reminiscent of our schoolyard spats. Neither one of us backed down or gave an inch.

"They always fought," Bolin told Jake, "even as children. Oil and water, I guess. Well, this time I'm taking sides. Your idea is a good one, Eja. Just be careful."

No one, even Deming, dared argue with Bolin Swann. He was Zeus incarnate, a force of nature.

"There's one issue I'll handle personally," he said. "This judgeship."

"Did you know about it, Dad?"

Bolin shook his head. "Nothing concrete, just rumors. I would have expected a call from Prescott Lewis before any formal offer was made. Matter of courtesy. I'm surprised that he approached Cecilia first."

"Huh!" Deming snorted like Secretariat at the finish line. "That creep! His interest in CeCe was more than professional. I warned him off, believe me. He wanted her, but not enough to face me."

"Looks like I should speak with Prescott," Bolin said. "He'll make a condolence call. Count on that. When he does, I'll ask him to contact you, Eja. For your essay."

"Not without me," Deming growled. "No woman is safe being alone with that man."

I ignored him. "You're crazy, Deming. Prescott Lewis is Mr. Milquetoast. Don't worry. I'll handle it. By myself."

No one noticed that the study door was ajar. We were too busy jockeying for position and swilling Krug. Suddenly Anika stood before us.

"I'll join you, Eja," she said. "I want to help."

The men in the room froze as she glided toward us and poured herself some Krug. Mrs. Swann was a teetotaler no more.

"What did I miss? Tell me." Her flowing hair and unadorned face made even tragedy seem sublime. For the first time in my recollection, Bolin Swann lost his composure. He folded his wife into his arms and kissed her forehead.

"Leda, I thought you were sleeping. Don't mind about all this. We'll handle it."

"Mind? She was my daughter too. I want to help. I have to, Bolin. Please."

He said nothing, just stood holding her, tenderly stroking her hair. I was transfixed, a voyeur who couldn't turn away. He'd called her Leda, his pet name for her. Bolin was a fan of Greek mythology, especially that business between the goddess and a swan. CeCe chortled about the eroticism, feigning horror at parents who still liked sex with each other. I'd had a different reaction. Their love for each other, the intensity of their passion—I yearned for that in a relationship. Wanted it but had never found it. CeCe had searched for that as well. Maybe she'd finally gotten lucky.

After we'd settled down, Anika repeated her question. "What can I do? Don't discount a mother's instinct. It's special, you know."

Deming glared at me as if I were a bad influence on her. "Ah, come on, Mother. We've got everything covered."

Bolin touched his wife's shoulder. "Okay. Work with Eja, darling. You two can sort through Cecilia's things before the police get there."

Anika nodded and headed for the door. "I'll get dressed right away. Po can drive us."

"Now? You're going now?" Deming's nostrils flared. "Stop her, Jake. She's not well."

Jake Harris shrugged. "You really should rest, Mrs. S."

Anika pivoted and faced the men in her life. "Enough. All of you. You mean well, but I'm not some hothouse flower. There's no good time to do this. Might as well be now."

Anika had no doubts. She buttoned her jacket and beckoned to me. "Come along, Eja. We've got work to do."

Six

WE RODE TO CECE'S flat in companionable silence; two women absorbed in private thoughts. Po drove the monster Mercedes as cautiously as if it were Cinderella's coach. He was a man of so few words that I'd never heard him utter a complete sentence. In English, that is. He and Bolin chatted quite easily in Mandarin, and the rest of the Swann family was also fluent in the language. I'd always suspected that Po absorbed every conversation he heard, English or not, and recounted it word for word to Bolin.

Jaime practically genuflected when he spied Anika. That didn't surprise me; I'd seen it all before. Anika had a quality that reduced adult males to quivering little boys. Beauty, charm, a whiff of vulnerability? If I could bottle and sell it, I'd never have to work again. I'd never be lonely, either.

As we boarded the elevator, I thought of the engraved ring. Maybe CeCe's middle name was Leda. That would explain the *L*. She'd always claimed that she had no middle name. If even I didn't know it, this Raven person must have been exceptionally close to her.

"Mrs. Swann . . ."

"Anika. Please, Eja. We've known each other too long to use titles. Especially now."

It felt strange, but I forced myself. "Anika, what was CeCe's middle name?"

She blinked. "Middle name, whatever for?" She exhaled and started laughing. "I'll bet she told you she didn't have one, right?"

I nodded.

"She loathed it, and you know Cecilia. What she didn't like just disappeared." Dimples surfaced as she recalled her daughter. "Her name was Lenore. For her Grandmother Lind."

"Lenore?"

Lines of poetry swam before my eyes. Of course! How could I forget Edgar Allen Poe's poem, *"The Raven."* The hero ached for his lost love: Lenore. CeCe must have connected with a guy who appreciated those sentiments. Hence, Raven. That didn't sound at all like a lawyer. They crafted odes to billable hours, not lost loves.

"Eja?" Anika watched me closely. No wonder. The elevator must have been stopped on the second floor for some time.

I felt myself flush. "Forgive me. I . . . I was stuck in the past."

Anika touched my shoulder. "Ah, yes. It's a great temptation, isn't it? Retreating into the past. Since we heard . . . that's just what I've been doing. It's comforting thinking of Cecilia that way."

She reached into her handbag and produced another set of keys with the distinctive CS monogram. "I kept these for emergencies. Never even thought of using them." A dimple surfaced in Anika's cheek. "Bolin didn't know, and Deming would have been livid. It's a girl thing."

I heard her gasp as she swung open her daughter's door. "I keep waiting for her to rush out. You know Cecilia was always running." Tears pooled in Anika's eyes.

To my surprise Cato went right to her and offered his paw. No ankle biting or growling for the lovely Mrs. Swann. She charmed all species of males.

She buried her face in the spaniel's soft fur. "My daughter loved this dog. I guess you know that, don't you?"

I nodded. "I told Deming I'd take him. Unless you want to, of course."

Anika Swann giggled. "Ooh no. Cecilia talked about that—just joking of course. She wanted you to have Cato. Said he'd protect you from harm." She turned away suddenly as if the memory was too much to bear. "She really loved you, Eja. Said you were her *laotong*, her friend for life."

I knew that expression. CeCe recounted tales from her Chinese grandma about old-world customs both frightening and exotic. Female friendships resonated with us. Foot binding—not so much. We'd done enough damage stuffing our tootsies into sexy shoes.

"She looked up to you," Anika said. "Depended on you."

I was too astonished to speak. "Me? I was always in her shadow."

Anika took my hands and squeezed them. "No, Eja. You're smart and talented. Cecilia envied that. Even your marriage."

"Huh! My spectacular failure, you mean. I couldn't even keep my own husband."

I thought of the huge diamond and Raven. "You saw that

engagement ring, Anika. Did you know anything about it?"

"Nothing. Cecilia had a lot of male friends, but no one special. Not that I knew of."

"The name—Raven. It doesn't ring any bells. CeCe had lots of nicknames for her dates, but not Raven. I'd have remembered that one."

Anika played with her wedding ring, moving it up and down her finger. "That's the connection with Lenore, isn't it. Poe's poem?" She grabbed my hand and squeezed it. "Did he do it—this Raven person? Did he take her from me?"

I shrugged. "I really can't say."

"But it's a clue, isn't it? Something to make them investigate."

It fit my theory, but Euphemia Bates might react differently. Botched love affairs could make a woman desperate. Might even make her commit suicide. I remembered Deming's analysis of his twin's life: no man, no kids, and no hope.

Anika cried again, weeping softly into a lace hankie. She clutched an ornate silver frame with a graduation photo of Deming, CeCe, and me. "You have courage, Eja. No one ever gave you anything. You earned it. That's what my daughter envied. Your friendship meant the world to her."

"No, no. I was the lucky one. You're all so special." I took her hand. "I'll find out. I promise."

Anika cocked her head. "What dear?"

I swallowed hard. Should I say it? Pour salt in the wounds of a grieving mother?

"I'll find out who killed CeCe, Mrs. Swann. Promise."

Her hazel eyes sparked. "You mean who *murdered* her, don't you? Stole her from those who loved her. That's okay, Eja. Say the word."

I didn't dare. It was harsh and unrelenting, the type of thing no mother needs to hear. Anika Swann stared at me, looking like an angry Athena.

"Yes, Mrs. Swann. CeCe was murdered. We . . . I . . . will avenge her."

She snapped her purse shut, jumped up, and sprinted for CeCe's bedroom. "Good. That's settled then. We'll work together on it. I can help."

I started sputtering. "But Deming . . ."

Anika waved her hand. "Don't worry about him, darling. He's so protective of you. Always has been. Right now, he's troubled and afraid."

My brows rose skyward. "Afraid? Deming? Whatever for?"

Her smile was gentle as sea mist. "Losing control. He needs to protect you and me, and he's worried. He always played that role, even as a small boy. His name means *virtuous* in Mandarin, you know. He can't help himself." She flung open CeCe's closet and sighed. "She loved clothes, didn't she? And purses . . . dear Lord, that girl loved leather."

That was an understatement. By last count, CeCe owned eighty purses, worth a small fortune. She'd cared for them, stuffed them with paper, and stored them in their own cotton sleeves.

"They're yours now, Eja."

My jaw dropped, and my mouth formed a perfect *o*.

"You didn't know, did you?" Anika shook her finger. "Cecilia left everything to you."

"Me? But why?"

"There was only one proviso. Cato. You have to keep Cato."

I hung my head, mopping tears that wouldn't stop. "I'd keep Cato anyway. She didn't need to do this. It's too much."

Anika shrugged. "Of course she didn't have to. She wanted to. Cecilia loved you, Eja. You were her *laotong*, her sister for a thousand years. Remember?" She patted her chignon. "Besides, we certainly don't need the money. I won't have some stranger pawing through her belongings or living in the house she loved. So it's settled."

"But I already have a condo."

Anika had seen my shoebox home. CeCe's place was five times larger and twenty times more luxurious.

"We'll put it on the market right away. Bolin can handle that. Use the money to pay upkeep on this place. Makes sense, no?"

Before I could answer, she sped into CeCe's bathroom and opened the medicine cabinet. "Grab one of her tote bags, will you Eja? We need to clean out this shelf." Anika dumped several prescription bottles in the bag.

"Maybe you should leave that, Mrs. Swann. It might be evidence tampering."

Anika Swann lost her ethereal look. "Frankly, I don't care. If the police find antidepressants, they'll swear that my daughter killed herself. Say she was despondent."

"They'd love a simple solution," I agreed.

"They won't get the chance. Cecilia got these when she was seeing that therapist about her acrophobia." She pointed to the vial. "See. Wesley Townsend. He's a friend of Bolin's from some business group. Cecilia saw him for years, for all the good it did her. She was still scared out of her wits by anything higher than a stiletto."

"Oh, yeah. I remember that guy. CeCe liked him at first. Then something changed her mind. Might be a good idea to question him."

Anika furrowed her perfect brow. "Hmm. Better let Bolin set it up. You know how touchy doctors can be. Just keep my son away from him. Dem acts like the Grand Inquisitor and gets everyone's back up. This calls for a woman's touch." She brightened. "I know. We'll do it together."

"Yes. No. I guess so."

As a rule, I'm fairly glib, but the events of the past two days had confounded me. I needed time to plan a strategy and collect my thoughts—about Deming Swann.

I SPENT THE evening in my own home, cuddling with Cato. Admittedly, it was a far cry from the opulence of CeCe's place, but the little spaniel seemed grateful for lodging. My head was buzzing from the day's revelations. Was it possible that I now owned CeCe's grand residence? Anika's calm assessment of Deming was another jolt.

I dozed off, wondering why in the world he'd protect me when he'd always considered me a pest and worse. Hours later, the shrieking phone awakened me from a particularly satisfying dream.

"I've got news."

"What . . .?" I groped blindly for my alarm clock. "Do you realize what time it is?"

"Stop whining." Deming's crisp tones were unmistakable. "Put some coffee on. I'll be right over. This can't wait."

He disconnected before my synapses began to fire. It was barely five a.m., and even the sun had the sense to catch extra zzzs before rising. Cato gave me a sharp look with disgust written all over it. CeCe regarded beauty rest with the reverence some give to Sacred Writ. She'd probably never risen before six in her privileged life.

I leapt into the shower and did a modified beauty routine. I'm no sybarite, but I have my pride. Deming Swann would never see me with bed head if I could help it.

When the buzzer rang, I was ready. I wouldn't win any beauty prizes, but at least my hair and clothes were clean. He, on the other hand, strode into my living room looking like cover art for *GQ* magazine. I caught my breath as I surveyed him: black leather jacket, white turtleneck, and disturbingly tight jeans. His thick dark hair was combed straight back and tamed with a touch of gel. To his credit, Deming came bearing gifts. He clutched a red porcelain pan of some heavenly substance.

"Here," he said, thrusting the plate at me. "Breakfast."

"Wow! Where'd you get this?"

He shrugged off his jacket and scowled. "Po made it. Mother insisted that I take it with me. She knows how you like spinach quiche."

This was the Deming I knew so well: gruff, gorgeous, and far from gracious.

I waved him to a seat at my small dining table and poured each of us an espresso.

"Get any sleep last night?" I asked.

He snarled an answer. "Why? There'll be plenty of time for that later on."

I arranged the quiche on a serving tray and dug in. No sense pretending around a man who knew for certain what a chowhound I was. Between forkfuls of egg, I prodded him. "Okay. You've got my attention. Let's hear it. What's this big news flash?"

His eyes shot angry sparks my way. If Cato had been on the job instead of snoring in bed, Deming's tender ankles would have stung.

"Swann Security did the matchup. You know, on the residents of that condo."

"Yeah?" A chill started at my scalp and traveled quickly down my body. Something big was coming, and I wasn't ready.

Deming paced himself, parsing each word as only a gifted lawyer can. "My sister knew one of the residents. Very well."

He slowly forked a mouthful of quiche into his mouth while I inhaled caffeine and reached for more. If he expected drama, Deming was disappointed. I sipped the heavenly brew and stayed silent. Two could play this game. My only challenge was staying awake.

I thought of CeCe, envisioned her diving into that quiche, spreading crumbs everywhere. She never worried about it, never gave it a second thought. Now here we were cleaning up after her, making things right. Deming and I.

I didn't mind. After all, we were the terrible trio, scourge of playground bullies everywhere. CeCe and I stayed even closer as adults, sharing triumphs and tragedies about the men in our lives. Deming went his own way, cutting a swath through the social register, pulverizing females in five states.

Everything had changed in the blink of an eye. My best friend, loving, generous CeCe was gone. The Terrible Trio was now two with one more service to perform: avenging her death. Like it or not, Deming and I were partners, and I needed information.

"Tell me. Who was it?" I grabbed his arm before he could shovel any more food into his mouth. "Please, Deming."

His face flushed, whether from fatigue or emotion, I couldn't tell. Deming removed my hand and said the name.

"Jem Russell. That bastard lives in the building, and he murdered my sister."

Seven

"JEM RUSSELL! Are you sure?"

Deming narrowed his eyes and growled. "Apartment 2810. That's how sure I am. When I finish breakfast, I'm heading over there. I'll beat a confession out of him if I have to." His muscles tensed, leaving no doubt in my mind that he'd do just that. I recalled my promise to Anika.

"Think for a minute. Jem would love brawling with you. He might even win."

"You're insane." Deming erupted like Vesuvius. "I'll have you know . . ."

I grabbed his arm. "Yeah, yeah, yeah. I get it. You've got black belts up the wazoo. So does he, if I remember correctly. You met at a karate competition, right?"

He nodded. For a moment, his eyes held the same bruised look they'd had in my fantasy. "Don't you see? I introduced them. I brought that killer into my sister's life."

His pain and guilt were palpable. No use reminding him that CeCe fell for Jem the second she'd laid eyes on him. Even I could tell he was a loser—a sexy, charming cad without an ounce of ambition. Bolin and Anika pleaded, even tried paying him off. Nothing worked. Cecilia Swann had gotten what she wanted all her life, and she wanted Jem Russell.

"They'd been seeing each other recently. At least I think so." I released his arm and sat down. "Wait a minute. That doesn't explain the engagement ring or this Raven character."

Deming wore his game face now, a smooth impenetrable mask that could air-condition hell.

"So what? Russell probably calls himself Raven. Not that he's a big reader. Comic books are more his style than poetry." He threw down the fork and grabbed his jacket. "For your information, he'd been calling her for the past three weeks. We got a printout of her cell phone records."

"Hold on. I'm going with you." I raced into the bedroom and wrestled that worthless cur Cato into his harness.

Deming stood in the doorway glowering at me. "No way. Both of you stay right here. Don't think for one minute that we're some kind of team."

"I promised your mother."

He gritted his teeth and uttered a particularly vile obscenity. Like every other male in existence, her surly son adored Anika.

"Move it." Deming charged the front door with his usual charm. "He's probably sleeping off a drunken binge right now. We need to catch him."

We rode to the lobby in sullen silence, each of us spoiling for confrontation. Cato was the only exception. He cavorted about the front desk in surprisingly high spirits. I saw Deming's Porsche parked in front of the building next to a fire hydrant. He'd escaped a ticket, but even Deming couldn't escape every downside of parking near a hydrant. Cato happily decorated the Porsche's tire and the hydrant.

"Don't you even try to obey the law?" I pointed to the No Parking sign. "You're an officer of the court, for heaven's sake."

He shrugged. "I care about some laws, like the ones against murder. Everything else is up for grabs."

Despite our tiff, good manners triumphed. Deming opened the passenger-side door for me and scooped Cato into the backseat with one fluid motion.

His arrogance infuriated me. How dare he act as if I were invisible? Typical. He'd done that since we were children.

"By the way," I said. "How'd you get that phone information? Don't you need a subpoena or something?"

He gave me the full eye roll. "Not when your head of security is the former police commissioner, you don't."

"Okay. What about her other calls? Anything interesting?"

"Who knows? No time to analyze it yet." He laughed. "My dad's on the case, so don't worry. It'll get done right."

No doubt about that. When Bolin Swann spoke, everyone jumped. CeCe was the apple of his eye, but he'd been much tougher on Deming. Maybe that was some father-son thing. CeCe had an entire comic routine called "my dad and his lectures." Apparently, settling Deming down into family mode had been number one on Bolin's to do list. He'd failed to convince his son of the urgency.

I shuddered as we sped through the financial district, reliving Sunday's horror. It was early, barely seven a.m., and most of the banks and buildings were still deserted. When we reached Jem Russell's building, I suppressed a strong desire to bow my head and howl. The area had been tidied up. No crime scene tape or lurking press to torment us. If only the crater in my heart could vanish as easily. I raised my head slowly, looking toward that roof garden, thirty-two stories up. I was transfixed, unable to look away. I felt CeCe's terror as she faced the end, and I prayed. *Please God maybe she didn't suffer. Maybe she was already gone before she fell. Please God.*

Tears coursed down my cheeks in rivulets of grief. I tried to suppress them before they became sobs. That's when it happened. Deming put his arms around me and gently stroked my hair. I felt the supple leather of his jacket, the strength of his grip, and the comfort of his words. Gone was his cynicism. Tenderness replaced his anger.

"Don't cry." His lips brushed my forehead. "We can still help her. Help her clear her name." He lifted my chin and stared into my eyes. "We'll find who hurt her. I promise you that. And when we do, I'll deal with him."

At that moment, my doubts vanished. I made a silent vow to CeCe and St. Thomas More. Until this was over, she'd never rest in peace. Neither would I.

THE CONCIERGE was nervous. She blinked furiously, arranging and rearranging every pen and paper clip on her desk while Deming and I waited patiently.

"I can't answer any questions," she said, in a wobbly high-pitched voice. "I'll lose my job. Legal warned me."

Deming nodded and produced a notarized document from Swann Industries. It was standard, a hold harmless agreement absolving the property owners and building management of liability for CeCe's death.

The woman blinked as she perused it. "You mean you don't want to sue us? I'm no lawyer, but that's what it seems to say."

Another patient smile from Deming, accompanied by a nod. "Of course, we won't quote you on any information you share. This is strictly between us."

"But your client . . ."

The muscles in his jaw tensed. "My sister was the victim. My twin sister. My only clients are those who loved her."

I chimed in. "We just wanted to know your procedures. About the rooftop gardens, I mean." I saw indecision and fear flit through her mind, accompanied by a shot of empathy.

"Please," I said. "Cecilia Swann was my dearest friend. We think she was murdered."

The concierge reared back, opening her mouth so wide I feared she would scream.

"Murdered! But how can that be? We heard it was a suicide."

Deming flinched. "That's untrue. My sister came to visit a close friend who lives here."

"Here? One of our residents?" A hint of caution crept into her eyes.

A distraction was definitely called for. It didn't require much acting; tears filled my eyes whenever I thought of CeCe. Fortunately, Deming played right along. He flourished another of those pocket squares, put his arm around me, and blotted my tears.

"It's okay, Eja. Once we speak with Jem, you'll feel much better." He leaned forward. "James Russell, apartment 2810. Will you buzz him? Please."

Hysterical women are bad for business; they breed uncertainty and confusion among paying customers. As tenants exited the elevators, briefcases in hand, they eyed our little tableau with undisguised interest. The befuddled concierge made a quick decision to put public relations over privacy. I stifled the sobs and smiled bravely through my tears.

"Let me ring him," she said, as she shoved a thick sheaf of co-op regulations our way.

Within two minutes we boarded the elevator for our meeting with Jem.

WE'D ALMOST reached his floor before I realized—I was still clutching Deming's hand. After exchanging startled looks, we retreated to opposite corners of the elevator.

Just thinking of Jem Russell made me crazy. My heartbeat scaled Everest before beginning the downward trek to normalcy. The last encounter I'd had with him had ended badly. How polite should a woman be to the selfish, scheming scoundrel who breaks her best friend's heart then laughs about it? Jem sailed blissfully through life, fueled by boyish charm and a line of blarney that would shame a leprechaun. I had no idea how he'd weaseled back into CeCe's life, but I'd soon find out.

As we stepped off the elevator, Deming donned his inscrutable face. I'd seen that look in court when he represented some corporate scumbag demanding leniency. If Jem Russell hurt CeCe, I'd demand the death penalty myself. Hell, I'd administer it. Otherwise, we needed his cooperation.

"Remember our plan," I said. "Be cool."

"Plan?" Deming's eyes were opaque.

"The tribute. I'll tell Jem I'm writing a commemorative tribute for your family." I gritted my teeth to avoid screeching at him. "We went over this last night."

He folded his arms, looking like a handsome mule. "That's your plan. Not mine."

"Your father didn't think so." I squeezed his shoulder. "Come on. Give it a try."

Bringing Bolin into the mix was a low but effective blow. Deming gave me a brusque, grudging nod and sped down the corridor.

Before we knocked, Jem Russell, clad in rumpled terry robe and striped pajamas, flung open his door and waved us in. Despite his attire, Jem's demeanor had a kind of dignity. He stood with his arms outstretched, a tragic sculpture frozen in time. For a moment, I almost believed that his grief was genuine.

"Deming, Eja, come in. Believe it or not, I just heard." He gestured toward his living room. "Please come in."

Deming took one step forward, balling up his fists. "You mean you didn't know? The media certainly gave it enough coverage."

Jem gave his charming shrug. "You know me—totally self-absorbed."

"We hoped you'd help us," I said, stepping between them. "I'm compiling a tribute for the family. After all, you knew CeCe as well as anyone."

Jem slicked back his auburn curls. "Yeah, I guess. I mean, I'll do anything to help. It's just . . . I still can't believe it. Why would CeCe kill herself?"

"That's still being investigated," I said. "What did she tell you that morning, Jem? Anything that aroused your suspicions?"

He plopped into a mustard leather lounger. "Huh? Forgive me for sounding dense, but I didn't see her that day. I haven't seen CeCe for two weeks."

Deming stood propped against the wall, his hazel eyes glued to Jem's face. "Oh. We hoped you'd spoken with her or something. As you can imagine, this is hard for my parents. It's killing my mom."

Jem closed his eyes and swayed back and forth. "Anika. Oh God, I need to call her."

He hadn't answered the question, and that made me curious. "So you guys hadn't spoken? CeCe told me you were back in town. In fact, she wanted to invite you to brunch with us that day."

One of Jem's strengths is mental agility. He read the storm signals and deftly called a different play.

"I've got coffee ready," he said. "CeCe bought me one of those Nespresso machines. You know the kind, Eja. Housewarming gift."

"Great! Point me to the kitchen, and I'll fix some." I bustled into the galley kitchen and powered up the machine. Deming stayed in his perch, a winged predator stalking his prey. He used a jot of silence, his favorite weapon to unnerve Jem.

"Were you two dating again?" Deming asked, his voice a silky purr. "We found a picture of you at her place." He waved the crotch shot at Jem.

"Nah. Nothing serious. Just friends. I can't believe she kept that thing. We were goofing around. You know how it is."

Deming took one step forward. "No. How is it?"

I played hostess by bringing both men a round of espresso. Jem downed his in one big gulp. Good thing I'd given him a saucer. His hand was shaking.

"How long have you been back in Boston?" I asked. "I thought we'd lost you to Las Vegas."

Jem had bright blue eyes that he knew how to use. He trained them on me and shrugged. "Vegas! That place gets old in a hurry. Makes you appreciate your roots."

Properly translated, he'd probably left Nevada under a cloud. Jem was used to that. With an endless supply of wealthy widows, he was golden. Throw a disgruntled husband or lover into the mix, and things got dicey.

Deming replaced his cup and made his move. "Cecilia died in this building. Why would she come here if not to meet you?"

I'd seen the good, bad, and ugly of James Russell. His puzzled expression seemed genuine this time.

"Gee. I don't know. That's what got me. Her going out on that rooftop and all. Last time I saw her, I tried to coax her out there. It's real nice in the spring. Romantic, you know. Anyhow, she got halfway through the door and bolted. Vertigo acted up, I guess. She dragged me to that shrink's office one time. Moral support, she called it." Jem shrugged. "I just hung out with the receptionist."

"Did she seem depressed when you two spoke?" I touched his hand to steady it.

"Hell no! She was on top of the world. Something about a big announcement. Promotion of some sort." He scratched his head again. "At least I think it was about work."

"Nothing specific?" I asked. "You know how CeCe got when she was excited."

Jem Russell hung his head. "Tell you the truth, I kind of tuned her out. See, I had this business deal cooking . . ."

Deming's muscles tensed. "You wanted money, didn't you?"

"No, no. You got me wrong. We'd have been partners. Fifty-fifty."

"How much did my sister give you?" Deming's voice was more of a growl.

Jem leapt to his feet and began pacing. "That's just it. She didn't give me a dime. We planned to meet Sunday night to firm things up. I hung around the bar for two hours, but she never showed."

Deming clenched his fists as if he were aching to use them. "You have witnesses, of course?"

"Wait just a damn minute. You think I killed CeCe? That's really sick, man. I loved your sister. Maybe I didn't treat her right but . . ."

"Maybe?" Deming was in front of him in two long strides. "You broke her heart, humiliated my family, and you have the gall to say that."

Jem hung his head in a rare moment of self-reflection. He spun around and stood toe-to-toe with Deming. "Listen here, big brother. I did her a damn favor. I wasn't good enough for you sister and everyone knew it but CeCe."

I intervened before things degenerated into bloodshed. "Hey, you two. This is no time to be settling old scores. The important thing here is CeCe."

Deming growled an unintelligible reply and stalked back to the other side of the room.

"What else, Raven?" I asked.

"Huh?" Jem looked genuinely perplexed.

"Raven. Isn't that what she called you?"

He laughed and scratched his ear. "Are you kidding? CeCe called me a lot of things but not that. Does it mean something?"

I hung my head in submissive female mode. Given Jem's antediluvian concept of women, it worked every time.

"Nothing special. CeCe called her fiancé that."

"Fiancé? You're kidding? She didn't act like she was in love with anyone." He licked his lips. "Not around me, anyhow."

In a flash, Deming closed the distance between them and pounced. "Bastard! That's my sister you're talking about." With one violent shove, he grabbed the collar of Jem's robe and knocked him to the floor. By the time I got over there, they were wrestling on the floor, locked in mortal combat. Kicks, punches, and plenty of oaths were exchanged, but I didn't see blood. That seemed like a good omen.

"Cut it out, you guys. Think of CeCe." I folded my arms, summoned my meanest frown, and waved the printout at them. "According to these condo rules, they keep that rooftop locked. Only tenants can access it."

That stopped both combatants. They rolled apart, gasping for breath as my words sunk in. CeCe must have been meeting someone; otherwise she couldn't have accessed the roof. She'd hardly choose that spot to end her life on the off chance that it would be unlocked.

Deming sat up as the message sunk in.

Jem did the same. "Hold on! She wasn't meeting me. I can prove where I was Sunday morning." His confidence faltered as he met Deming's murderous glance.

"Oh, yeah?" I said. "Where were you? Put up or shut up."

Deming said nothing. He seemed to know the answer already.

Jem stood up, adjusted his clothes, and turned away. "I was with someone. A girl."

I knew immediately it was the truth. No sane man would invent that story with Deming's punishing fists nearby. "Who is this . . . woman?"

He shrugged. "You don't know her. It doesn't matter anyway. I didn't hurt CeCe."

Deming straightened his jacket and nodded to me. "Come on, Eja. We're out of here."

"Wait!" Jem Russell held out his hand. "I want to help. I'll do anything. Please."

Before Deming hustled me out the door, I locked eyes with Jem. "I'll call you."

Eight

WE RODE IN silence to the lobby, each of us absorbed in our thoughts. Deming's mood was turbulent. There'd be hell to pay if Cato had munched on the Porsche's leather seats for a breakfast snack. Luckily, we found the little devil nestled in the backseat sound asleep.

"Not your finest hour," I told Deming, "although CeCe would have loved seeing you roll around the floor with Jem. What were you thinking?"

His eyes narrowed as he spit out a response. "I don't regret one thing. Mind your own business."

I fastened the seat belt, trying mightily to contain my rage. "You don't get it! This *is* my business. I'm part of this, whether you like it or not. Deal with it."

"You are the most stubborn woman . . ." Deming started a rant that lasted for two blocks.

"What next?" I asked, with my sweetest smile.

His expression hinted that he planned to dump Cato and me at the earliest opportunity. "I'll drop you off. I'm meeting Jake for lunch."

"No problem," I said. "I'm starving."

"You aren't up to it," he said, clutching the steering wheel. "Jake's got the preliminary autopsy findings for us. I can't have you causing a scene in the restaurant."

"I promise. No scene. It's early yet, anyway. Let's drop Cato off with Jaime."

Deming stared at me with menace in those hazel eyes. "My mom told you, didn't she? I guess you'll be moving in there soon, taking this mutt with you."

The anger in his voice surprised me.

"I . . . I didn't ask for anything, Deming. Why? Does that bother you so much? I'm not trying to take her place."

"I know." He shook himself. "Don't mind me, Eja. Losing her . . . it's like a knife in my gut. Twins are part of each other. Another self."

It was unsettling to witness such naked vulnerability. For a moment I feared that Deming might weep, but by the time he swung into the driveway of the Tudor, he was as stoic as ever.

"Give him to me. I'll find Jaime." He reached into the backseat for Cato's lead.

I said nothing, but Cato had other ideas. He lunged at Deming, leaving a vicious tear in his fine leather jacket. Perhaps Cato was also acting out his grief. From the string of curses Deming hurled at the spaniel, he wasn't buying that excuse. Leave it to CeCe to find a one-woman dog with a bad attitude.

He took his sweet time situating Cato. I leaned back and rested my eyes, envisioning the battle plan we'd crafted last night. Our lunch with Jake would provide vital information. Like it or not, we'd know how CeCe died. Why she died was another matter entirely. Was Jem telling the truth, or had he lured CeCe to that rooftop? He was a lying, cheating cretin, but try as I might, I couldn't conjure up a motive. Jem hoped to worm money out of CeCe, and knowing her kind heart, he probably would have succeeded. In that scenario, killing the golden goose made no sense. Unless—was it possible? With his track record, Jem Russell was the perfect patsy. Had someone set him up?

I screamed as a hand touched my arm. I hadn't seen or heard Deming until he was sitting next to me. Maybe I'd done more dozing than planning. "Ready?" I asked. "Cato's okay, I presume."

He grunted and aimed the Porsche toward Arlington Street. Against all odds, Deming snagged a parking space across from Legal Sea Foods. I love the place, but it seemed an unlikely choice for the elegant Mr. Swann. He's more a Clio kind of guy.

"Yum," I said. "I love the bluefish here. They do it in this mustard dill sauce that . . ."

Deming yawned. His rudeness was nothing new, although it seemed wildly at odds with the spurts of tenderness I'd just witnessed. In a way, it was comforting: I understood this version of my childhood nemesis. That other guy, gentle and loving, was a total stranger.

He swung his long legs out of the Porsche and sped over to the passenger side.

"Come on, Sleeping Beauty. Do I have to carry you?"

"Don't bother. I'm fine, thank you very much." I straightened my shoulders and launched toward the restaurant at a dignified trot. A long line of hungry patrons had already queued up in the waiting area, but Jake Harris was nowhere to be seen. Deming glided to the front desk and conferred with the hostess. Despite groans and glares from the masses, we were immediately ushered to a choice booth where Dr. Jake Harris sat.

"Hey, Dem," Jake said. His dark eyes lit up when he saw me, and he rose immediately. "Eja, what a treat! Dem didn't tell me you'd be here."

Dr. Jacob Harris was quite a hottie. He was Deming's height with a broad build that was more football than fencing. His hair fell in soft ringlets that framed a smiling face with perfect white teeth.

"Ignore her, Jake. She's just an observer." Deming laced his hands around a steaming cup of tea and cautiously sipped. He plunged into the fray as soon as we ordered.

"Well. Did you get anything?"

Jake lowered his eyes. "Yes." He withdrew a folder from his briefcase and hesitated.

"It isn't easy to hear. Try to pretend it's some television show." He took a deep breath and read the information in a dry doctor's voice. "Okay. Official cause of death is the hard part. There's a lot of medical gobbledygook that precedes the final conclusion."

Deming clutched his fork as if it were a weapon. "Go on. Massive trauma or something like that. I can take it."

"That's just the thing." Jake paused. "CeCe didn't die from the fall."

Despite my promise to Deming, I felt a flush that went all the way from my toes to my head. *Don't faint, Eja. Remain calm.*

"What are you saying?" Deming croaked. "That must be a mistake."

Jake shook his head. "No. CeCe was dead before she fell. The police are on that rooftop right now, looking for forensic evidence. Your sister was murdered, Dem."

"Murdered!" Deming shuddered as his friend continued reading the report.

"Of course, they'll do toxicological tests, but that won't change anything." Jake's warm brown eyes oozed compassion. "Someone must have lured her there to kill her."

"That explains a lot," I said in a small voice that even I didn't recognize. "I knew she wouldn't harm herself."

Deming seemed stunned, his eyes glazed and unfocused. He stood abruptly, upending his water glass. "My parents. Do they know?"

Jake shrugged. "I think that lieutenant—Euphemia Bates—was on her way over."

"I've got to go. Take Eja home, will you?" Deming staggered toward the exit, oblivious to everything.

I pushed back my chair, preparing to follow until Jake Harris stopped me with a gentle touch.

"Let him go, Eja. It won't do any good when he's like this. Better that we finish our lunch and plan our next move."

"But . . ."

He was right. I knew it, but I still felt guilty. CeCe blamed it on the nuns. They loved inducing guilt in their hapless charges. Thrived on it.

"Were there pictures? Of the roof, I mean, not CeCe."

"Some. Enough to prove that no one could fall accidentally. A mesh fence borders the edge of the roof. It's at least three feet high. Too high for any accidental fall."

I mouthed a silent prayer of thanks that my friend had been spared the worst. At least she didn't feel the terror of falling into space. That was a blessing. It wouldn't take much to push CeCe's willowy form over the ledge. A man, even a strong woman could do it. Jem Russell's bright eyes flashed in my mind. He was more likely to charm a woman to death than murder her. Still, Jem was a taker, ruthless in his own way. Maybe she'd turned him down. Maybe he'd lost his temper. Lots of maybes and no certainty.

"What about her shrink?" I asked. "Wesley Townsend, that's it. Anika said he's some type of family friend."

Jake gave me that neutral look that they must bottle and sell at med school. "Let's not get ahead of ourselves, Eja. I'm not sure what help he'd be."

I finished my bluefish, taking care to wipe dill sauce from the corners of my mouth. Hottie or not, Dr. Jacob Harris was a royal pain. Surely, a graduate of Harvard Medical School wasn't this obtuse. Was he pretending for some reason?

"Listen, Jake. Let's get one thing straight. We can't afford to wait for the cops, or to stand on ceremony with anyone. For all we know, this Townsend might be Raven. Maybe CeCe dumped him, or threatened him with a restraining order. Maybe he's a quack."

Suddenly he laughed. Dr. Jacob Harris guffawed so loudly that heads turned. "You are really something. Cecilia was lucky to have a friend as loyal as you. Anyone would be."

He reached across the table and squeezed my hand. "I get the message, okay? I don't know this guy Townsend personally, only by reputation. He's solid. Well respected. How about this? I'll do some digging. Talk with some of the guys I went to med school with who might know him. You need ammunition before you tackle him. Okay?"

"It'll have to be." I gathered my things as Jake paid the bill. "Can you drop me off at the Swanns' house? If not, I'll grab a cab."

"No problem. I plan to pop in there anyhow to see how Anika's holding up."

"What about Bolin?"

Jake unlocked his Jeep and helped me in. "Bolin's tough. He'll channel his grief into action. Then, watch out. Whoever did this better be saying his prayers right now."

A CLUSTER OF cars blanketed the Swanns' driveway. I recognized a patrol car and Mia Bates' black sedan. As always, Deming's Porsche was splayed defiantly across the path, making a statement.

"Come on," Jake said. "Things must be heating up."

I grabbed his arm. "Wait a minute. Who's that woman?" I pointed to a sinewy blonde who appeared in the doorway, draped over Deming. Her long manicured nails moved up and down his arm as if she owned it.

"Oh. That's Pam Schwartz. She's the managing partner at CeCe's law firm." Jake surveyed her from stem to well-toned stern. "She and Dem are close."

My reaction made no sense. I had no claim on Deming Swann. One simmering night between the sheets—if it even happened—didn't confer any rights. Somehow my blood pressure and heartbeat didn't understand that. My insides plummeted straight to my basement as I watched him hold her close and stroke her hair. My faded makeup, chipped nails, and windblown hair were no match for such blonde perfection.

"She's older than him. In her forties at least."

Jake put his arm around me and squeezed. "So what? You know how crazy love is. Besides, Pam's a special case. Brilliant, sexy, and driven. A femme formidable." He chuckled. "Kind of like a female version of Dem himself."

"Love? I didn't realize . . ."

"I've known him for a long time, and lately he's changed. Must be

Pam's influence."

Jake guided me toward the front door. "Come on. Let's find Anika and leave these lovebirds alone."

Deming didn't look at all pleased to see me. His scowl was deep enough to darken the skies. "What are you doing here, Eja? I thought you'd gone home."

"Darling, you're being rude." His companion playfully elbowed his ribs. She stepped forward and shook my hand. "Eja Kane. I've heard so much about you I feel like we're old friends. I'm Pam Schwartz."

I felt shy and inadequate next to this womanly paragon. She was impeccably dressed, a corporate warrior; I was a midlist author in faded denim. Luckily, Jake ladled on the charm, and Pamela Schwartz soon forgot my existence.

"Why are you here?" Deming hissed. "My parents are in with the cops. Stay out of it."

That snapped me back to reality. Deming Swann could have his golden cougar for all I cared. Served him right. My goal was to help CeCe. Nothing more. I ignored him, brushed past Po, and knocked on the heavy walnut door to the study.

Bolin appeared and waved me inside. "Eja. You've probably heard the news. Lieutenant Bates was just briefing us." He gestured toward the sofa, where Anika sat dry-eyed and alert.

Euphemia Bates nodded to me. "Nice seeing you, Ms. Kane. I was just saying that you raised some very good points yesterday morning. Your faith in your friend was amazing." She spread her hands. "The reality of big city policing is too many victims, too little time. But we get there eventually. Yes, we do."

Anika clutched my arm as if to steady herself. "Tell us, Lieutenant. Do you have any suspects yet, or a motive?"

The language of crime sounded odd coming from those elegant lips. Bolin Swann walked over and put his hands on his wife's shoulder.

Mia managed a wintry smile. "Actually, we have a very promising lead. Someone with motive and opportunity who knew your daughter quite well."

Bolin stood soldier-straight, his hands balled into tight fists. "Who is it, Lieutenant?"

"I think we all know who she's talking about." Deming had noiselessly entered the room. "Jem Russell. That's the name. Right,

Lieutenant?"

Euphemia Bates rose to her full height and faced Deming. "I keep those things to myself, Mr. Swann. Avoids complications."

I noticed that Pamela Schwartz was shadowing him, her eyes slithering up and down his body like a serpent as she murmured into his ear. The startled look on his face convinced me it was some lewd, anatomically improbable suggestion.

"I thought you had an urgent appointment," Mia Bates said to her with an unconvincing grin. "You lawyers are all so busy."

Pamela tossed her perfect bob to the side. "Of course, but nothing's more important than Cecilia. If I can offer any more insights . . ."

"I'd prefer to speak privately," Mia said. "In your office if possible. How's your schedule tomorrow at eight?"

"In the morning?" Her eyes registered shock.

Deming gave a rakish grin. "You see, Lieutenant, Pamela doesn't do anything before nine." They locked eyes. "At least on the business front."

I turned away and counted to ten. Twice. How dare he parade his conquest before Anika? And me. CeCe told lots of tales about Pamela Schwartz, none of them flattering. She'd named her she-wolf, a predator who'd strip the meat from a rival's bones then send flowers. If Deming liked that sort, so be it. They deserved each other.

"You look tired, Leda." Bolin bent down and kissed his wife's cheek. "Nap?"

There it was again, that exquisite bond between husband and wife. You'd think Deming would have learned something from his parents, or that I'd stop dreaming.

"Go on, Mom. I'll finish up with the lieutenant." Deming turned to Mia. "Eja and I were at that building today. We have something to share."

Pamela's face ballooned into a major pout until she gave me the once over. After starting my day at five, I was more waif than wanton. No woman would call me a threat.

"If you're sure you don't need me," she said, "I'll be at the office."

Jake Harris followed Pamela out the door, using Harvard charm to jolly her along.

As Bolin led her upstairs, Anika stretched out her hand. "Eja, call me tomorrow. Okay?"

Nine

EUPHEMIA BATES took her time, easing into a leather wing chair and examining her notes. A thirty-something sergeant with a walrus mustache sat behind her, armed with a laptop and a miniscule tape recorder.

"Okay Mr. Swann, why don't you start? Tell us what happened today."

Deming acted like a racehorse at the starting gate, frothing at the mouth and pawing the ground. His zeal to neutralize Jem Russell was unnerving.

"Ms. Kane and I went to his apartment and . . ."

"Hold on." Mia held her hand out traffic-cop style. "How'd you know he lived in that building? You never mentioned it when we met."

Deming maintained his composure by evasion and half-truths.

"My father told me. He stayed with my mother, and I went in his stead." He nodded to me. "Ms. Kane knows him too, so she went along."

Mia crossed long, elegant legs and nodded. She wore that flat cop look like a custom suit.

"We confronted him, and he admitted that he'd been seeing my sister. Trying to get money from her." Sparks flew from his hazel eyes. "He even said he'd tried to lure her out on the roof before."

"That sound about right, Ms. Kane?"

I met Deming's withering gaze and shrugged. Lying to the police was not my style. Misleading them was equally dangerous. If Jem Russell was innocent, they'd waste valuable time while the real killer skated.

"I'm not sure he *lured* her. You have to understand Jem, Lieutenant. He's a facile liar who barely knows the truth when it hits him. To me, his story was probably true, at least most of it."

A neutral nod from Mia convinced me that she must play a fantastic game of poker.

"We did some checking on him, once we found the connection

with Ms. Swann." She donned reading glasses and read from a printout. "Seems he had some trouble in Las Vegas. Local PD was involved but let it slide."

"What kind of trouble?" Deming asked.

The corners of her mouth twisted in an impish grin. "The usual. Parting rich women from their money. In this case, it was a rich, married woman whose husband was not amused."

Deming reached into his jacket pocket and produced the crotch shot. "Here's the kind of man he is. My sister took this last month. Can you imagine?"

She gave that photo a thorough examination. "I see. No wonder he's successful with the ladies. Doesn't make him a killer though. Just a sleaze. Tell me this, did he confess?"

"Of course not!" Deming threw up his hands. "After I throttled him, he came up with some lame alibi about spending Sunday with another woman."

"You believed him, Ms. Kane. How come?"

I paused. Words are my chosen profession, but I struggled to explain myself.

"I've seen Jem lie before. He's a simple-celled creature, kind of like an amoeba. Always figuring the angles. What's best for him. Why kill CeCe before getting what he wanted?"

"She turned him down! Then he got mean." Deming clenched his fists until the knuckles paled. "He lured her out there and . . ."

"Hold on," I said. "Think of that security tape. She looked happy! If she expected a confrontation, she'd look tense. Plus, she invited him to join us for brunch."

"Interesting," Mia said. "It still doesn't answer this question: Why choose that building and why the roof?"

Neither one of us had an answer. Even Jem said CeCe balked at entering the roof garden. No surprise—her vertigo had been an ongoing battle since childhood. She'd been the only kid on the playground who avoided both the slide and monkey bars.

Mia looked at her notes and frowned. "This whole business about the roof garden bothers me. It's supposed to remain locked at all times, and only residents have keys. Limits access and avoids problems. Of course, if they're careless about it, no one in management will admit it." She smiled at Deming. "Lawsuits, you know."

My thoughts felt fuzzy and unfocused, as if I were navigating through a marshmallow haze.

"Wake up, Eja," Deming snorted. "Stop dillydallying."

"Sorry. Did I miss something?"

Mia shook her head. "I asked if Mr. Russell said anything incriminating. Anything at all."

Both of us said no.

"Okay then." Mia gathered her things and signaled to her sergeant. "I'll be in touch."

"Great move, Eja. Letting that murderer skate." Deming seethed like a boiling kettle. "I thought you were Cecilia's friend."

I bit back the feelings that welled up in me. Tears wouldn't help right now, so I substituted anger for angst.

"Fine. No more partnerships. Take your girlfriend with you next time. You're birds of a feather anyway."

"What? Are you daft?" Deming crossed the room and leaned down until we were nose to nose. "What's this girlfriend shit?"

I averted my head, refusing to meet his eyes. "Pamela Schwartz, that's what. Not too respectful, making out in front of your parents."

He laughed. The bastard laughed!

"Pam and I are old friends, if you must know. Served on a couple of ABA committees together. She's like that with all the guys. Loves flirting."

I ignored the sensation inching up my spine. His arms felt strong and comforting. So good. I fought the urge to lean in and get closer. Everything was suspended in time, floating toward a rainbow sky. Could it be true? Had Deming Swann, my childhood nemesis, made my heart flutter?

"What's wrong with you? Are you having some kind of fit?" Deming scrutinized me as if I were a circus freak. He backed away and flopped down on the sofa. "Everything's haywire. Someone killed my sister, and no one knows why. It's a disaster."

I bounced back to reality with a sudden brainstorm. "Time for more detective work. CeCe logged an incredible number of hours at the firm. Maybe she found out something—something incriminating."

Deming curled his lip. "What the hell does that mean? Did she mention anything about a litigant? Any threats from a coworker?"

I summoned my sweetest smile. "That's where your friend Pamela comes in. After all, she'd know that stuff. Isn't that what the managing partner does? Ask her."

He raked his fingers through his hair. "They worked together on some charities, but Pam's removed from the real action. She oversees the in-house side. You know, wills and trusts, estate planning, and taxes. CeCe liked trial work. It turned her on. Especially pro bono cases."

"She was a real tiger." Bolin Swann smiled as he spoke of his daughter. He'd slipped into the room while we were arguing. "I wanted her at Swann Industries, but she refused. Said she could do more good at the firm. Probably just as well. She and Deming were polar opposites. Went at it hammer and tongs about almost everything."

Deming nodded. "My sister was an idealist. Some of the shenanigans lawyers pull made her mad. We had a . . . disagreement . . . last month. Since then she'd avoided me. We barely spoke."

His eyes showed raw pain and something else. Guilt. Even as a child Deming valued control. Craved it. CeCe and I had fought him every step of the way, from playground games to college majors. Now when he needed it most, he was powerless to avenge his twin's murder. I felt a strange, unsettling urge to hold him close and comfort him. It quickly passed, leaving me confused and out of sorts.

"I still think you need to ask Pam," I said. "Snoop around the firm. I'll bet CeCe's paralegal and secretary know something."

"She's right, son." Bolin Swann spoke calmly but emphatically. "For all we know, Cecilia found something that wasn't right. She wouldn't just walk away from trouble. You know how she was. We called her the Avenger."

Deming folded his arms, bulldog style. "I'll speak with Pam, but I refuse to chat up the staff. I'm no good at that sort of thing. That's more Eja's department."

"Thanks. I think."

"Tomorrow an important visitor will stop by. Condolence call." Bolin managed a wry grin. "Before you ask, Deming, it's Prescott Lewis. He extended his sympathy to your mother, but asked if he could stop by. Naturally, I agreed."

"When? I want to be there."

Bolin's handsome face softened. "No, son. Let me handle this. I know how to deal with men like Prescott. Threats won't get you anywhere. You need finesse."

"May I make a suggestion?" I wasn't sure how he'd react, but I had to try. "Maybe you could tease him a bit about this Raven thing. You know, show him the ring and mention the inscription. Catch him off guard."

"Excellent, but I think I'll have Anika handle it. Prescott adores her, you know. He'd never suspect anything if she mentions it." Bolin rose and headed out the door. "Will you join us for dinner, Eja?"

"No, thanks. I need to get Cato and go home."

"Hold on," Deming said. "You can't use CeCe's flat until the locks are changed. It isn't safe."

"I almost forgot," Bolin said. "Anika had that done this morning." He sped over to his large bureau plat and retrieved a set of keys. "Here, Eja. I promised my wife I'd deliver these to you personally."

"Thanks. I'll catch a cab and leave you alone for now. Poor Cato will be lonely."

"No need." Jake Harris stuck his head in the doorway. "I'm going your way anyhow. Maybe we can have dinner or something."

Deming made a noise that sounded suspiciously like a growl. "Just a minute. I still have a few more questions for you, Jake."

"No problem, Dem. Shoot." Jake clapped his friend on the back and waited.

"Why did my sister want to see you? Was she sick or something?"

"Ah, come on. I can't violate medical privilege. You know that. You're a lawyer, for Christ's sake."

Deming whirled around and faced his friend. "Enough of a lawyer to know that privilege ends with the patient's death."

"Son . . ." Bolin Swann sounded a warning.

"CeCe never kept her appointment," Jake said. "I told you that already. But if you're asking about her frame of mind, I can only speculate. She seemed on top of the world. Never happier."

I turned to Bolin. "That brings us right back to Raven, whoever he is."

DINNER WITH DR. Jake was great therapy. I overcame my shyness, stopped moping about CeCe for a while, and had a good time. Even Cato liked the medicine man. He kept a civil distance from Jake but eschewed the usual round of growls and bites. That passed for puppy love in his book.

"Dem seems positive that Russell's our man." Jake raised his eyebrows. "Do you agree?"

I shrugged helplessly. "We have no real proof, and Jem never struck me as the violent type. Too much effort. He might break a woman's heart or rob her blind, but I don't see him doing this. CeCe liked him. She'd finally figured him out, but she still liked him."

"Hmm. Still stuck on this Raven stuff, aren't you? Even if you find him that might not prove anything." Jake sipped his scotch and looked pensive. "Funny that CeCe didn't tell you about him though. I thought she told you everything."

"Apparently not. She said she was in love, but that was no big deal. CeCe fell in love with a different guy every month."

He laughed. "You know, you're right. That engagement ring might help. Maybe the police can trace it or something."

I was no jewelry expert, but that ring looked old. Classic. If it was a family heirloom, we'd never trace it.

"Can't your dad help? You said he was a diamond merchant."

"Sadly, no. He passed three years ago. Finest man I ever knew, except for Bolin Swann." Jake looked down, avoiding my eyes.

We stayed silent for a bit, honoring the past. I hardly saw my own father. True to conventional wisdom, he'd remarried fast and moved away, as if my mother had never existed. Forty years of marriage dismissed. I thought about her every day, but now I had no one to share memories with. Only CeCe had cared.

"Enough of this sadness," Jake said, as we left the restaurant. "Do you need help moving your things? I'm stylistically challenged, but my back is strong."

I didn't answer right away. Couldn't. Moving into her flat was too final. Almost predatory. Despite Anika's wishes, the place wasn't even mine yet—legally or morally. CeCe would still inhabit her home until we found her murderer. Only then could she rest in peace.

"Thanks for the offer," I said, "but I'll take Cato to my place for a while. It's unseemly. Deming was right about that. Like expunging every trace of her."

Jake squeezed my hand. "I know. I think Anika sees it differently though. Almost as if you'd be keeping CeCe alive by living there. That's why she's so keen on it."

"Anika's in the denial stage. I guess I am too. Sometimes, when I get one of my brainstorms, I forget CeCe's gone, and I start to dial her number."

He nodded. "I know, but cut yourself some slack. It's only been a few days. I'm certainly no detective, but I keep wondering about motive. It makes no sense. Why would anyone want to harm her, even this Raven guy? It wasn't a shotgun wedding. People break up without resorting to violence."

He was right, of course. CeCe was a breakup specialist who pined for a while then quietly moved on. She'd never agree to meet someone she feared in a place that terrified her. The murderer knew a lot about CeCe: fears, friends, and what made her tick. It had to be someone close to her, a cunning, ruthless planner who traded on trust and exploited it. Even worse, it was someone cool enough to implicate that sad sack Jem Russell. This was no crime of passion. It was an execution.

When we reached the Tudor, Jake pointed toward the driveway. "Look who's here—good old Deming."

His Porsche was there, defying rules and good manners, hogging two parking spots.

"Want me to go up with you?" Jake asked.

I shrugged. "Naw. Cato probably has him treed by now anyway. I've got my keys. Deming can give the two of us a ride back to my place."

"Okay then." Jake leaned over and kissed my cheek. "Keep your chin up. I enjoyed dinner. You're everything CeCe said you were and more."

I EXCHANGED smiles with Jaime's replacement, an ample woman whose name eluded me. I admit it; my mind was focused on Deming Swann.

Control yourself. Stop acting like a child. You've known him thirty years! I shivered as memories of Sunday evening swirled in my head. *Forget it. It never happened. You were too drunk to remember anything.*

My heartbeat quickened as I sped down the corridor and fumbled with the lock. Damn! The new Medeco was as worrisome as the old one. I'd make a rotten burglar. Despite my attempts at stealth, Cato the Wonder Dog heard everything. A furious spate of barking erupted as my new roommate flung himself at the door. Right on cue, Deming turned the lock, draping himself against the doorjamb.

"About time you got back. What'd Jake do, have you for dessert?"

My face got that crimson hue I'd always loathed. Deming was masterful when it came to pushing my buttons. Over the years, he'd honed his skills on countless playing fields from grade school through graduate school. I chose hauteur over anger and responded in kind.

"Me? What about you? Pammy stand you up?"

His lips twitched into a half-sneer. Instead of a withering retort, he surprised me by laughing. "Touché, Eja. Come on in."

He seemed to have reached détente with Cato, through luck, bribery, or brute force. They eyed each other like opposing counsel in a contentious divorce and retired to opposite corners. I understood Deming, but Cato's behavior had me stumped. The feisty spaniel acted weird, bombarding me with doggy wags and kisses.

"Well, you certainly won him over," Deming said. "What's your secret?"

"Clean living and a pure heart." I walked toward the living room and stopped. It was so disheveled I felt like Dorothy after the tornado. "What the hell! Who did this?"

"You can thank the long arms of the law for the mess. Lieutenant Bates sent her minions over to search for clues. They carted a bunch of things away. Nothing important."

"What about the papers in her storage room?"

Deming gave a superior smirk. "They didn't ask, and I didn't volunteer. They teach you that in law school. I thought you'd know that."

"Where'd you stash them?"

He walked over to the bay window and pointed. "In the Porsche. Quite the elegant filing cabinet, wouldn't you say? Bates can't get at them without a search warrant, and I'll make sure she never gets one. Hiding in plain sight. That's something Sherlock Holmes would appreciate. Your idol."

As a member in good standing of the Baker Street Irregulars, I knew chapter and verse of anything in the canon. Deming Swann was merely an amateur. I whirled around, expecting to field another zinger. One look at Deming stopped me in my tracks.

He looked feverish, as if those hazel eyes might burn a hole in his heart. My throat felt parched and arid as I struggled to speak. Silence seemed an intolerable burden.

"What's next," I whispered, well aware of the double entendre. "What should we do?"

He turned toward the wet bar and poured two snifters of cognac. "Rémy Martin okay with you?"

I nodded, remembering what happened the last time we'd tried this.

Deming clinked glasses with me and sat down. "To truth." He looked into my eyes, searing my nether parts with one glance. "I propose that we review everything in those boxes. Are you game?"

"Of course." A sip of cognac scorched my throat, giving me false courage. *Self-control. That's all it takes. I can handle things. No problem. As long as he doesn't touch me.*

"It might take a while." He sat far away, at the opposite end of the long white couch. "Maybe all night."

Silence was my greatest ally. I didn't trust my voice.

"I'll run out to the Porsche and get the stuff." Deming leapt up in one fluid motion that made my heart race. His sculpted body, encased in tight black jeans, was a moving violation, possibly a felony. I was ready for a life of crime, willing to be a repeat offender.

As soon as the door slammed, I ran straight into CeCe's bathroom. My hair was a tangled mass of curls that no brush could adequately tame. I did my best by spritzing it with hair spray and dipping into CeCe's Kiehl's stash. A dab of shadow, slash of lipstick, and a pinch of blush completed my toilette. I was no beauty, but at least I looked better.

When the buzzer sounded, I hurried to the door. Deming stood there, but he wasn't alone. Bolin Swann was at his side.

Ten

"HOPE I'M NOT intruding, Eja," Bolin said. In jeans and a sweater, he looked like Deming's sibling, not his dad. Same tall, lean body, thick black hair, and sculpted features. Only the eyes were different. Bolin's Asian heritage was more prominent; Deming had only a slight upturn to his hazel eyes.

"Anika took a sleeping pill and went to bed. I was so restless, I just had to get out and do something." He slapped his son on the back. "Somehow I figured Dem would be over here with you."

Was this Providence intervening, saving me from a disastrous mistake? It made sense, although my raging hormones begged to differ. I phonied up a smile and welcomed Bolin.

"We were just getting started," I said. "Reviewing the documents, I mean."

My social skills had taken a nosedive. Passion will do that to you. That's what it was, pure animal passion, nothing more. It was no big mystery. Deming had been part of my life since I was five, and having him near reminded me of CeCe. They were twins, after all. Once my grief subsided, so would my longing for him. Maybe.

I turned to Bolin. "How about some cognac?"

"Sure. Think you can handle two lawyers, Eja? We may drive you crazy."

Deming and I locked eyes. The fire in his had vanished, but I was less sanguine.

"Don't worry. One writer versus two lawyers is a fair fight. Besides, we weren't doing anything special."

Deming had stuffed almost everything into CeCe's Vuitton suitcases. She had every style imaginable, from the hatbox to the steamer trunk. I'd chided her about that hatbox. I mean, who even wears hats these days? She'd shrugged it off, saying she was in her Grace Kelly phase at the time. The steamer trunk was another matter entirely. I'd always coveted that trunk. It conveyed impossibly romantic images of the Orient Express, first-class travel in the halcyon days when luxury, not security, was paramount. Even at auction, they cost a fortune. CeCe had once promised it to me, knowing I'd use it as a fabulous coffee table rather than a suitcase.

"Stop dreaming, Eja, or we'll never get done." Deming loomed over me; just close enough to brush my arm. An electric current shot through my skin, awakening every nerve ending I had. He felt it too. I could tell by the way he jumped back.

"Sorry. I was reminiscing."

Bolin's laugh was bittersweet. "Oh Lord, CeCe and her luggage. Does it ever bring back memories. That girl kept Vuitton in business, collecting every piece." His beautiful eyes filled, and he turned away. For a moment I'd forgotten why we were here. Her father had not.

We divided the spoils and each took a bag. I spread the contents of the hatbox on her dining room table and started sifting. In typical CeCe fashion, what had initially seemed like clutter had a strange sense of order. My stack contained financial transactions from her sessions with Dr. Wesley Townsend. She'd had plenty of them, two a week for three years. That added up to a tidy sum if my math skills were still functioning. Well over $100,000.

"Did this shrink do CeCe any good?" I asked Bolin. "She told me she quit going after a year, but these bills show that her last session was the Thursday before she died."

Bolin raised his thick dark brows. "I have no idea. Anika might know something. I just dealt with Wesley on boards and fundraisers. Seemed like an okay guy to me."

From the thundercloud on Deming's face, I sensed that he disagreed.

"Have an opinion, Deming?"

"You bet I do. That guy is a Freudian. You know, everything, including acrophobia, had a sexual meaning. Unresolved Electra complex is what he told my sister."

"What!" Bolin's scowl was a thing of beauty. "That's disgusting . . . how dare he. You know, he asked me and Anika to stop by. Said he liked to know the parents of his patients. I couldn't make it, but Anika went. She actually had a few sessions with him herself. He used hypnosis to help her stop smoking."

CeCe thought Wesley Townsend was a quack. At least that's what she'd told me. Why then had she paid his ridiculous fees for three years? It made as much sense as her willingness to meet someone on that rooftop. I bundled the paperwork back into the hatbox, determined to have that chat with Anika as soon as possible.

I sipped my cognac and thought about the gun. It belonged with Euphemia Bates, no matter what Deming said. I knew it and so did he. Suppose someone had used it in a crime? Something CeCe witnessed. That might explain the whole sad story. There was another possibility too foolish to contemplate: Had CeCe used that gun herself?

"We found something else the other day," I said. "It's up to you guys, but I think it belongs with Lieutenant Bates."

Deming shot me a look so venomous it would have stunned a serpent. "Not now, Eja."

His father hadn't scaled the financial pyramid by missing signals. Bolin spun around and quietly sighed. "Okay. We're a team here. What's the big mystery?"

I knew enough to keep my big mouth shut. That left Deming holding the bulging bag of snakes he'd fashioned. He was brilliant and headstrong, but when it came down to it, paternal fealty trumped everything else.

He answered his father through gritted teeth, pointedly ignoring my existence. "A gun, Dad. Cecilia had a gun in her safe. A Walther, not one of ours."

I admired Bolin's composure. His lips formed a firm, straight line, but his features didn't change one bit.

"Where is it?"

Deming's shoulders sagged slightly. "In the Porsche. Don't worry, the cops won't find it. I've got a secret compartment under the seat."

Bolin gave a sharp intake of breath. "Give it to me when we leave here. I'll take it to Lieutenant Bates myself in the morning and tell her the truth—that we found it among Cecilia's possessions. Is that clear?"

"Crystal."

I refilled our glasses, hoping a swallow of prime cognac would dissipate the tension. Luckily it seemed to work. We continued the sad task of delving into the private life and personal papers of someone we loved. It was hard work, heartbreaking too. CeCe had never heard of a paperless society. She'd committed everything to hard copy.

Bolin grimaced as he opened a red, silky sleeve tied with a ribbon.

"What's wrong, Dad? What'd you find?"

"Calm down, son. Unless I'm way off base, I've found Raven."

Deming had the agility of a cat. He sprang over to his father's side like a prowling feline.

"Let me see them. What does he say?"

Bolin turned the letters facedown. "This feels very awkward. Intrusive. Cecilia kept these private. They must have been very special to her."

"Dad . . ." Deming kept his temper on a taut leash. "Murder victims don't get privacy. I'm not suggesting we hand them over to the cops, but if we can find him . . ."

He didn't have to finish that sentence. I'd been there when Deming launched himself at Jem Russell. Poor Raven would suffer a similar fate when Cecilia Swann's crazed brother confronted him. Feathers would definitely fly.

"They're love letters," Bolin said. "Mostly poems. Some original and some classics. You know how much Cecilia loved poetry, Eja. Tell him."

Fathers! They see their little girls through rose-colored glasses long after the truth surfaces. Poetry had bored CeCe to death. She'd been a philistine who buried her nose in law books to the exclusion of the arts. We'd once had a spirited debate about the manliness—or lack of—that most poets displayed. CeCe scoffed at Keats, Shelley, and Whitman. Called them effete. I countered with Thomas, Frost, and Poe. We'd both agreed that Lord Byron was an anomaly who set the bad boy bar impossibly high. Even Malcolm Cates, her staid secretary, was enthralled by the infamous lord and his exploits. After all, his hijinks led the sexually stunted Brits to ban him from burial with his peers at Westminster.

CeCe had dismissed Poe as an inebriated lout who had squandered his talent. Something—or someone—had changed her mind about poetry in general and Edgar Allen Poe in particular. All those Lenore and Raven references meant something to her. Raven must be quite a man—literate enough to write and quote poetry, virile enough to capture my spirited friend. I closed my eyes, mourning what might have been.

Bolin's hand patted my cheek. "Are you okay, Eja? I've been inconsiderate. Forgive me." He returned the letters to their silken sheaf.

"Hold on," Deming said. "Eja's the best person to decipher this stuff. It's mumbo jumbo to me. Something a guy uses to seduce a woman, or I guess he'd say, a maiden. She can read it and find clues."

"Poetry is food for the soul," I quoted. "Don't worry about me. You guys do your thing while I unmask Raven."

When they finally agreed, I settled into her favorite French chair and started my task. It wasn't sadness that I feared; it was the impact of erotic poetry on my fragile libido. I was needy for the physical and emotional components of love. Some would say horny, but it was much more complex. I'd never admit it to anyone, especially Deming Swann.

They left before midnight, promising to update me after Prescott Lewis's visit. Somehow I dozed in the middle of Raven's exquisite love letters. The imagery was flawless, but I found myself yearning for a flesh-and-blood man to hold me and kiss away the pain. CeCe had died alone without the loving family she'd dreamed of. Would a similar fate befall me?

At one a.m., Cato's muffled growls awakened me. I'd planned to go home, back to my own cozy nest, but someone had other ideas. It was a scene worthy of Poe with the rapping, tapping on my chamber door. I shivered, too terrified to quote poetry.

"Who's there?" I tried, unsuccessfully, to sound menacing. In reality, my quivering voice mimicked a strangled mouse.

"I'm coming in. Chain up that hound."

The key turned quietly in the Medeco lock, reminding me that I hadn't latched the door. He was in the hallway before I could scream, surrounding me with a firm embrace.

"I had to see you." Deming gently swept the hair from my eyes and touched my cheek. He bent down and kissed me, softly at first, then harder. "I borrowed my mother's key."

I moaned as his lips brushed the hollow of my neck and collarbone, gliding like a feather down my skin. His long, elegant fingers, worthy of an artist or surgeon, stole slowly downward, exploring the hem of my chemise. I stood on tiptoe, moving closer as I felt his heat.

"I wanted this," he said. "So many times."

"You did? I thought I imagined it."

Deming muttered something I couldn't hear and led me toward the guest bedroom. "I couldn't wait any longer. I had to be with you."

My fears were eradicated by a hot blast that consumed me like lava flow. His lips and tongue were everywhere, teasing long forgotten parts of me that begged for closure. I floated in a sea of shifting tides and crashing currents, guided back to shore by the sound of his voice.

Deming switched on the lamp, watching my reaction as he made me whole. For once I was too needy to care. Afterward, he swept aside the sheets and surveyed every part of me as if I were a sculpture.

"You're beautiful," he said. "So lovely."

"Don't mock me," I said, scrambling for my clothes. "Not now. I can't take it."

Deming shook his head. "Me? You're the one who always puts herself down. Why is that? Don't you own a mirror?"

I turned on my side, replaying those long-ago marital tapes I knew by heart. *'No other man would want you. Inner strength counts more than glamour, Eja. Not every woman can be a beauty. That's just not you."*

"Don't pull away from me, Eja." Deming put his arms around me, planting a gentle kiss on my ear. "I care about you. Don't you see? I always have."

"I thought you hated me. We've always fought like cats and dogs."

He pulled me close. "It wasn't you I was fighting. CeCe understood. She always thought we'd get together, even when you married that weasel."

"Gabriel?"

"You've only had one husband, unless you disposed of the others." Deming reached into the table drawer for a cigarette. "Ah. I see my sister kept her stash of Gauloises."

That triggered another CeCe moment. "She said she only smoked after having sex."

"Humph! Then she must have bought them by the caseload. Let's face it, Cecilia loved a good time." Deming inhaled, smiling at the memory. "Raven would have had a hard task keeping my sister in the corral, no matter what kind of poetry he wrote."

"You should talk! I don't see you with a wife and kiddies. CeCe believed in love and fidelity. She was just being careful this time." I couldn't muster evidence to refute what he said, but I knew that CeCe had been on the cusp of a major life change. She'd been coy about her new love—a major first for her—but had left no doubt how serious it was.

Deming bent down and offered me a puff of his Gauloises.

"No thanks. I've never smoked."

"Jesus, you are a little prig. I'll bet you never even did drugs."

I'd done my share, but he'd never know. "Why? Is destroying brain cells some mark of distinction? Skid row is full of adventurous types, if that's what you like."

Deming tilted my chin toward him. "Feisty, aren't you, Ms. Eja? Is that what good sex does for you?"

"Who said it was good?" I threw back the covers and sprinted toward the bathroom.

He caught me before I got there and bundled me back in the sheets. "Hold on. We have unfinished business. I won't let you go until you change your mind."

AFTERWARD, I crept out of bed and fired up the espresso machine. It was barely sun up, but the sudden immersion in passion had left me sleepless. I'd forgotten the joys that tenderness and lovemaking can bring. Forgotten how desperately I wanted them.

Watch yourself, Eja Kane. For you it was lovemaking; for him it was probably screwing.

I knew the score, for heaven's sake. At thirty-three ingénue roles were far behind me. Deming was a skilled practitioner of erotic arts who had his pick of women—young, beautiful women, not bashful scholars like me. Someday he'd settle down and sire a clutch of beautiful Swann babies. His union with me was temporary, born of convenience and shared circumstance. I had no illusions about him. Like that famous description of Lord Byron, Deming was "mad, bad, and dangerous to know." By next month, he'd be a fond but distant memory, and I'd revert to the status of old childhood acquaintance. It didn't hurt when I intellectualized it that way. Not too much.

"What's going on?" Deming appeared wrapped in a fluffy Turkish towel and nothing more. His golden skin glowed from the sting of cold water and the liberal use of a loofah. In short, he was an erotic dream designed to quicken any woman's pulse. I passed him an espresso, watching as he greedily inhaled the magic brew.

"I finished Raven's things. They gave me a pretty good picture of him."

He gave me the lawyer's gimlet eye. "Oh, yeah. Tell me."

"Okay. I know you'll scoff, but nevertheless . . ."

Deming's lips twisted in a mischievous grin. "Scoff, will I? Maybe I'll surprise you. I have a sensitive side too. You know that better than most."

My cheeks felt a bruise of color as I bent down to consult my notes. "Okay, here it is. Raven is cultured, knowledgeable about poetry, and extremely creative in his use of metaphors and similes. He has excellent penmanship—odd for any man, so he can't be a doctor—and isn't afraid to pour out his heart to the woman he loves."

"That's it? My God, Eja, we live in Boston. The best universities in the world pump out liberal arts majors by the gross." He shook his head. "Sorry, but that doesn't help one bit. Did he mention their marriage? Anything about a wedding?"

"Not a specific date, but his letters presume they will soon be married." I considered that for a moment. "Oh, and he tells her not to worry about her family. That your parents and his mom will come around. One more thing: He uses her middle name. Lenore."

That got me a world-class smirk. Before he could speak, his iPhone sang out. Deming held up one finger, turned his back to me, and took the call. "Okay. See you soon."

He chug-a-lugged his espresso and gave my cheek a hasty peck. "Hey. Gotta run. Client meeting at nine that can't wait."

I'd glanced at the caller ID right before he picked it up. Big surprise. His *business meeting* was with Pamela Schwartz.

LATER THAT MORNING, Cato and I took a brisk trot around the Common. Exercise reportedly releases endorphins that elevate your mood and mask pain. You can't prove that by me. I can truthfully say that I've never felt euphoric after grunting, groaning, and gasping, unless there was a man involved. Sweating is a disgusting spectacle that should be criminalized, or at least confined to the bedroom.

Cato seemed to share my sentiments. He was happier sniffing and sniping at passersby than bounding after sticks. I kept my head high and my tear ducts sealed. Deming didn't owe me anything, not even an explanation. He hadn't forced himself on me. I'd savored every minute and longed for more.

Some men feel obliged to pretend they love you after a session between the sheets. *N'importe*, the French say, and they know all about romance. I could never in a million years compete with a siren like Pamela Schwartz. I've always been shy around men. Not in the classroom, of course, but in every other arena. I'd fight tooth and nail on academic issues and compete with anyone. Socially—not so much. CeCe was the social butterfly, gliding gracefully from man to man, always part of the in-crowd. I was her shadow, a perpetual understudy who never quite knew her lines.

I had no illusions. Deming needed someone familiar to give him comfort, someone who had known and loved his sister too. Who better than Eja Kane, loyal friend and family retainer? We were both hurting, mourning the loss of someone special. It was the least I could do for her brother.

I felt better after that dab of introspection. The next time we met, I'd shake Deming's hand as if nothing had ever happened. Maybe it hadn't. Things would get back to normal soon enough, and our nights of passion would fade to black. I cursed myself for ever thinking otherwise.

Eleven

I PROMISED CATO that after one more turn around the Common we'd pack up and catch a cab for my place. Deming had no key to my apartment, probably sneered with Pam at its compact size and downscale location. No matter. It suited me, and Cato seemed to like it just fine. That's all that mattered.

My cell phone rang as we headed toward the lobby. Despite the sensible self-talk, my heartbeat skyrocketed. *Maybe it was only business. Maybe he did love me . . . Maybe I'm a credulous fool.*

"Eja—what's up?" Jem Russell's voice was loud enough to evacuate the building. He was proud of it, once said he had *stage presence.*

"Nothing. What's going on with you?" *Haven't they arrested you yet?*

"We need to talk."

"Kind of busy right now, Jem. Have to get dressed and take Cato back to my place."

"I'll help. Are you at CeCe's?"

"Yes, but . . ."

"I'll be there in thirty minutes. Wait outside for me."

Shit, hell, damn! Vulgar language is the refuge of the intellectually bereft. I've said that many times, but today I just couldn't catch a break. I'd earned the right to wallow in Anglo-Saxon expletives.

Jem's call intrigued me. Who knew what that simpleton might disclose? If I wormed some information out of him, it was worth the inconvenience. There was also an added bonus: It would drive Deming mad when he found out. I plunged into CeCe's luxurious shower, lathered up with honey cream, and did my daily minimum. After plundering her makeup and closet, I managed to make myself look human again.

Deming's words rang in my head. *You're beautiful. Don't you own a mirror?* I took a chance and peered warily into CeCe's looking glass. Typical of her, it had special bulbs and merciless lighting. I didn't look too bad. Not beautiful by a long shot, but passable, good enough for the likes of deadbeat Jem Russell.

Anika called as I was rushing out the door. Her voice was hushed, as if she were whispering.

"It's me, Eja."

"Is everything okay, Anika? Isn't Prescott there yet?'

She lowered her voice even more. "He's on his way. I don't want Po to hear me, or Bolin. Listen, can you meet me this afternoon at Dr. Townsend's office?"

"Of course, but . . ."

"Great. See you at three."

I'd always believed that Anika was key to finding the murderer. Wesley Townsend could easily rebuff me with secrets and self-serving lies, but he couldn't turn away a grieving mother, especially a former patient. I had plenty to ask him about his billing practices and CeCe's acrophobia.

When we reached the lobby, Jaime was waiting, shifting from side to side, his eyes bright with excitement. He dodged Cato and beckoned to me.

"Miss Eja, he's waiting for you. Outside."

"Who?"

"Miss Cecilia's friend. The one who was just here."

I resisted the urge to grab his collar and shake him senseless. "Oh. You mean Mr. Russell? You saw him recently, Jaime?"

"Oh, yes. The day Miss Cecilia . . . the day she died. That morning."

My pulse throbbed like a castanet. Cato sensed the drama and growled.

"You said you didn't work that day. How could you have seen him?"

Jaime hung his head like a penitent. "I wasn't. I stopped by first thing to get my check. Thought I'd lost it."

I remembered the security tape from Jem's building. CeCe entered at 8:30 that morning. If Jaime was correct, Jem had seen her much earlier, or more likely, had spent the prior night with her. Suppose CeCe had refused his plea for money? That gave him a compelling reason to push her off the rooftop. Jem was volatile, quick to anger and forgive, like a petulant child. He was also cagey enough to omit any details that might incriminate him. Plenty of women would provide an alibi. Foolish females abound.

I patted Jaime's arm. "You've been a big help. Make sure you contact Lieutenant Bates and tell her what you saw. I know the Swann family will be very grateful."

Jaime's eyes brightened as he contemplated the type of gratitude that implied. I grabbed Cato and hustled out the door, more eager than ever to confront Jem Russell.

He was parked on the corner in a splashy red vehicle they call a muscle car. My uncle had owned a similar one, a Camaro Z28. I'd seen pictures of him polishing that beast, grinning with a teenager's optimism. When he died, fresh out of college on foreign soil, my grandmother couldn't bear the sight of it. She'd sold that car and destroyed every trace of it except some photographs.

"Wow! That's some car," I said. Cato sniffed suspiciously at the tires and then decorated them.

The grin never left Jem's face. "Yeah, she's a sweet ride. Restored it myself. Every part."

"Sure it's okay for Cato to get in? We can catch a cab."

Jem opened the door and waved us in. "Don't sweat it. CeCe brought him with her all the time. She took that mutt everywhere."

His manner was subdued, and that made me suspicious.

"Turn left at the light," I said. "I'll direct you from there."

His reaction was swift. For a moment, Jem dropped the genial mask he habitually wore. "Don't bother. I know where you live, Eja. Thought we'd take a little ride first."

I forced myself to remain calm. Jem Russell was an irresponsible cad but not necessarily a murderer. I glanced out the window, hoping to see a patrol car, fire engine, or even an ambulance. My deliverance came in the form of a phone call. I grasped my phone as if it were a lifeline. It may very well have been.

"Where are you?" Deming barked. "I've been trying to reach you all morning."

"Nice to know," I said. "Jem was kind enough to offer Cato and me a ride home. We're with him now."

Deming's answer was crude, ungentlemanly, and very reassuring. "I told you not to get mixed up with him. Don't let him into your apartment. I'll be right over."

I raised my arms helplessly and plastered a big faux smile on my face. "Change of plans, Jem. Deming wants me to go right home. He's on his way, and you know how excitable he is."

Jem Russell was physically strong but feckless. He had the skills to challenge Deming but not the will. Without saying another word, he swung his muscle car around and headed toward my condo. His weakness fed my spirit. I felt empowered, bold, and sassy.

"You lied to us, Jem. You saw CeCe the day she died."

He curled his lip in a bad imitation of an Elvis sneer. "Prove it."

"I don't have to. It's on the security tapes from CeCe's condo. What'd you do, spend the night with her?" My building was in sight. That pumped even more courage into my veins. "She said no, didn't she? Turned off that financial spigot."

To his credit, Jem kept his face an unreadable mask. I reached into my purse for the super sharp tweezers I always carry. They're hell on stray hairs and anything else in their path. If he grabbed me, he'd get more than he bargained for.

Jem braked at the stoplight and turned toward me. "Listen, Eja, you got it all wrong. CeCe liked my idea. Said it had potential. She told me to whip up a business plan and meet her at that bar." He shrugged. "I made it, but she never showed."

Surprise, surprise. I believed the big lug. Still, I'm old school. "Trust but verify" always works for me. As he swung into my driveway, I summoned my iciest stare.

"Email me a copy of that business plan," I said. "Then we'll talk. Otherwise, my next chat will be with Lieutenant Bates."

I DOUBLE-LOCKED my condo door and switched on every light in the place. CeCe would have called it paranoid yet the facts spoke for themselves: Someone had murdered my friend, and Jem Russell might well be the guy.

Moments later, Deming pounded at my door. It was barely eleven o'clock, and I hadn't even caught my breath. The forthcoming session with Anika and the shrink weighed heavily on my mind. I needed time to compose myself, but I knew he'd batter down the door if I ignored him.

Deming swept into my hallway like a new age angel, all glistening ebony locks and superb tailoring. Apparently his nine a.m. *business meeting* had only been a quickie. I got a perverse satisfaction out of that.

"Where is he?" Deming barked. "Are you okay?"

"Jem's gone." My voice was a bit shaky, but I breathed deeply and soldiered on. "He had me worried though."

He was at my side in three quick steps, glowering down at me. "I told you not to go near him. What's wrong with you? Are you some kind of adrenaline junkie? Do you have a death wish?"

I grimaced and turned my face away from him. A man who played Don Juan had no right to give me orders. Who knew how many females the great Deming Swann had in his thrall? One less wouldn't matter a bit.

"I can take care of myself, thank you very much. Jem insisted on giving us a ride, and I thought . . . that is I hoped . . . to trick him. You know, a damaging admission."

"Fuck! Do you think you're Nancy Drew or something? This isn't one of your mystery stories. My sister's dead. Don't you get it?"

I expected fireworks when I told him what Jaime had seen. True to form, Deming exploded. "I told you! I knew that scumbag killed my sister. Wait 'til Dad finds out!"

Until CeCe's death, I'd never seen the volatile side of her brother. He'd always played the aristocrat—cold, dispassionate, and arrogant. CeCe laughed when I'd told her that. "You don't have a clue about Brother Bjorn," she'd said. Naturally a sister's perspective differed wildly from an outsider's. My immediate goal was to calm him down and shove him out the door before he bulldozed my session with his mother.

"See if Jem produces that business plan," I said. "Admittedly he's a sociopath, but I think he cared about CeCe. In his way."

Deming snorted something unpronounceable. "I want you to stay put until we figure that stuff out. Dad called a meeting for six tonight. With all that went on today we'll have plenty to discuss. I'll pick you up at five thirty."

"Don't bother, I'll meet you there. I've got things to do."

He clenched his fists as if anger had curdled into full-blown rage. "Don't do this, Eja. Please. The cops are indifferent, Dad's unavailable, and my mom floats around the house like a wraith. It's been almost four days." Deming closed his eyes. "They say the first forty-eight hours are the most critical. After that, the chances of catching anyone are close to zero."

This was something new for him—helplessness. Most of us learn to live with it, but Swanns are accustomed to controlling people and events. CeCe would have winked at me, glad that even Deming must occasionally feel mortal.

It should have pleased me to see him humbled, but that didn't happen. I kept my arms at my side, afraid that I'd reach out to comfort him. Touching Deming had become a habit, one that grew harder to break each time we were together. He wasn't serious about me, he couldn't be. He was merely seeking comfort in the first available set of arms. I'm the one who sizzled when he touched me and dreamed of what might be. He was the brother devastated by loss who clung to his sister's best friend until the horrors receded.

"Promise me you'll be careful." Deming blinded me with his glance.

I retreated to the safety of my old persona—calm, sensible Eja, truth-seeking missile and family friend.

"What about her work life?" I asked him. "Did Pamela have any ideas?"

His cheeks flushed with emotion—anger or embarrassment—I couldn't tell.

"I really didn't have a chance to question her," he said.

I fussed with my shoelace to hide my confusion. From personal experience, I knew that Deming got right down to business where lovemaking was concerned. Maybe Pamela demanded more foreplay.

"I suppose the cops have already sealed CeCe's office."

He nodded. "It got testy. You know, privacy of client files, that kind of stuff. As I understand it, Cecilia was working on some fairly important cases. Of course, she would have handed them over if that federal appointment came through."

"Of course." I edged a safe distance away from him, far enough to break the spell.

Deming rose slowly, gathered up his things, and headed toward the door. "I guess I'll see you tonight."

"Okay."

If he left now, I had just enough time to make myself presentable and research Dr. Wesley Townsend before our meeting. No sense in glamming it up. Anika would laser in on any changes in my person or behavior and draw her own conclusions. Lately I'd detected a certain amusement in her eyes whenever Deming and I were in the same room.

It was easy in the old days when we were enemies and I was my nondescript, asexual self. I'd never felt awkward with him then. True, our conversations were often heated and always acerbic, but they were comfortable. Sort of like a worn pair of sheepskin slippers. I was out of practice navigating the twisted corridors of the male mind without CeCe as my spirit guide. On my best day the bar was set low. Without my friend, it was non-existent.

I stroked Cato's silky coat as a diversion. "See you then."

Deming nodded briskly and marched through my door without another word.

WESLEY TOWNSEND'S office was comfortably situated in the middle of a shady Beacon Street neighborhood only blocks away from the Tudor. Small wonder that CeCe found it so tempting to nip in to see the good doctor whenever her demons surfaced.

I'd never consulted a shrink. In fact, I'd never even considered paying someone an exorbitant fee to tell me what I already knew. Chalk it up to my middle-class roots. CeCe couldn't believe it. Everyone in her social set had a therapist on speed dial. Only dull, sensible Eja plodded through life doing the best she could.

Researching Dr. Wesley Townsend wasn't easy. I tried the Boston Medical Society website, even scanned Angie's List and Yelp, hoping to find something—anything—to substantiate CeCe's feelings about him. I learned that no malpractice claims had been made against him in the past twelve months. Of course, anything that had been settled informally wouldn't show up anyway. The only hint of trouble surfaced in the *Boston* magazine "Top Docs" section. Townsend had been a fixture on the list for years. Curiously enough, his name had been omitted the last two years. Maybe it meant nothing. After all, they must maintain a Shrink Emeritus list somewhere. Maybe I was boxing with shadows.

I stumbled into the corner Starbucks, guided by a thirst for caffeine and Anika's frantic waves. She looked wan despite her impeccable attire and perfectly painted face. No wonder Deming called her a wraith.

"Oh, Eja, thank heavens you made it." She clasped my hands in hers, giving them a gentle squeeze. As our fingers touched, I jerked away. Anika's grip was frigid, encapsulated in ice.

"Are you okay?" I asked. "Your hands . . ."

"Just fine." Her eyes acknowledged the lie on her lips. "It's just . . . I feel so distraught every time I come in here." She shook her head. "It makes no sense. I know. Wesley cured me when all those nicotine patches and shots didn't help at all. Bolin was ecstatic."

She took a healthy swig of espresso. "Don't mind me. We're here for Cecilia. It's just that I was never comfortable with hypnosis. The loss of control, you know."

"What about Dr. Townsend? Do you like him?"

Anika shrugged. "He's okay. Insincere. Somewhat obsequious. You know the type."

"CeCe wasn't his biggest fan," I said. "I guess Mr. Swann . . . Bolin . . . told you about this billing issue?"

"Yes. Very curious. Cecilia loved spending money, but she was tight as a tick about getting value. She'd never pay someone unless she was satisfied with him."

"I might introduce that into our conversation. Think it'll work?"

Anika flashed that complacent smile only a beautiful woman can manage. "Bolin says Wesley likes me. Too much in his opinion. That's why I didn't mention this visit to him. Why complicate things when it can work for us? Let me broach the subject."

She pushed back her chair and winked. "Ready?"

Twelve

SOME COLORS HAVE the power to soothe. In the sixth-floor office of Dr. Wesley Townsend tranquil pastels were king. Baby blue, mint green, and cream predominated in both paint and upholstered pieces. The color scheme repeated itself in the tropical fish swimming calmly through the large tank and in the tasteful mauve suit of the receptionist. If I hadn't been anxious, I would have taken a snooze.

The doctor himself ushered us into his office. He embraced Anika and shook my hand, looking all the while like a bereaved healer. There was nothing wrong with his appearance either. Wesley Townsend was a middle-aged white man who had the whole tall, dark, and distinguished thing down pat. He was practiced at his art, full of gentle touches and soft words that emitted a faint whiff of insincerity.

Anika explained my role as CeCe's best friend and biographer. Then in a daring lie that took my breath away, she added that I was also her future daughter-in-law.

"How wonderful," Wesley said, displaying perfect teeth. "I understand you want to talk about Cecilia."

While Anika dabbed at her eyes, I jumped in. "We told the police about CeCe's acrophobia, doctor. There's no way she would have jumped off that roof. It's impossible!"

He tut-tutted and cast a wary eye on Anika. "Nothing I knew suggested that Cecilia was suicidal. She seemed in very high spirits, other than some issues at work."

"When did you last see her?" Anika asked, turning those hazel orbs his way. "I know how much she relied upon you."

"Whew!" He ran manicured fingers through his razor cut. "I'd have to check my files, Anika, but it was a while ago. Cecilia was very strong-willed, as you know. She'd decided to tough things out without professional help."

Wesley Townsend favored us with a practiced smile and sighed. "She was something special, your daughter."

"You're so right, Doctor. CeCe told me just the other day that it was still a big issue. Her thing with heights, I mean." I shrugged. "We told the police, but they disregarded it."

Right on cue, Anika stifled a sob. "I knew you'd understand, Wesley. Bolin always mentions your kindness."

Bolin Swann's name worked like a cattle prod. Townsend's leg twitched as he shifted in his seat. "Of course. Anything I can do."

Anika plucked a Hermes notepad from her bag. "We've been sorting through Cecilia's things, Eja and I. It's very difficult . . ." No need for acting; her tears were genuine. "Anyway, I found something puzzling. My daughter wrote checks to you for the past three years, even though she said she'd stopped treatment." Anika shook her head. "I can't make heads or tails of it, but Bolin's counting on me."

I watched his reaction through lowered eyes. Townsend was cool under pressure, but human enough to show discomfort. Was it guilt or confusion?

"Some of my patients keep secrets, Anika. Even from their mothers. Anyhow, I don't deal with the finances. That's Brenda's job." He rose and put his arm around her. "Ms. Kane, could you give us a minute? I need some time alone with Mrs. Swann."

After Anika nodded, I left for the reception area. The lady in mauve, who wore a discreet nametag with Brenda on it, glanced up immediately. She was slim, impeccably groomed, and on the sunny side of forty. Her large chestnut eyes radiated intelligence and empathy, making her a perfect choice to calm the roiled seas of shrinkdom. I sensed a kindred spirit.

"I'm so sorry about Ms. Swann," she said. "She was different from most of our patients—very in charge but charming. So charming. Stylish too. Her purses were to die for, especially that Hermes one." Brenda sighed. "Mine are fakes from street vendors."

CeCe's fixation with fine leather was the stuff of legend. My heart lurched as I pictured her strutting around her condo, savoring her treasures. "Lawyers can be quite challenging, I guess. All that confrontation."

Brenda rolled her eyes. "Amen. My sister works with them every day. You should hear the stories she tells."

I tested my hypothesis. "What did you think of her new hair color? Personally, I loathed it, but you know CeCe. So bold."

Brenda frowned. "I'm sorry. Wasn't Ms. Swann a natural blonde? Why would she change? It's been so long since I've seen her."

I laughed. "She must have come in on your day off. You see so many people, I'm not surprised that you'd overlook something like that."

"Not likely." Brenda's tone was emphatic. "I'm here every day. She spoke with the doctor quite regularly but not in person. Not here."

Brenda had no reason to lie. None that I could think of. We'd learned nothing that explained why my razor-sharp pal had paid Dr. Freud a small fortune for phantom sessions. The checks I saw were endorsed by him and cashed immediately. Hardly uncommon, not illegal, but somehow suspicious. Unless, of course, he was Raven. The missing money might constitute love offerings to her fiancé.

"Must be kind of fun. I mean, working with a doctor who's so cultured. A regular renaissance man! Poetry and all. I'm a writer, and I appreciate a man like that."

She was accustomed to crazies, so Brenda didn't challenge me. Not outright. "Dr. Townsend is a very smart man. But poetry? No way. He's more the medical journal type."

My people skills are sound. They told me that Brenda was nobody's fool.

"She didn't do it, you know. Kill herself, I mean." I approached her desk and whispered. "Someone lured my friend to that rooftop, and I won't rest until I find him. Or her."

Brenda's gaze was calm and untroubled. "Good. I never believed that girl would harm herself, no matter what anyone said."

I handed her my card.

"Ah, you're a writer. How nice." She must have been one hell of a poker player. Her expression was smooth as steel and equally impenetrable.

This was an opportunity I didn't intend to waste.

"I'm creating a tribute for the family. You know, a memoir of Cecilia. If you think of anything—anything at all—give me a call."

Brenda nodded. When the doctor's doors swung open, she was busily tapping her computer keys, and my card had magically disappeared.

Anika's pale face and grim expression worried me. I nudged her toward the elevator, wincing as she gripped my arm in a vise.

"Everything okay?" I asked.

We were wedged in a space crammed with office workers thirsting for freedom and that first evening cocktail. Neither one of us said a word until we'd cleared the building and found a table in Starbucks.

I checked my watch. "That meeting's at six. We don't have much time."

She laughed. "I told Bolin we were going shopping. You know, girl stuff. He won't expect us 'til then. He needed to chill out anyway. Our session with Prescott made him crazy." She put her finger to my lips before I could ask. "We'll discuss that tonight. Let the boys have the stage."

It sounded way too flippant. Shopping after a horrific murder—your daughter's murder? Who does that? Was this some bizarre palliative of the uber-rich?

"We have no packages. He'll know something's up."

"Eja, Eja. No one carries packages anymore. It's tiring and attracts muggers. Bolin knows I have things sent home." Anika grabbed my arm again. The woman was far stronger than she looked. Sneakier too.

"Something happened with Wesley. He tried to hypnotize me again. To relax me, or so he said. It didn't work, mostly because he was so distraught. Our questions about Cecilia really shook him."

I closed my eyes, replaying the scene at his office. Dr. Wesley Townsend was a piece of statuary until I mentioned money. For some reason that spooked him. Medical practices get in trouble all the time for overbilling insurance companies or Medicare, but neither category fit the Swanns. Plus, CeCe was paying him for sessions she'd never had. Brenda was certain about that, and I believed her. Moreover, the checks weren't made out to the practice. They were personal checks made to and endorsed by Wesley Townsend. It was weird, as if CeCe were paying hush money or blackmail. Had her shrink been blackmailing her?

"He's pretty free with that hypnosis, isn't he?"

Anika laughed. "He's had great results with it. Of course, my daughter absolutely refused. That's why Wesley called her a difficult patient. I agreed to almost anything he suggested. Not CeCe."

I sipped my latte while Anika shared more memories of my friend. She rambled a bit, but I didn't mind. It was good therapy for both of us. When I heard Pamela Schwartz mentioned, I almost spilled my drink.

"What's the story with Pam?" I asked. "Deming wouldn't tell me much. I know for a fact that she was no favorite of CeCe's."

There was that enigmatic smile again. Anika crossed her elegant legs and wagged her finger at me. "You know Dem. So secretive, especially about his social life."

I felt that full body flush. Maybe Dr. Jake was right. Deming was in love with her and too ashamed to admit it. My boon companion, that mile-wide streak of masochism, asserted itself. I had to know, no matter what the cost.

"Are they . . . involved? CeCe never mentioned it." I dove into my purse for a tissue. Anything to avoid her probing stare.

"My son is like catnip to women, Eja. Always has been. All ages, colors, and types throw themselves at him, and most are really nice. I pity them."

"Why?"

"Because inevitably, he'll leave and break their hearts. Deming has never been in love, or at least, he's never acknowledged it. I'm his mother. Trust me, I'd know."

I felt deflated, like a punctured, rimless tire. What made me think for even one minute that he cared for me? No matter. My loyalty was to CeCe. I'd do whatever it took to help, then slowly disengage from the Swanns. All of them. It made sense in a sick, gut-wrenching sort of way and would spare me pain in the long run. If I avoided him, the ache would subside.

"We need to check out CeCe's workplace," I said. "Deming wasn't keen on the idea, but you and I could pull it off. You know, chat up the office staff. Speak with her colleagues. I'll pretend I'm writing that memoir about her. You can give me cover."

"Okay," Anika said. "I'm in. It makes me feel less impotent. Like I'm doing something to help my daughter." She gathered her purse and rose. "But Eja. Keep this between the two of us. Bolin and Deming mean well, but . . . you know men. So emotional."

THEY WERE WAITING for us when we arrived: Deming, prowling around the room with a brandy snifter, Jake Harris hunched over a computer, and Bolin paging through *The Wall Street Journal*.

"It's about time! Where were you two?" Deming whirled around, scowling as if I were the sole culprit.

His mother patted his cheek and kicked off her shoes. "Sorry. Time got away from us, you know." She walked over to her husband and hugged him. "I could use a drink, darling. Eja looks thirsty too."

Bolin's arms clutched his wife's side. "Everything okay, Leda? I was worried."

"You never said you were meeting my mother." Deming shot

hazel daggers at me.

"Didn't I?"

Jake Harris put down his paper, watching the verbal gymnastics. "Can we discuss your meeting with the senator? I'm anxious to hear what he said."

"We can do better than that," Bolin said. "The whole thing was recorded." He pressed a button, summoning Po. "Our security system is state of the art, but I normally wouldn't infringe on anyone's privacy."

Deming growled. "Nothing about this situation is normal. Let's see it."

We sat facing the giant plasma screen as Po inserted the disc and doused the lights. Bolin was right—everything was state of the art. The Swanns welcomed their distinguished visitor and observed the usual proprieties. Senator Prescott Lewis had bearing, looks, and a voice that any casting director would covet. When he said CeCe's name, he hung his head and gulped. Either his grief was genuine, or he was the most jaded sociopath on the planet. I favored the former explanation. Whenever I'd seen him with CeCe at some social event or political rally, he'd shown a tenderness toward her that defied a simple explanation. I knew for a fact what Deming only suspected: Prescott Lewis had once been her lover. CeCe had shown the bloodless Brahmin a vivid slice of life that was foreign to him. Passion, both emotional and erotic, soon enslaved him. He offered everything—his name, fortune, and future, but it hadn't been enough. CeCe set him free and reclaimed her life without losing a step. Prescott loved her, but he wasn't Raven. His mind was too conventional for poetry. That didn't get him off the hook though. He might have traded obsession for murderous rage.

When Anika slipped the Raven word into the conversation, Prescott looked more blank than usual. His reaction seemed genuine, but he was a politician, cunning enough to lie whenever it served his purpose.

"You'd mentioned a federal appointment for my daughter." Bolin's patrician features were granite smooth. "That was kind of you, Prescott, but wasn't it premature? Cecilia was just thirty-three."

Prescott fingered a shock of steel grey hair. "Just what we needed on the bench. Youth, enthusiasm—she had both. We looked at others. In her own firm even, but no one was a better fit than Cecilia. Not even Pamela Schwartz."

Anika inched closer to her husband, clasping his hand. "Would she . . . was it a sure thing?"

"Absolutely. She would have been perfect." He looked away for a moment. "Honestly, I had no idea she was distraught. Cecilia loved the idea. You know how enthusiastic she'd get. Clapping her hands and laughing, almost like a little girl."

"She wasn't distraught." Bolin pressed his lips into a tight smile that never reached his eyes. "My daughter didn't kill herself. She was murdered."

Prescott blanched. "But the police . . . I had assurances at the highest levels. They said things would be handled. Laid to rest with a minimum of publicity."

"You're right," Bolin said. "Things will be handled. I'll handle them. Can we count on your help too?"

Prescott Lewis, family friend and spurned lover, suddenly morphed into Senator Lewis, politician. He spread his hands wide in a gesture common to cowards, weasels, and candidates.

"Of course. You understand I have to be discreet. I hadn't seen Cecilia in weeks. But anything I can do . . ."

Bolin gave him an amiable nod that fooled no one. "Thanks. I'll hold you to that. Anika and I have always admired your integrity and dedication to truth. I hope you'll be running for office again next year. You'll have the support of the Swann family, of course."

Prescott bowed his head. "That means a lot. Thank you." He shook Bolin's hand, kissed Anika's cheek, and fled the room.

No one spoke until the lights went on.

"What the hell!" Deming's eyes gleamed with hate. "That phony bastard wasted our time."

"Language, Dem." Anika nodded toward me. "Eja's here."

"She knows me," he said. "Too well." For a second our eyes connected, telegraphing a very different message.

Color stained Anika's cheeks as she leaned against her husband. "I'm not sure we learned anything except the obvious. Prescott was being Prescott."

Jake raised his brows in inquiry.

"He's always been a wuss," Deming spat. "I told her to stay away from him, but she never listened to me. He used her to suck up to our family. The man has a cash register for a heart."

I had to tell them despite the consequences. CeCe wouldn't mind. Deming was right about one thing though. Corpses have no right to privacy.

"You're wrong," I said. "Prescott Lewis loved CeCe. Wanted to marry her in fact. He was willing to scrap his career, go through a messy divorce and all the attendant publicity just to have her. She dumped him instead."

I expected something—anger, disbelief, surprise. What I got was silence. Dead silence. Anika was the first to recover.

"Glad to see my daughter had good sense. Prescott's not nearly smart enough for her. Plus, Cecilia was no home wrecker."

"He's nothing but a gigolo," Deming said. "Willing to trade wife number one for a younger, richer model. What could she possibly see in him?"

I couldn't suppress a sudden cough. Once again, all eyes were on me. "I think . . . that is, CeCe said . . . the Senator had hidden assets."

"Nonsense," Deming huffed. "I ordered a full financial report on him. Plus his holdings are in that annual disclosure report they all file. Everything he has is in his wife's name."

Anika caught on right away. She smiled up at him. "Eja's being discreet, dear. She means physical assets. You never know with a man until it's too late."

Deming turned crimson, Bolin looked away, and Jake Harris grinned broadly.

"Well, what do you know," Jake said. "Senator Lewis is a stud."

Thirteen

WE ADJOURNED TO an exquisitely presented dinner of broiled lobster and fresh vegetables that tempted no one. Deming usually wolfed down anything Po put in front of him. But tonight he listlessly picked at his food, just like the rest of us.

"I have a confession to make," Anika said as we finished dessert. "Eja and I did some investigating." She touched Bolin's hand. "Nothing dangerous, darling, but instructive. Very instructive."

Deming's frown lacerated me. He clenched his jaw as he spoke. "Snooping, you mean. All right. Tell us."

Anika summarized our encounter with Dr. Wesley Townsend. "I know we should have waited, but I just had to do something." She turned to Jake. "You understand, don't you?"

He nodded. "I did some snooping of my own. Spoke with a few colleagues about Wesley."

Deming glared at his friend. "Well. Let's have it, man."

Jake dabbed the corners of his mouth with his napkin. "It's nothing conclusive. Mostly gossip, and you know how unreliable that can be."

"Get on with it!" Deming walked the tightrope between anxious and rude, drumming his fingers on the table.

Bolin touched his son's arm and leaned forward. "Don't keep us in suspense, Jake."

"Okay. There's nothing formal. Wesley's too clever for that. It's just . . . a few things that concerned me. Whispers. Just hints, nothing more. Some of it's probably prejudice. You know how conservative our profession is, and Wesley's always been keen on hypnosis. He's written any number of journal articles on it."

"So?" I controlled my impulse to shake the good doctor until he spilled his guts.

Jake turned to Anika. "I know he helped you, but I don't think you should see him again. Not if it involves hypnosis."

She shuddered, turning an even whiter shade of pale. "Say it, Jake. You're scaring me." Anika grasped her husband's arm as if she were drowning.

"Okay," Jake said. "One of his patients claimed that Wesley molested her. It was never proven, and she'd been under hypnosis. Had a history of delusions. I understand that such accusations are not uncommon in that field."

Bolin's eyes gleamed with a ferocity I'd never seen before. "Just one, Jake?"

Jake avoided his eyes. "More than one. They said their clothes were rearranged, that there were other signs of . . . interference." This time Dr. Jake looked really uncomfortable.

"Were the authorities involved?" Bolin's voice was low and lethal.

"I understand that they did a rape kit on one of the women. No evidence whatsoever of sexual contact."

"Not surprising," Bolin said. "He'd use a condom."

My confusion mounted as they debated the forensic aspects of sexual congress.

"I don't get it," I said. "CeCe refused hypnosis. It's one of the reasons they had a blowup."

"I didn't," Anika said. "Wesley hypnotized me every time."

A small bomb imploded in the room. At least it seemed that way. Deming shot out of his seat, upending his plate and savaging his crystal goblet.

"That bastard! That dirty rotten bastard!" He averted his eyes from his father's anguished face. "If he touched her, I'll . . ."

"Hold on, son," Bolin said. "Take it easy. We need proof before we charge in."

"No matter what, it still doesn't link him to my daughter's death, and that's all I care about." Anika was strangely calm as she sat upright, sipping her wine. I couldn't shake the feeling that she was hiding something.

"I wish there were some way to find out," she said. "All I remember is feeling uncomfortable. No other physical symptoms."

I'd been mulling over the same issue, and a plan was germinating in my head. It wasn't foolproof, and it might not mean anything. But it might explain those checks CeCe wrote and even the gun in her safe.

"I have an idea," I said. "We'd need independent corroboration. Someone with insight into Townsend's operation. Maybe we can trap him and contact Lieutenant Bates."

Deming's frown rivaled the wrath of Zeus. "Absolutely not. I forbid you to endanger your life running around like some addlepated gumshoe."

"Let her speak, Dem." Bolin turned to me. "Go on, Eja. What's your plan?"

I explained the contact with Brenda the receptionist and my feeling that she might want to help. "She knows something. I'm positive about that, and she was very fond of CeCe."

"There's more, isn't there?" Jake asked. "Might as well tell us."

I took a deep, cleansing breath. My plan was risky, and Deming's reaction would be volcanic. But it just might work.

"Okay. Here it is: I'll become Dr. Townsend's patient. Any story will do. Grief or guilt over CeCe, general anxiety—you know the drill. Anything to make him hypnotize me."

"We could say you're nervous about your wedding," Anika said. "You know, premarital doubts based on poor self-image."

Deming's face darkened. "Wedding? What the hell . . ."

"That was my idea, darling. I told Wesley that Eja was my future daughter-in-law." Anika beamed. "It explained her connection quite nicely, and he totally bought it."

Bolin furrowed his brow. "Hmm. We'd need some help from Jake. A referral. Townsend doesn't take just anyone."

"Dad! You're not buying this nonsense, are you? Eja thinks she's some kind of sleuth. She spends so much time reading and writing that crap that she's delusional."

Bolin grinned. "Maybe fiction is stranger than truth for once. How about it, Jake?"

Jake nodded. "But how will you trap him? Remember Eja, hypnosis is a very effective tool. Most people can't resist it."

"I know. But I can have some type of recording device in my purse. Then when he tries something, we'll have proof."

Jake grimaced. "I don't know. That sounds like entrapment. And what if it doesn't work? You could be very vulnerable." He shook his head. "He's not Raven."

"Heaven no. His assistant said Townsend has absolutely no interest in poetry. Plus, there's another complication. He already has a wife." I stole a glance at Deming, who looked almost comatose.

"So, how about it? If CeCe found out what he was up to, Wesley Townsend had a big fat motive to kill her. Plus, as her shrink he could lure her to that rooftop. You know, say he finally found a cure. She was desperate to conquer her fears. It might have worked." I choked back a sob. If only my friend had waited for me. We could have figured something out.

"It's highly unethical, a risky proposition. Very risky." Bolin's lips turned up in a faint smile. "I like it."

"Dad!" Deming stalked out of the room without saying goodbye. Bad behavior was getting to be a habit with him. I preferred the aloof, predictable Deming Swann of old to this volatile stranger. Once again, CeCe had been right: I had no clue about Brother Bjorn.

"Don't worry, Eja." Anika showed the serenity of the Mona Lisa. "Dem always reacts when people he cares for are threatened. It's one of his most endearing traits."

My cheeks burned, and I feigned interest in my napkin. He'd probably think I manipulated his mother, pushed my way into the family circle. No doubt he'd fled to the welcoming arms of Pamela Schwartz or one of her surrogates.

"I'll have my security people work it out," Bolin said. "They'll know the equipment that we need. I'm expecting a call back from Lieutenant Bates anyway. Won't hurt to check in with the authorities in case they have any leads. Meanwhile, we'll need your help, Jake."

The two men huddled together, devising a plan that would pass muster with Dr. Wesley Townsend. Anika's eyes brightened as she discussed a strategy of her own.

"Tomorrow, Eja. We'll visit my stylist. You'll just love Harpo, don't worry."

"Stylist? Mrs. Swann . . ."

She waved off my protests. "Now, now. You've got to look and act the part of Dem's fiancée if we want this to work. Don't worry. My treat. Wesley is very sensitive to nuance. If he senses a trap, he'll back off in a minute."

I loathed the idea of a major makeover just to claw my way up to Deming's standards. Wild curls and an unadorned face were part of my charm. Why not accept me for who I was?

Anika entwined her hands like the Gordian knot. "Indulge me on this, Eja. Please. It's one last thing we can do for Cecilia, you and I. Her burial will be low-key—family only—to be followed by a celebration of my daughter's life later on." Her eyes filled as she said the words. "I won't have any public gathering until Cecilia has been vindicated. You understand, don't you, Eja?"

I'm not the clingy type. Never have been. But before I knew it,

Anika and I were holding each other, sobbing for the daughter and friend we'd lost. Tears are cleansing forces that can sweep away pain and clear the mind. By the time I left, we'd charted a path that might mean justice for my friend.

SLEEP ELUDED ME that night. I was assailed by makeover nightmares that rivaled any horror film. Upscale hair salons give me a rash. Always have. I feel awkward and inadequate entering a beauty temple where even shampoo girls can show me up.

The next morning I agonized over my wardrobe, makeup, and hair. I finally settled on a black ensemble, last year's Christmas gift from CeCe. With any luck, I'd fade into the woodwork, eclipsed by Anika's radiant beauty.

Promptly at nine a.m., Po swung the Mercedes into my driveway and hopped out. Anika, resplendent in crimson, beckoned me into the back seat.

"This is exciting, Eja! I feel so . . . what is that word . . . empowered! Bolin liked the idea. About the salon, I mean. You know how men are. Girly stuff comforts them."

I had to ask, even though I shouldn't have.

"What about Deming?"

She shrugged. "No clue. He never came back last night. Probably hunkered down at his place, playing music. My boy loves Mozart. Beethoven too."

Probably hunkered down all right—with Pamela Schwartz.

"You look lovely, by the way. Armani suits you." Anika chattered on, briefing me on the day's beauty agenda: highlights, cut and blow-dry, followed by a mani/pedi and professional makeup application.

"Gee, I don't know about that, Anika. I've never had much luck with makeup. CeCe tried to show me, but I flunked the course."

She patted my cheek. "Nonsense. You'll be a natural. Afterwards, I suggest we pop into Cecilia's office. You know, chat up the staff. The timing should be just right."

That part of the plan appealed to me. If I encountered Poison Pam, at least I'd look my best. The thought buoyed my spirits all the way to the salon.

To my relief, the surroundings echoed the name. *Piao-Liang*, the Mandarin word for beauty, was serene and understated, awash in soothing earth tones with occasional accents of cherry. No sneers or looks of thinly veiled contempt from the staff. Harpo Chan was a Chinese man of about my age with a kind manner and discerning eye. He sized me up immediately, asked a few questions, and made suggestions. It was obvious that Anika doted on him and that the affection was mutual. In order to placate her and survive the ordeal, I gave him carte blanche to work his magic. I'm open-minded. Maybe I'd enjoy playing queen for the day after years of a no-frills, low-maintenance lifestyle.

I averted my eyes as Harpo snipped, foiled, and puffed my hair into submission.

"My friend praised you to the sky," I said. "No one else could touch her hair. She wouldn't even consider it."

He bowed. "A number of my clients are lawyers, but Ms. Swann was unique. One of my favorites. She worked so hard. Too hard. I was pleased to see her finally relax."

My antennae rose like antlers. Many women confide personal things to their stylist. Did Harpo know something important?

"I'd never even seen her engagement ring until . . . afterwards."

He gave me a measured look. "It was beautiful. Five karats. Flawless."

"Only the best would do. CeCe loved jewelry," I said. "I suppose you met Raven?"

Harpo shook his head. "She mentioned him. Told me about him. I never saw him, though." He held the mirror up for me to admire his handiwork. "He made her happy, this Raven. I know that."

I swiveled the chair around to face Harpo. "Did she describe him, or tell you anything that might help us identify him? Please. It's important."

He hesitated as if he were debating the issue with my murdered friend. "She worried how her brother would react. Not her parents, just him. Brother Bjorn, she always called him. She said he was very protective."

"You got that right!" I smiled as I recalled those flashing eyes and taut muscles.

"One thing more." Harpo lowered his voice. "Raven was someone she'd known for a while. She said it would surprise everyone."

My stomach clenched. Oh, Lord! Two names popped into my head: Jem Russell and Wesley Townsend. That explained those recent photos in her condo. Jem was a Neanderthal who lacked the Irish gift for wit. Wesley Townsend had a sinister side, but at least he could claim a distinguished academic pedigree.

The whole beauty experience was exhausting, a waste of time that I could have spent writing. Then I saw the results.

No more stolid, wholesome Eja. The new me was sleek, sophisticated, and almost sultry. I was beginning to get the hang of the spa experience, and it was awesome!

Anika's cries of approval were echoed by Harpo's brisk affirmative nod. I'd passed the test and for once in my homespun life I felt glamorous.

"Wait 'til Dem sees you," Anika said. "He'll just explode."

I hoped that was hyperbole, but knowing CeCe's twin, it was probably accurate.

Fourteen

WE PILED INTO the Mercedes for the brief ride to Sevier, Miles and Swann. Anika kept her comments to a minimum in recognition of the probing gaze and big ears of Po. I'd gained insight into her modus vivendi over the past week. After thirty-six years of marriage, Anika Swann kept her smoking hot hubby by a wily combination of femininity and cold calculation. There was much to learn from this woman.

Anika adjusted her scarf and did a quick time check. "Okay. Our first target is Meribeth Foye, Cecilia's paralegal. You chat with her while I handle Emerson. He's the managing partner. Naturally, we'll spend some time with Malcolm. You've probably met him a hundred times, Eja."

I nodded. "Her secretary. Yes, I got to know him fairly well. Great guy." I lowered my voice. "Remember. We need information on two fronts: personal and professional. Anything, even if it's a rumor. They've already spoken to the cops, but I'll bet everyone was very discreet."

"You know lawyers, don't you? Bolin said they're paranoid about anything that might sully the firm's reputation."

"I guess murder falls into that category," I said. "Pamela Schwartz is another matter. Let's hope we can avoid her until the end. You may have to get dramatic, Anika. Draw her attention away from me."

Her smile was fraught with sorrow. "That won't be difficult. I'll faint if I have to."

We slapped hands. "That's the spirit."

A PILE OF VENERABLE grey brick housed Sevier, Miles and Swann. The firm was large, over eighty attorneys, an offshoot of the original enterprise founded by CeCe's grandfather and his late partners. From the portraits adorning the lobby, I learned that Grandpa Swann had the same good looks and sinewy form as Bolin and Deming. His partners looked like many lawyers, earnest, amiable, and unremarkable.

We were escorted to the elevator by a deferential security guard who stopped just short of kissing Anika's ring. His heartfelt tributes to CeCe seemed genuine, however. As we ascended to the thirty-third floor, Anika freshened her lipstick and winked at me.

"We're on, Eja. You look fantastic!"

He was waiting for us. Malcolm Cates, CeCe's assistant and trusted right hand, drew us close and hugged us. With his neatly trimmed hair, navy suit, red tie, and white shirt, he could easily have passed for an attorney. Malcolm never cared for that. His most endearing trait was dignity and a sense of pride that transcended status. CeCe adored and trusted him. If she'd hidden any secrets, I'd bet Malcolm knew them.

Anika described my cover story and left for the corner office in the lupine grasp of the grand pooh-bah, Emerson Michaels. Malcolm waved me into CeCe's office and poured espresso from her machine. "I'm at your disposal," he said. "Orders from on high."

"Great! I have lots of questions." I resurrected my peppy cheerleader act from high school. Since I'd never made the squad, it was total fantasy and a bit rusty.

"Tell me about these cases she lost. You know, product liability ones."

Malcolm blanched. "That's confidential. Propriety information. I don't think . . ."

"Orders from on high?" I glared at him, hands on hips. "Bolin Swann must have been mistaken."

That name worked on Malcolm like a lightning strike. He gulped a slug of espresso and nodded. "Okay, I'll have Meribeth brief you on that. What else?"

His discomfort made me wonder how big a deal those lost cases really were. I'd chalked CeCe's outrage up to her fierce competitive spirit. Swanns never lost, and they never accepted second place in anything. What if there was more to it? CeCe would stamp out impropriety like a demented flamenco dancer.

"Let's make one thing clear," I said. "CeCe didn't kill herself. If I'm wrong, tell me. Otherwise, let's cut to the chase."

Malcolm grinned. "So. You're not writing a memoir."

"Not so fast," I said. "I am a writer, as you know, and I will tell CeCe's story. But it may end up being more true crime than memoir. That depends on getting facts from the people who knew her best."

He thought about it for a moment, then closed the door and loosened his tie. "Very well. How can I help?"

WE SPENT THE next hour trading memories of CeCe, recalling her generous heart, crazy laugh, and fierce ambition. Malcolm had been the prototype "office husband" who did whatever it took to lighten his boss's load. He understood her, appreciated her many strengths, and compensated for her weaknesses.

"Did you know about Raven?" I asked. "Even I didn't know she'd gotten engaged."

Malcolm smiled. "Ms. Swann kept her personal life to herself. Mostly. But over the past few months, she was just so . . . jubilant, I guess you'd say. She asked me how I felt about married life. You know, all the trade-offs and rewards." He sighed.

"Did he call here? Maybe leave a number?"

His clenched jaw told me this was a touchy subject. I understood but didn't back down. "Please, Malcolm. It's important."

He tapped his iPad and accessed a file. "He called from this number several times. Kind of weird, because I think it's an answering service or something." Malcolm shrugged. "I must be wrong. No one uses those these days."

"What made you think that?"

"Just a feeling. I could hear pages, you know, like in an airport or train station."

I looked at the number. Was this innocuous set of digits the key to Raven?

"How about at work? You guys probably knew her big news. The federal appointment?"

"You know offices, Ms. Kane. Word of mouth and all. When Senator Lewis showed up, people talked."

That jolted me awake. "Wait a minute. Prescott Lewis came into the office to see her? Recently?"

Malcolm tapped his iPad once more. "Yep. He met with her and Pam Schwartz last month, and he had lunch with Ms. Swann on Thursday."

"Thursday. Three days before she died?"

That lying sack of shit said he hadn't seen her in weeks!

"Yes, there was a bit of fuss about that."

I gained a new appreciation for dentists. Questioning Malcolm was like pulling teeth.

"What kind of fuss?"

His face grew ashen, highlighting the sprig of freckles on the bridge of his nose. "It's only hearsay. You'd better ask Meribeth Foye. She heard everything."

"You were the one she trusted," I said. "You monitored her messages, made all her appointments. What about Dr. Townsend?"

"Townsend?" He'd perfected a blank, unreadable stare.

Discretion is fine. Commendable. But Malcolm Cates was pissing me off. "She's gone," I said. "You can't protect her now. We both know she was seeing a shrink. Acrophobia's nothing to be ashamed of." I jabbed my index finger at him. "Tell me everything you know."

Malcolm swallowed hard and sipped his latte. "She kept it quiet. Didn't want to show weakness. This is a cold, harsh place, Ms. Kane." He stepped over to CeCe's computer and accessed her calendar. "Ms. Swann went once a week to Townsend for six months. Then she stopped. Wouldn't say why."

I raised my eyebrows skyward and stayed silent, willing him to crack. Malcolm was a tough customer, but he finally relented. "Okay, it may not mean much, but she and Dr. Townsend spoke on the phone."

"Often?"

He shrugged. "Once or twice, maybe. I heard her raise her voice one time, and that was unusual. Ms. Swann was always a lady . . . very self-contained."

A good detective knows when to quit. I thanked Malcolm and gave him my card with instructions to call me directly.

He squeezed my hand as I left and whispered to me. "She'd found what she'd been searching for. She was happy, Ms. Kane. At peace."

ANIKA JOINED ME this time. She accepted Meribeth Foye's teary condolences and introduced me, trotting out that "future daughter-in-law" fiction.

CeCe seldom spoke of her paralegal, not out of animus, but because the poor thing was so damn dull. She even dressed like the Catholic schoolgirl she'd once been: buttoned-up white shirt with Peter Pan collar, pleated plaid skirt, and lumpy, ill-fitting blazer. The oxfords were missing, but I bet they held pride of place somewhere in her closet. Frumpy women like Meribeth make stringy hair and mottled complexions a point of honor. It's a welcome reprieve that makes wallflowers like me feel almost sultry.

I'd never swallowed her selfless serf pose. It was too facile an explanation for a very complex woman. Meribeth radiated subservience and piety, but I'd seen the mask slip more than once. Her brand of salvation entailed sprinkling nuggets of malice everywhere while exposing her victim's every vice to relentless scrutiny. I envisioned her in seventeenth century Salem, brandishing a torch as she led the mob to the gallows.

"Eja wants to ask you some questions," Anika said. She hesitated, drew a beautiful lace hanky from her purse, and dabbed her eyes. "It's difficult to talk about. I know that. But having a memoir—something we can turn to—might give us comfort."

Meribeth's avid little eyes glistened. They were her best feature, a rich shade of chestnut that enabled her to skirt the line between plain and ugly. "Naturally I want to help, Mrs. Swann. Anything I can do." She fumbled with a file folder on her desk. "We were close, you know. Very close."

I forcibly restrained myself. Instead of slapping the lie off her chipmunk cheeks, I smiled tremulously. "Do you have time now? I have only a few questions."

Anika rose and patted Meribeth's shoulder. "I'll leave you girls alone while I go speak with Pamela." She walked unsteadily toward the door, teetering on her stilettos. I could tell by the way she clutched the doorframe that Anika wasn't faking. She and CeCe had been allies as well as mother and daughter, joining forces against the male Swanns. The enormity of her loss was staggering, and Anika was barely holding on.

"So sad," Meribeth said. "The Swanns were like a second family to me."

More lies. Anger subsided as curiosity overwhelmed me. Why was this pompous mouse pretending? Was she delusional or just a cunning liar?

"You were a great comfort to her," I lied. "Especially in the past few months. She barely confided in me anymore."

Meribeth nodded. "I told her to tell the cops. So many nuts run around these days that you can't take chances." She folded her arms in self-righteous glee.

Holy shit! CeCe had a stalker. Meribeth would clam up if I asked direct questions, so I opted for sheer cunning. "Did you keep them?

You know, the things the stalker sent?"

Meribeth Foye set her lips in a mean, firm line. "She told me to destroy them."

I played a hunch. "Good thing you ignored that. Sometimes CeCe had no common sense. She needed someone to take charge of things like that."

Meribeth rewarded me with a tight smile.

"Where are they? I'd really like to see them."

She reached into a capacious knitting bag and pulled out a packet of letters. "I hid them here so the police wouldn't find them. You'd think even stalkers would use email these days. This feels like some convoluted mystery novel."

Don't get insulted, I told myself. After all, mysteries weren't everyone's cup of poison. Besides, threatening letters were a tried-and-true literary device that still worked even in the Internet age.

I handled the letters gingerly, although any fingerprints were long gone. Meribeth had neatly grouped a series of six letters with envelopes. All were uniform size and shape, the type of cheap lined stationery stocked by every CVS or Walgreens in the Bay State. Each was directed to Cecilia L. Swann, Esquire. That was curious. The sender was educated enough to address a lawyer properly and intimate enough to know her middle initial. CeCe never used that initial—claimed that she had no middle name. Even her diploma from Harvard Law School didn't include it.

The message was printed in block letters that would be difficult to identify. Its tone was hostile but marvelously simple. *Back off, bitch or you die*. Each message escalated the threat until the final one said, *You die tomorrow.* It was postmarked last Thursday in Boston. The date stamp from the mailroom confirmed that CeCe received it on Friday, two days before she died.

"Wow! These don't seem like office pranks. They're serious." I gave Meribeth a winsome smile. "Who would do something like this? I'll bet you have a hunch. CeCe always said you were shrewd."

Actually, she'd called her a shrew, but why quibble.

Meribeth swelled with self-importance. "I have suspicions. Nothing more." She leaned forward, her voice barely audible. "Some people around here think only lawyers have brains. Ms. Swann was different. She listened to everyone, even me."

"I'll bet Lieutenant Bates would be interested in these letters. Let me take them to her. That way you won't get in trouble with the firm."

She hesitated for a moment and checked her watch, no doubt weighing the merits of playing hero with the downside of unemployment.

"Wow!" I said. "Your watch is terrific. I love a Rolex."

The compliment unleashed a tide of resentment that threatened to swamp any further conversation. Meribeth's chest inflated like a pouter pigeon. "Rolex! That's a laugh. Do you know what they pay me around here? It's a fake. I'm lucky to have a Timex." She gathered the notes and thrust them at me. "Here. Take the nasty things if you think they'll help. Ms. Swann wasn't bothered one bit. In fact, she laughed. Said they were only a ruse. I got the idea she knew exactly who sent them." Meribeth wrinkled her nose. "I remember when the last one came on Friday. Ms. Swann tossed it right in the trash."

I tried subtly. "I'll bet she made some quip. Just like CeCe."

The paralegal froze. "She said something, but it didn't make sense. Something about a rook trying to be a queen."

CeCe and her chess metaphors! Even I knew that rooks didn't have the power of the chess queen. That wouldn't stop one from trying some upward mobility by capturing the queen. I summoned every ounce of hypocrisy in my body. "Lawyers are used to confrontation, I guess. They seem to enjoy it."

Meribeth gave another supercilious smile. "You've got that right."

"What was bothering her, Meribeth? You'd know better than anyone."

Appeals to vanity often work. They're especially effective when the target is delusional law firm chattel. Meribeth swelled with pride and a touch of malice.

"There was one thing that drove Ms. Swann absolutely bonkers." She paused theatrically and said, "Losing. She hated losing a case. Wasn't used to the downside like most of us."

That surprised me, but I decided to play along. "She seldom lost. Not CeCe Swann."

Meribeth sniffed. "You'd be surprised. Ms. Swann lost three big cases recently. Product liability issues. Major clients. Mr. Michaels was livid. Lots of business lost there."

"But surely that's expected. Can't win them all, you know."

The paralegal glowered at me as if cursing my abysmal ignorance. "There was a big brawl, I can tell you. Opposing counsel accessed privileged information somehow." She curled her lip. "Some people blamed Ms. Swann."

"CeCe told me she'd had a nasty encounter with another lawyer just last week." I shrugged. "She blew it off immediately. Personally, I'd have been upset."

Meribeth slouched down in her chair after checking to see if we were alone. "Nothing scared Ms. Swann. Most of us, well, we avoid Ms. Schwartz if we can. Sometimes she's as sweet as pie, but you never know when she'll erupt. Last week she went wild."

I threw her a conspiratorial wink. "Men adored CeCe, and she reciprocated. I suppose that's what they quarreled about."

Meribeth nodded. "Senator Lewis is a real flirt. He joked with all the girls when he visited here. Even me." Meribeth's expression morphed from sad to smug.

Something clicked in my mind. On the videotape, Prescott Lewis said he'd considered other lawyers for that judicial slot, including Pamela Schwartz. No wonder she'd pitched a fit when CeCe, a woman ten years her junior, was selected.

My heart palpitated, and my palms felt sweaty. I yearned to fly out of the office and find Deming. He'd know what to do, unless he cared for his lover more than justice. I yearned for the softness of his Kiton suit and the comfort of his arms around me. I was acting like a fool, and it didn't faze me one bit. That was truly frightening. I kept dreaming, oblivious to time and place until Meribeth Foye's violent gasp awakened me.

Pamela Schwartz stood in the doorway, oozing the synthetic charm of a road-stand cobra.

Her eyes widened as she gave me a quick, expert appraisal. My buffed and polished image left her temporarily speechless. That felt good!

"Why Eja Kane, you look marvelous. Whatever have you done to yourself?" She stepped closer, giving my curls a quick tug. "These highlights are superb! Who did them?"

"No one can fool you, Pam." Anika slipped into the office, putting her arm around me. "Eja and I had a session with Harpo. He's a wizard, don't you agree?"

Pamela nodded, showing a predator's grin. Her teeth were enormous—perfectly formed, soldier-straight, and blazing white. Made for ripping and tearing prey.

"I understand congratulations are in order, Eja. Such a shock! Dem never mentioned anything about you two. He'll pay for that when he stops by. Count on it."

Color flooded my face. "Nothing's official yet," I stammered. "Everything happened rather quickly."

She blocked the door. Otherwise, I would have stampeded headlong toward the elevator. Deming would be furious when he heard. He'd think I was trying to trap him into a relationship he neither wanted nor needed. Anika's well-intentioned ploy no longer amused me. It was humiliating.

I focused on a seascape adorning the far wall. I'd always loathed that dreadful painting, but today it provided a welcome distraction.

Anika choked back a sob that seemed genuine. "Oops! I shouldn't have said anything. Bolin will be so cross. It's just . . . since we lost my daughter, Eja has been such a comfort. She's already a member of our family."

"Let's leave," I said, gathering my things. "These ladies both seem very busy."

I was desperate to flee the tasteful, hermetically sealed prison where nothing was as it seemed. Somehow CeCe had thrived here. She loved the palace intrigue and the sweltering egos. I was made of simpler stuff, content to hunch over my computer, crafting fiendish murders in the solitude of my living room.

"Nonsense," Pamela purred. "Come have a latte in my office. You've had an exhausting day. I'm sure you could use the caffeine." She swept out of CeCe's area with Anika and I trailing in her wake.

Pamela's office was a large corner space with stunning views of the Boston skyline. The modern décor and stark black-on-white color scheme sent a chill up my spine. It was a pristine blend of leather, chrome, and glass that flirted with sterility. No signs of disarray: Not a paper clip, magazine, or pen out of place in Pamland. I wondered if she was equally tidy in her most intimate moments. Deming Swann knew how to ravage bed linens and their inhabitants. Maybe she made an exception for him.

"Did you hear me, Eja?" Pamela had that strained smile on her face again. "Whole or skim milk in your latte?"

"Skim is fine. Thanks. I was so busy admiring your office that I got lost." I looked around for Anika.

Pamela nodded to her assistant and joined me on the couch. "Anika took a break. Now, what can I tell you about Cecilia? For your memoir, I mean."

A sudden surge of adrenaline swept through my veins, making me more Wonder Woman than street urchin. I flashed my newly lined eyes at her, feeling a healthy jolt of self-esteem.

"How about describing CeCe to me as if we were strangers."

She paused then tapped her finger on the glass cube. Her hands were perfectly manicured today. She'd repaired that broken nail and chipped polish.

"Cecilia was . . . fearless. Bright, ambitious, and bound for glory. She was younger than most of our partners by quite a few years, but that never stopped her." Pamela smiled. "If she had something to contribute, she'd do it. Her favorite phrase was, 'Have you considered . . .'"

That tugged my heartstrings. I'd heard my friend say those words in countless academic debates. More often than not her suggestions were brilliant. Unorthodox, sometimes shocking, but right on the money.

"How did clients react? You've got some old-line Bostonians on your list."

"She charmed most of them—especially the men. Cecilia was hell on wheels in front of a jury. Until recently she got astounding results on corporate cases I thought were hopeless."

That intrigued me. Meribeth had mentioned the same thing.

"CeCe didn't like to lose," I said. "She was such a competitor. Wouldn't that make her a liability to the firm—losing cases, I mean?"

Her expression mixed pity with contempt. "Every lawyer loses cases, Eja. Even Clarence Darrow lost a few." Her smile was one notch short of a sneer. "Of course, since you're a writer you probably judge everyone by Perry Mason."

I reminded myself that this was a mission. Any pleasure I'd derive from pummeling Pamela's surgically sculpted nose would pale in comparison to achieving my goal. Maybe a well-placed lie would save the day.

"I wonder why CeCe was upset about it then. Bolin said it really bothered her."

"Bolin knew about it?" Pamela stiffened. "They were corporate cases. Sure bets until the other side anticipated our arguments. She lost only three. Three big clients."

Pamela's lizard eyes darted back and forth, never leaving my face. "Of course there were downsides to her energy too. Cecilia could be intrusive. She spent far too much effort meddling in other people's cases and their personal business."

I took a risk and played hardball.

"I've heard that the two of you quarreled. Violently."

She burst out laughing. "You bet we did! That was the only way we could communicate. Two ambitious, strong willed-women. It was a recipe for disaster."

I glanced up from my notebook. "So you didn't mind then . . . about the judgeship?"

Tricking lawyers is hard. They're duplicitous by nature and never afraid to lie. Pamela Schwartz fended off my feeble efforts without raising a sweat.

"Mind? I was happy for her." She ruffled her perfect bob. "Besides, I'd already turned Prescott down. I simply don't have the temperament for wearing the robes. Frankly, I doubt that Cecilia had it either. She liked the limelight way too much."

I was peddling downhill at astounding speed while Pamela scaled the heights. She was an Olympian; I was the towel girl. That didn't stop me. What I lacked in finesse, I made up for with grit.

"Death threats are commonplace in your firm? That surprises me."

Her composure dipped for just a moment. "Death threats?"

I resisted the temptation to check my mirror. Mirror! What was happening to me?

"Don't worry. I'll ask Lieutenant Bates. Now, what other memories of CeCe would you like to share? I suppose you two played chess together."

She laughed and shifted in her seat. "You're really something, Ms. Eja Kane. Not quite what you appear to be. No wonder Deming kept you under wraps. To answer your question, I don't play games. That includes chess. CeCe was the game player in the firm. Always, always trying to finesse things."

I steadied my hand by foraging in my purse. A vial of eye drops provided a temporary diversion. "Excuse me. Chronic dry eye."

Pamela Schwartz was a Sherman tank demolishing my defenses. "So," she drawled. "When's the big day?"

"Pardon?"

"Your wedding day. To Deming. You know. Tall, dark, and dreamy."

A deep baritone sliced through the dead air. "Yes, darling. Tell Pamela. Don't be a tease."

Fifteen

HE STOOD IN THE doorway, smirking while my heart lobbed back and forth like an errant tennis ball. This scene would never make it in my novels. My heroes were paragons who inspired passion, not abject humiliation. Deming raised his eyebrows, doing a double take when he saw Harpo's handiwork. He recovered quickly, glided over, and planted a quick kiss on my cheek.

"Cat's out of the bag, Pam. Discretion was called for. You understand." Deming kept a firm grip on my wrist. "Come, my love. Time to go home." He steered me out the door, while Pamela fumed.

"Let go of me," I hissed. "I'll scream if I have to."

His eyes sizzled as he spun me toward him. "Don't cause a fuss, dearest. We're in love after all." He pasted a phony smile on his face and muttered in my ear. "What the hell are you playing at? And what kind of mess did you drag my mother into?"

"There you are!" Anika floated toward us, her smile radiant. "She's something, isn't she, Dem? So lovely."

He urged us toward the elevator, saying through gritted teeth, "Let's discuss this at home. Dad's waiting."

Deming helped his mother into the Porsche, leaving me to scramble into the back seat. Deming stared straight ahead, refusing to meet my eyes. Some fiancé he was! I forgot my woes and chuckled.

"I guess our engagement is over. Who said relationships can't last?"

"Funny, Eja. You're quite the comedian." Deming stuck out his lip the same way he'd done as a boy when CeCe called him Mr. Sulky Pout.

Anika patted her son's arm. "Oh, darling, don't be an old meanie. It was my idea. You know, to throw them off the scent. Eja uses it all the time in her books. Red herring. That's the term."

He rolled his eyes. "That's just the point, Mom. This isn't one of Eja's convoluted plots. My sister's murder was real."

"Convoluted! I'll bet you never even read my books."

Now it was Deming who flushed. "I may have glanced at one or two of them. My sister left them strewn around the house."

I felt rather smug after that admission. Not many authors my age have written four traditionally published books. Besides, despite my pitiful royalties I was steadily building a fan base, and sales were inching up. Deming Swann could just stuff it!

I whipped out my notepad and updated my findings. "We did pretty well today, didn't we Anika? You'll be surprised."

"Huh!" I've learned to ignore Deming when he throws a tantrum. Silence is the gold standard when arguing with a lawyer.

I stole a quick glance at his profile. Deming was in full stone-faced mode, cold and unyielding. Hard to believe that those same lips, soft and pliant, had rocked my world a few nights ago. When we arrived at the Swann manse, he helped his mother alight and hustled me toward the door.

"We need to talk," he growled. "Wedding plans and all."

"Not now, Dem." Anika linked arms with me. "Come upstairs, Eja. I have a surprise. We can change into something comfortable."

"I didn't bring anything, Mrs. Swann. Plus, I'm worried about Cato. He'll get hungry."

A hungry Cato was a fearsome spectacle. One I didn't care to face.

"Don't worry. Give Po your keys, and he'll get Cato for you."

Swann magic—an answer for everything. I bowed to the inevitable and trudged upstairs to her dressing room. It was just as I expected, airy and elegant with silk-flocked coverings, a patterned chaise, and closets lining each wall. Anika padded toward a column of custom built shelves and pulled out a prize.

"This would look amazing on you, Eja." She motioned toward a floor-length leopard print silk with the store tags still on it.

"Oh, I couldn't. It's brand new."

Anika choked back a sob. "I bought it last week for Cecilia." She handed it to me. "Take it. Please."

She left me there, fingering a beautiful garment that seemed like a shroud. After a few adjustments, I wiggled into it and stole a glimpse in the mirror. Good grief! Could that sultry woman actually be me, Eja Kane, MFA? My life hovered between charade and farce. I was either Raggedy Ann or Cinderella sans prince, waiting patiently for salvation.

A sharp rap jolted me back to reality. Deming cracked open the door and poked his head in. "Get a move on. Stop preening, for Christ's sake!"

"What's the matter? Don't you like the new me?"

He curled his lip. "There was nothing wrong with the old you, although I have to admit that you look . . . nice. The way you looked when you married that slug."

There it was again. For some reason Deming fixated on my ill-fated marriage and the husband who dumped me. "Get a grip, Deming. After all, you never even saw me that day. You were too busy to attend the wedding, if you recall. Something about a fishing trip."

For the second time that day, I achieved the impossible—making Deming blush.

"Mother has pictures. You know how sentimental she is. Cecilia too. They were blinded by that guy's looks. Thought he was charming. Ugh!"

We locked eyes and quickly turned away.

Deming waved me toward the stairwell. "Come on. Don't keep my Dad waiting. Jake's here too, in case you plan to faint or something."

"No danger. I'm much tougher than I look."

THEY WERE IN the library sipping brandy; Bolin, Jake, and Anika with Cato curled around her feet. The two men looked up at me, did a double take, and quickly slipped into neutral. Cato ignored my existence.

"Wow," Jake said, admiration in his eyes. "You look fantastic!"

"I second that. Looks like your handiwork, Leda." Bolin smiled fondly at his wife.

Deming's frown erased every bit of good will. "Don't encourage her, Dad. The two of them played detective today and stirred up trouble. For no good reason."

"Whoa. Hold on a minute." I cut him off in mid-rant. "First, listen to what we found. Then judge us."

"Sounds like a plan, son." Bolin nodded at me. "Go on, Eja."

I summarized our exploits, focusing on the major players and our objectives. When I concluded, even Deming wore a look of grudging admiration.

Bolin leaned forward, gripping the arms of his chair. "You actually found him? You found Raven?"

"Well, not quite. But we've got at least one number for him and a few clues." I ticked off each point on my fingers. "We know he's a longtime acquaintance, someone all of you are familiar with. Plus, for some reason, CeCe worried that Deming might oppose him."

"Damn straight," Deming barked. "Jem Russell, or our senior senator. Not to mention some of those other jokers she found."

I sprang up. "You're missing the point. She knew her parents wouldn't mind. Just you. That means something." I turned toward Bolin. "You've made your feelings about Jem and Senator Prescott pretty clear. Raven is someone you know and like."

Anika clutched her throat. "She's right! Oh, Bolin, we're getting closer."

"Keep in mind that Raven made her very happy," I said. "Harpo, Malcolm, even Meribeth Foye said so. Maybe we're on the wrong track. Raven, whoever he is, loved CeCe. Why would he hurt her?"

Deming tapped his toe like a castanet. "Maybe she changed her mind, and Raven went bonkers. Loved her to death."

Anika buried her face in her husband's jacket. His reaction was immediate, a withering look that stopped Deming in his tracks.

"Anything else, Eja?" Bolin asked.

I hesitated, trying to balance hard truth with compassion. "There was some trouble at the firm. Did CeCe ever discuss any threats she'd gotten?"

The room grew tomb-silent. Even Cato stayed frozen in place.

Bolin recovered first. "Threats?"

I reached into my purse and handed the letters to him. "Someone sent these to her. It's probably some crank blowing off steam, but I think Lieutenant Bates should see them."

Bolin's face masked any show of emotion. He spread the letters over the coffee table as Deming and Jake hovered behind him. Anika neither spoke nor looked at the letters.

"How the hell did you get these?" Deming asked. "Torture or the third degree?"

"Confidential source," I said. "Pamela didn't seem to know anything about them, and CeCe never mentioned them to me either. Maybe she didn't take them seriously."

Jake moved beside Anika to take her pulse, but she shrugged off the attention.

"I'll contact the lieutenant tomorrow morning," Bolin said. "She'll probably know something about that gun by then." He sighed. "Anything else, Eja?"

"Actually, yes." I glanced at my notebook. "This is rather

awkward."

"Like that would stop you," Deming said. "Come on. Give it your best shot."

Bolin and Jake exchanged worried glances, but Anika held up her hand. "I'm fine. Don't worry. The important thing is finding our daughter's murderer."

I paused to regroup. "It may be nothing, but Senator Prescott lied when he said he hadn't seen CeCe recently. He had lunch with her the Thursday before she died."

To their credit, no one gasped or cursed. Even Deming remained calm.

"Hard to hide something like that," Jake said. "Pam must have known about it."

"She did. In fact, she said she'd bowed out of contention. Had no interest in it at all."

Bolin turned to his son. "You're close to her. Do you believe that?"

I trained my eyes on the room's elegant Sarouk.

"Maybe," Deming said. "We don't discuss office politics, Pam and I. And thanks to Mom's little marriage scheme, she probably won't even take my calls."

Jake choked back a devilish grin. "Ah, come on, Dem. You should be honored that a hottie like Eja would go along with it when she could do so much better." He tugged his tie. "Like an eligible, compassionate healer."

"Stuff it, Jake." Deming glowered, but his heart wasn't in it.

I was momentarily lost, meandering through a delightful maze. A hottie? Me? Men always admired my brains, loyalty, and wit, never my looks. I ducked my head, awash in superficial splendor.

"We're going to put you on the firm's payroll if this keeps up." Bolin's jovial manner was a facade, a futile attempt to distract us from the pain of CeCe's murder. I yearned to console him—all of them—but came up empty.

"Meribeth mentioned one other thing. It's news to me, but maybe you guys heard about it."

Four pairs of eyes turned my way, warily, expectantly.

"This was a work thing. About CeCe losing some important cases. Anybody know about that?"

"She mentioned it," Deming said. "No big deal. Well, she was pissed, but you know how she was. CeCe expected to win every time."

Bolin threw a sideways look at his wife. "We spoke about it. Naturally, her pride was hurt, but more than that she was puzzled. She reviewed every action in those cases, trying to find where she'd missed a step. No luck."

"Maybe that's it," Jake said. "Could this whole tragedy be work related?"

My fantasy solution had Pamela Schwartz murdering CeCe out of jealousy or because she'd hurt the firm. It was an absurd but alluring way to dispose of a rival.

A swath of fur swept past me as Cato headed toward the door. I knew from experience what that signaled.

"Come on, Cato. Let's head home."

Anika leapt up. "No. You can't, Eja. It isn't safe. Stay here tonight."

I was wedged between compassion and independence, unable to assert myself without hurting CeCe's mother.

"No problem, Anika." Jake gave her a dose of charm therapy. "I'll watch out for her. Take her right to her doorstep."

Deming bristled at his friend's offer. "Don't bother, Jake-man. I'll drive them home and check out her place for bad guys. Okay, Mom?"

Anika nodded meekly, unable to hide the triumphant gleam in her eyes.

I ARRIVED HOME safely with my Praetorian Guards in tow. Jake and Deming checked out every crevice in my humble abode, finding nothing more sinister than dust bunnies, chew toys, and the odd shoe. When they left I felt bereft. I had no right to expect anything from Deming. I knew that. Ours had been a fleeting physical alliance. Nothing more. My head and heart waged a fierce struggle for control. Logic couldn't quell the dull ache I felt or still my longing for him. I was accustomed to solitude and rather enjoyed my own company. Deming, on the other hand, always had a roster of nubile women to squire around. CeCe and I had teased him about his little black book many times. Now the reality of it numbed me.

I fired up the Bose and curled up on the sofa with Cato beside me. Bonnie Raitt and Linda Ronstadt kept me company, wailing about that universal heartbreak: faithless men and shattered dreams. Until now, I'd spared myself such angst. My ill-fated marriage was long over, and I'd avoided the entangling alliances that cause trouble. Casual dates and lots of solitude sustained me. And CeCe. Her friendship had compensated for the void in my personal life. *Laotung*—sisters forever. Nothing much changes. That's just an ancient version of today's BFF. As loneliness overwhelmed me, I buried my head in the cushion and cried myself to sleep.

Sixteen

SHARDS OF LIGHT filtered through the curtains as I shook myself awake. That sound. Someone was battering down my front door. Cato the Wonder Dog never even stirred, but I leapt up, electrified by the hope that it was Deming. Sometime during the night I'd drifted into my bedroom and shed the leopard silk. Unfortunately, makeup was spread all over my face, and my tousled highlights looked like a hornet's nest.

"Coming." I donned a robe, swirled mouthwash around, and made some quick repairs. Then, abandoning every sensible precaution drummed into me since childhood, I flung open the door. My smile faded quickly when I saw my caller. Lieutenant Euphemia Bates, hands on hips, stood firmly planted on my doorstep.

"Finally." She flashed a practiced smile, but something told me mirth was the last thing on her agenda.

"Sorry. Did I miss an appointment or something?"

Sarcasm was wasted on Euphemia Bates. She was used to grilling far bigger fish than me. "May I come in? This is strictly unofficial. Just wanted to verify a few things. Check out some inconsistencies."

I waved her in and did a quick survey. Every inch of her was encased in charcoal from the paper-thin merino wool dress to her cashmere cardigan and pumps. A slim black belt and silver locket broke the monochromatic color scheme. Mia Bates looked stunning, and judging by her strut, she knew it.

"Espresso?" I mumbled. "I just woke up."

"Perfect." She gave me another meaningless smile that never reached her eyes.

Cato, that worthless cur, wiggled up to Mia, dispensing doggy charm.

"Oops! I need to walk him right away, or he'll have an accident."

"No need," Mia said. "My sergeant's right outside. He'll do the honors."

So much for a strictly unofficial interrogation; I'd been stalked and trapped by an expert. Without a double dose of caffeine, I didn't stand a chance. Fortunately, the Nepresso machine was close at hand. After a few sips of the deep, rich brew, my mental fog lifted. I steeled myself for whatever Mia had in mind.

"How can I help you?"

"Apparently you're trying to do my job," Mia said. "Doing pretty well at it, too."

I feigned innocence. "Pardon me?"

Mia flipped open her notepad and stared. "You got to all of them: shrink, hair stylist, secretary, paralegal, and ex-fiancé. Did I miss anyone, Ms. Kane?"

In my novels it's the amateur sleuth who confounds the cops. Obviously, Mia didn't follow that script.

"I'm writing a memoir about my friend at the family's request. Ask Bolin Swann if you don't believe me."

Mia daintily placed her cup on the saucer and dabbed her lips with the napkin. "I read one of your books, you know. Clever. Not terribly accurate though." She fixed me with a stony stare. "We know what we're doing, Eja. This isn't fiction. In real life things aren't tied up neat and tidy every time."

"Maybe I can help you. Compare notes, share information, things like that."

"No!" Her words stung like a slap. "I won't risk your life. Get it?" She took a deep breath. "Mr. Swann already gave me those poison-pen notes. He mentioned your other efforts too."

I had nothing to lose. "What about the gun? Any results?"

Her eyes narrowed to umber slits. "No information. The serial number was filed off, but at least there was no ballistics match to any crime."

That puzzled me. Where in hell had CeCe gotten that thing, and why had she kept it? Maybe she felt more threatened than she'd ever admitted. Why hadn't she trusted me, or her family? At the first hint of trouble Bolin Swann would have dispatched a squad of tough guys to guard her. That gnawed at me, festering like a sore tooth. Had I somehow failed my friend, or was this another in CeCe's endless quests for independence from the male Swanns?

"Did you hear me, Ms. Kane?" Mia looked one inch short of handcuffing me.

"Sorry. Missed it."

"Stay out of this. We're dealing with a clever murderer. Ruthless enough to throw your friend off a building. Imagine that, Ms. Kane, next time you feel curious."

Lieutenant Euphemia Bates gathered her things and stomped out the door.

THAT EVENING, I went into author mode for a book signing. When it comes to hawking my wares, I'm a perpetual wallflower, proud of my product, shamed by my tactics. Signings were part of the business to be endured, not anticipated. I pasted a bland, professional smile on my face and did my personal dog and pony show for the sparse crowd.

I stiffened, thinking of yet another CeCe moment. We'd established a ritual to commemorate book signings. After each one, CeCe would meet me at The Last Hurrah, the iconic bar named for the O'Connor novel. We'd eat a shameful number of snacks while toasting James Michael Curley, Parker House rolls, and Boston cream pie. That was over now, a treasured relic of my past.

As the final straggler left, I mentally calculated my take from the evening's proceeds and packed my satchel.

"Sign one more, lady?"

I looked up and saw him, a vision in black jeans so tight they left nothing to my very active imagination.

"What the . . .?"

"I understand we have a date at The Last Hurrah. Nine sharp." Deming's eyes looked suspiciously moist. "I'm a poor substitute, but I'll try my best."

I forced myself not to cry. Lord knows I'd shed enough tears lately. After years of teasing and fights, Deming's kindness was the hardest thing to accept. I moved in close and hugged his waist. "Thank you."

"Hey, what's this about? Not getting soft on me, I hope."

"Never." We walked silently up Newbury street, through the Common, and over to the Parker House site of the Last Hurrah. The first Christmas lights twinkled star-bright from tree branches along the path. Way too early. Grossly commercial. Utterly sublime.

Deming signaled the waiter, and we eased into a padded leather booth in a premium spot. Our booth. The one CeCe and I always claimed.

He gave me the eye. "You're not thirsty?"

"I know what I want." I flushed at the implication. "To drink."

The well-trained waiter took our order with a straight face.

"Pumpkin martini! Are you serious? That's disgusting." Deming made a rude remark and ordered Glenlivet XXV.

"We always drank those, CeCe and I. Martinis for the fainthearted. Plus they're tasty." I smacked my lips in anticipation.

"I'll take your word for it. I'm a scotch man. Always have been."

We clinked glasses and toasted her.

"She loved Christmas," Deming said. "Acted like a damn kid."

I nodded, thinking of CeCe's mad scramble to find just the right gift for everyone. She'd start in July and hide them all over her house until Christmas Eve.

"Wait a minute!" I startled our waiter into dropping the cutlery.

Deming moved closer to me. "Are you okay?"

I clutched his arm until he yelped.

"What the hell is wrong with you?"

"Don't you see? It's a clue. CeCe led us to it."

He stroked my cheek. "Slow down and tell me."

"It's just a thought, but knowing CeCe, she might have Raven's Christmas present hidden in her house. She always did stuff like that."

"It's only October, and so what if she did?"

"Okay, it's a long shot, but one worth taking. Even if the cops found the gifts, they wouldn't think anything of it. But it's a clue."

Deming shrugged, acting lawyerly again. "Highly improbable. Unlikely."

I gulped my martini and grabbed my coat. "Drink up."

AFTER THE MAD dash to CeCe's place our momentum stalled. We collapsed on her platinum couch, paralyzed by indecision and doubts. My bright idea of an hour before had lost its luster.

"Okay. Where do we start, Sherlock?"

"I'm thinking. Give me a minute."

I looked away to mask my real thoughts. Deming's black jeans and turtleneck distracted me from almost anything unrelated to sex. It was shameful and totally unlike me, a major sixth and ninth commandment no-no. The nuns would condemn me to hell for even considering it. Dull, loyal Eja transformed into a succubus by some carefully placed highlights and a brief taste of ecstasy. What next? It was weird, wonderful, and incredibly hot!

"Time's up," he said. "Put up or shut up, Ms. Kane."

If he said "put out" I might have jumped his bones. As it was I forced myself to focus on our task. Deming was hopeless at searching, too repressed to tear into closets and explore the seamy contents of his sister's lingerie chest. I assigned him the simplest task possible: dialing the number I'd gotten from Malcolm. The number Raven had called from.

The police search had been remarkably precise. They'd accounted for every item, bagged and tagged things of interest, and replaced the rest. The inventory sheet was no help at all. They'd chosen mundane but valueless things.

I'm no expert, but I had one big advantage: I knew my friend. CeCe had a system, a method to her madness, as my mom used to say. It was quirky and defied logic, but it worked for her. Each present was concealed in a place whose initial matched the recipient. My gifts, for example, were in the entry closet, *E* for Eja, and kitchen, *K* for Kane. If that logic prevailed, I had to search anything remotely related to *R* for Raven. I discounted "roof" since even CeCe had her limits. That left the Recamier couch, rugs, and the vast refuse in her storage locker. It sounded ridiculous the more thought I gave to it.

Deming hadn't budged from his perch on the sofa. He'd hunkered down in front of the fireplace as though mesmerized by the flames and the snifter of brandy he sipped.

"Hey! Are you going to help or not?" I ignored the stirrings in my nether parts and jerked the pillow from underneath his head. "Come on. I'm not having much luck."

"I can change that." He discarded his drink and gently pulled me toward him. We rolled off the couch, tumbled on the rug, and held each other close.

"What's wrong with you?" I gasped, praying that he'd never stop.

"Nothing. For once, everything's perfect."

He brushed his lips slowly down my neck, feathering them across my collarbone in a gentle, inexorable journey of exploration. I helped him every way I could, groaning encouragement each time he touched me. Deming's long slender fingers—artist's hands—unfastened my blouse, gently tugging the chemise over my head. We snuggled under folds of cashmere, savoring the sensuous pleasure of skin on skin, deferring release almost beyond endurance.

We made love by the firelight, to the sweet sounds of Thelonious Monk. Deming held me tight against his chest, calling my name, softly, urgently kissing every part of me while I slipped seamlessly into another realm where dreams came true and love was mine to claim. I surrendered myself, giving everything, expecting nothing. Afterwards, I closed my eyes, savoring the scent of Creed and the blissful sound of his heartbeat.

Deming drifted off to sleep, but I was not so lucky. Something, some kernel of forgotten lore, kept rattling around my head. Despite the bravado, my brainstorm was barely a rain shower.

Then it hit me! I'd forgotten the vagaries of Cecilia Swann's mind. She loved obscure things and words, relished the chance to confound her peers. There was one *R* place I'd forgotten to search. It was in her closet, hiding in plain sight. Her reticule, a rare auction find, was wrapped in a soft felt sleeve among her other purses. The drawstring pouch, a cunning blend of net, beading, and brocade, had been carefully preserved by a lady of the eighteenth-century French court, possibly even by Madame de Pompadour herself. CeCe paid a small fortune for it, indulging in informed guesses and wild speculation about its origins.

I swept aside the covers, sprinting half-naked toward the closet.

"Nice view, missy, but what the hell are you up to?"

I ignored Deming and opened her purse collection, reaching to the back of the drawer for my prize. The reticule, perfectly preserved, was as regal as its purported owner. Deming grabbed a robe and hovered over me as I carefully searched the crevices of the pouch. We both gasped as a small black velvet box tumbled out. I pried open the top with trembling fingers, praying that I'd found the key to Raven.

It nestled in a plush velvet bed, an exquisitely crafted gold tie clip with a ruby-eyed serpent wound sinuously across a rough club. It was so like CeCe, beautiful but obscure.

"What's wrong?" Deming asked. "You look disappointed."

"Puzzled, actually. What the hell is that thing? Some fertility symbol?"

He bent down and examined the tie clip. "Nope. You've got sex on the brain. What we have here is the final clue." He chuckled. "So typical. Anyone else would have found a caduceus and been satisfied. Not Cecilia."

"Wait a minute. I know what a caduceus looks like: two snakes, wrapped around a shepherd's staff. This thing is more primitive."

He pinched my cheeks. "Now you've got it. This little beauty is custom-made. A staff of Asclepius."

"Who?"

"Listen and learn, my little scholar. Asclepius was a legendary Greek healer and *this,* not the caduceus, is the correct symbol for physicians. Check out the AMA website if you don't believe me."

It took me a moment to process Deming's blather. "Hold on. Does this mean that Raven is a doctor? Oh my God! She fooled everyone. CeCe was hooked on that creepy shrink after all!" I felt ill just thinking of it. All my tender feelings about Raven evaporated.

Deming shrugged. "Her phone records didn't show any calls to Wesley Townsend. But we have another way to settle this." He walked over to the side table and grabbed his wallet. "Here's that phone number Malcolm gave you. Let's try it again."

I held my breath as he dialed the number, praying he was wrong, that CeCe hadn't loved Townsend. How would Anika ever deal with that? Bolin didn't worry me. Unlike Deming, emotion wouldn't cloud his judgment. He'd dispatch his daughter's murderer without a second thought no matter who it was. Revenge is an admirable trait in a man.

After an interminable number of rings, someone answered Deming's call.

"Whose number is this, please?" It was an order, not a request. Deming Swann, master and commander. "Okay. Thanks."

His eyes showed absolutely no emotion as he turned toward me.

"That number is a switchboard."

"Where?" I was wired, one inch short of clawing his face.

"Massachusetts General Hospital."

Seventeen

"CALL JAKE," I croaked. "He'll know what to do."

Deming nodded and scanned his phone directory. He spoke with Jake in clipped tones, telling him we needed his help to track down Raven. After a few grunts and monosyllabic replies, he hung up and pointed to me.

"Get dressed. We're meeting him at my parents' place in thirty minutes."

"Tonight?"

"You heard me. Unless of course you're too tired. I'll drop you home."

"No way. And don't be so bossy. I'm the one who found the clue."

He raised his eyebrows and snickered. "You'd have more authority if you weren't half naked, you know. Not that I'm complaining. I like the view just fine."

I grabbed one of CeCe's robes and fled to the bathroom to restore my makeup and composure. After a rendezvous with a brush, I felt reasonably calm, ready to complete the quest for Raven.

Deming broke every traffic rule on that mad tear through Back Bay. Under duress, he even agreed to stop and pick up Cato. That resulted in a snarl fest where canine teeth triumphed over brute strength. The feisty spaniel leapt into the Porsche while Deming issued a string of remarkably creative oaths.

"Jeez, I hate that little fucker," he said. "My sister was nuts to adopt him. He should have gone straight to the glue factory."

I wisely kept silent since Cato was curled up on my lap wearing a particularly smug expression.

Deming tossed an envelope in my lap as he rounded a corner. "Here. Someone taped this to your door. What's the matter, late on the maintenance payment?"

"Very funny." I slipped the envelope into my purse and focused on our forthcoming meeting. "Did Jake know anything? Give you any ideas?"

He shrugged, leaving me to watch his brooding face and draw my own conclusions. Deming Swann could ace any screen test for *Wuthering Heights*. He was Heathcliff down to the last Byronic scowl, a man with intellect, physical beauty, and uncertain temperament. On the other hand I was certainly no Catherine. Sulky males, no matter how sexy, were not my cup of Earl Grey.

As we pulled into Bolin's driveway, Deming cautioned me. "Be careful if my mom's around. Something about Wesley Townsend makes her nervous."

Just then, Dr. Jake Harris swung his silver Jeep to the curb. He grabbed his medical bag and trudged toward the front door without greeting us. Curious. Jake seemed sluggish, a far cry from the lively man I'd grown accustomed to. Deming locked the Porsche and sped up to join his friend. I was delayed by Cato, who took his sweet time, stopping to inspect and water every shrub in his path.

They were waiting for me when I reached the library, stiff and awkward, like bad actors in a drawing-room farce. Bolin was the first to break the silence.

"Seems like we'll finally get to the bottom of this."

Deming shared the basics then turned to his friend. "Jake did some digging. He knows the answer."

I tried not to stare, but Jake Harris looked shattered. What the hell would affect him that way? Dark smudges ringed his caramel eyes, and even his thick springy curls sagged into limp coils.

Bolin took the lead. "So. This man my daughter loved is a doctor. Based on everything we know that can only be one person. It pains me to even think it but . . ." Anika grasped his arm so tightly that he winced. "No, Leda," he whispered. "Relax."

Jake rose quickly and stepped forward. "I can clarify things. When Deming called, I gave it a lot of thought."

"For Christ's sake man, spit it out if you know who he is. Stop stalling." Deming's muscles tensed.

I met Jake's eyes, seeing in them resignation and deep sadness.

Bolin nodded, urging him on.

"You were right about this man. All of you. He loved Cecilia, and she loved him. She worried about your reaction, not because she was ashamed, but because she'd made so many mistakes. She was especially concerned about you, Dem. I should have told you before. I know that." He turned toward Anika when he spoke. "I am Raven."

No one moved or said a word. Even Cato was uncharacteristically silent. I scanned the faces of the Swann family, seeing shock, disbelief, and a faint hint of joy. Our long quest for Raven had ended in spectacular fashion.

"We wasted a lot of time looking for you." Deming's voice was flat and unemotional, but his clenched fists signaled tension. "Why the hell didn't you tell us?"

"I wanted to, but it never seemed like the right time." Jake turned toward CeCe's picture, his face awash with emotion. "No. That's a lie. Truth is, I was ashamed to tell you. You see, I'm responsible for her death."

"What!" Deming's voice rumbled, a low, menacing monotone. He'd never seemed more dangerous as he faced Jake, his body a coiled serpent.

"You killed CeCe?" I gasped, clutching the sofa for support. The beautiful room suddenly felt oppressive, as if all the air had been sucked out of it. Anika and Bolin stayed statue-still.

"No wait! Listen, please." Jake Harris spread his hands wide. "I'll accept your verdict after I explain, even if it means Dem beats the hell out of me."

Bolin held out his arm, blocking Deming's path. "Relax, son. Hear him out." His face betrayed no emotion, although I knew what to expect if Jake confessed to murder. Bolin Swann would avenge his daughter swiftly and decisively.

"I can't explain how it happened," Jake said. "We'd been friends forever and suddenly . . ." He shrugged. "We planned to go public after this judgeship was settled. Didn't want racial politics screwing things up for her. At least that's what I told myself." He gazed at me as if I alone might understand. "But you know Cecilia. Never could keep a secret, especially from her best friend. She planned to spring it on Eja at brunch that day." A smile stole across his face. "The Big Reveal, that's what she called it, like on those stupid reality shows."

"What happened?" Deming spoke with a stranger's voice, hoarse, almost guttural.

Jake's eyes moistened as he replayed the scene. "I was too busy, too self-absorbed, to go with her. Some damn seminar on public health at Harvard. That's what I traded her life for, three CME credits."

Anika's voice was shaky. "I'm confused, Jake. What happened?"

He sipped his drink and continued. "Cecilia begged me to go with her that morning. She said she had to make just one stop first. At Jem's building."

"Did she explain? Say what it was about?" Bolin's tone was deceptively mild.

"She just laughed. Cecilia Swann, mistress of intrigue. Said she'd clinch an important deal and make it a double celebration." Jake slumped in his seat. "If I'd been on that roof, she'd still be alive."

I now understood that silence can be deafening. The library reverberated with the sound of questions unasked and grief unquenched. Even Deming traded rage for a shocked silence that broke my heart.

It was Anika who acted first. I watched her glide over to Jake and envelope him in a firm embrace. "I'm glad you found each other, Jake. Even for a little while."

He looked down at her and closed his eyes. "Can you ever forgive me?"

"Nonsense," Anika said. "You didn't hurt my daughter, did you? Well then. Now that we've ended this Raven business we can focus on finding Cecilia's killer." She turned to the rest of us. "Are we in agreement?"

Bolin joined her and shook Jake's hand, but Deming stayed rooted to his chair. If things had been different, I would have gone to him, held him, done something. As it was, I had my own demons to wrestle with. Jake and CeCe! She'd never even mentioned his name to me. Oh, she alluded to her "family doctor" in that casual way that most of us do. Nothing more. My mind accepted it, but my heart rebelled. CeCe Swann, my best friend, had deceived me. I'd told her everything, confided every triumph and bruise in my pathetically dull life. Why hadn't she trusted me? I'm no racist. Jake Harris, a handsome, brilliant doctor, happens to be black. Bi-racial. Whatever. Any woman would feel lucky to have him. I wanted to weep, but I was beyond tears, too exhausted to even think. It was almost midnight. Time to go home, sort things out, and get some sleep. We'd eliminated one suspect tonight, and that was an accomplishment of sorts. Tomorrow, I'd chart a different course with Deming's help or on my own if it came to that. I owed it to CeCe, no matter what she'd done.

I gently rubbed my eyelids, trying to pry them open. The accumulated weight of several major shocks made that a thankless task.

"You're tired, Eja. Stay here tonight. Please." Anika held her hands out, palms up.

"See. Even Cato wants you to stay."

I glanced sideways at Deming. He sat stone-faced, unable or unwilling to acknowledge my existence. Jake and Bolin were hunched over, speaking softly in a deep rumbling of male voices.

"I'll stay, Mrs. Swann, if you can lend me some night things."

Anika's face brightened at the prospect. Perhaps she needed an ally in this male encampment, another woman who mourned for CeCe. At least that was my simple interpretation. Anika Swann was a complex woman with a full arsenal of beauty and charm at her disposal. A steely inner core buttressed those attributes. Her methods were indirect—hell, they were downright sneaky—but like it or not Anika got her way. Could I, with my dismal marital track record, dare to judge her?

"Come on, Eja. I've got everything set up." She pulled me into a large guestroom packed with every bit of feminine frippery I'd ever imagined. It was awesome, a magic kingdom for the stylistically challenged.

Anika latched the door. She spoke in a soft, urgent voice that was almost a whisper. "I didn't want the boys to hear us. You know how they overreact."

"But Deming . . ."

She waved her hand. "He'll calm down. He always does. It's up to you and me now."

"Pardon?" I gaped at her like the village idiot.

"You know. Our appointment with Wes Townsend. It's scheduled for tomorrow." She checked her exquisite diamond watch. "Well, it's really today. This morning. You get some sleep, and I'll keep Bolin occupied."

No doubt about that. I'd seen the way his eyes softened, following every move his wife made.

"But what's our cover story? We know Dr. Townsend isn't Raven."

"Naturally." Anika gave me her luminous smile. "That makes things easier. You see, I wasn't totally honest yesterday. About my sessions with him."

She smiled at my incredulous look. "I know my family, Eja. Deming's volatile. Bolin's cold as ice—about protecting me that is. If either of them knew the truth, he'd kill Wesley. Bolin would handle it personally. He has all the skills, you see." A hint of steel peeked through the soft silk of her negligee. "I won't put them at risk. We've already lost enough."

It was time to take off the gloves. No more hints and subtle winks. I had to know what the hell she was talking about.

"What happened to you at that office? Did he . . . touch you, Anika?"

I saw the first signs of vulnerability. Anika looked down, stemming the tears that threatened to spill. She gulped, straightened her shoulders, and faced me.

"At first there was no problem. None that I knew of. I relaxed and let him hypnotize me." Her smile seemed painted in place like a mannequin's. "For the first time in years, my craving for nicotine subsided. That bastard praised me, you know. Told me what a good subject I was. Bolin was so proud."

"And then?" It was cruel to prompt her, but I had to know.

"After I stopped smoking, Wesley had me come back for 'reinforcement' sessions. Once a week. That's when it started, I think. That's when I started having nightmares. Bolin was worried, so I increased my sessions."

Now her tears flowed freely. I felt like a voyeur, repulsed and fascinated, unable to turn away from this horror in Anika's normally charmed life.

"One day something went wrong. Maybe he skipped a step. Who knows? I wasn't really under. Do you know much about hypnosis, Eja?"

I shook my head.

"No one can be forced to do something inconsistent with her character like commit a murder or something. That's just Hollywood stuff." Anika took a deep breath. "I've always hated hot weather, even avoid the beach in summer. Wesley knew that. He told me it was sweltering, almost Sahara-like in his office. Then he took off his jacket and shirt and urged me to get cool. He had an entire routine about oppressive heat, and it worked."

I shivered, listening to a tale more grisly than anything I'd ever devised.

"Pretty soon he was naked, and so was I. When he tried to touch me, I screamed! Told him I'd have him arrested, thrown out of Boston."

"Oh, my God! You poor thing. What did he say?"

Anika hung her head and stayed silent, dabbing tears with her handkerchief. "Wesley? He laughed. Said he had something I'd be interested in. Part of my therapy." Anika hissed through gritted teeth. "He'd recorded everything, Eja. That bastard showed me cavorting around the office naked. Kept the discs right there in full view. He even showed me the camera. One of those hidden things concealed in a bust of Freud!" She was sobbing now. "He said if I told Bolin, he'd release it to an international porn site. Put it on the Internet so that all Bolin's friends could see what a whore his wife was. He said it was nothing new to me since I'd been a model. That I'd enjoyed it." Anika blotted her tears again. "Then he laughed. That bastard laughed! He said it was fun seeing what Bolin had for himself."

I rushed to Anika's side and hugged her. "You must have been terrified."

She swiveled around with the fierce look of a warrior queen. "Terrified? Oh no, Eja. I was angry. I could have easily killed him right then. My real concern was to protect my family, especially Dem and Bolin."

I covered my mouth with my hand. "Oh, my God! What did you do?"

Her smile was stiff and fleeting. "I bought a gun and got myself the best lawyer I knew. My daughter."

Gun! That explained the thing in her safe. Walther PK something or other. Typical CeCe behavior, trying to protect her mama. It also left one thing unanswered. Those checks she'd written. Were they blackmail or part of a structured settlement? Oh, God! It was catching. I sounded like a lawyer, not the elegant wordsmith I aspired to be.

I asked Anika, "Why was she paying him?"

"I'm not sure. Cecilia was 'negotiating' for the discs. Her word, not mine. She handled everything. Took my gun and said to consider it a business proposition and blot out emotion." Anika's lips curved in a sad smile. "She was good at that. That's what made her such a great litigator."

The whole thing puzzled me. I couldn't picture Anika, the model of femininity, as a pistol-packing mama!

"You don't know anything about guns, do you Anika?"

Those hazel eyes narrowed to fiery slits. "Wrong. Bolin insisted I learn when the children were born. Kidnappers, you know." She patted a stray lock of hair. "I'm quite proficient, actually. A natural."

My head was spinning from too much information. Good Lord! Why kill CeCe? After all, she was the golden goose unless "negotiations" had reached a deadly impasse. CeCe would never risk exposing her mother, but she might take a more direct route. She might kill the bastard herself!

SWATHED IN luxurious bed linens, I sank into a dreamless state. Midmorning, Cato awakened me by perching on my stomach. He radiated a blend of insolence and menace more potent than an alarm clock.

"Okay. Okay."

I gently pushed him away and toddled off to the bathroom to gape at the incredible array of pricey shampoos, potions, and emollients it contained. Anika's taste was high-end, unlike my own penchant for drugstore brands. Ever the good guest, I forced myself to indulge.

Some good elf—probably Anika—had draped a snuggly cashmere robe on the bed and left a steaming pot of espresso with two cups. Better and better! The ways of the fabulously rich were remarkably easy to endure.

A brisk rap on the door jolted me back to reality. My curly mop was sopping wet, my face scrubbed clean of makeup. In short, I looked a mess. Fortunately, my visitor was the lady of the house, not her gorgeous, grouchy son. Mrs. Bolin Swann was a model of perfection from her wafer-thin wool sheath to her tastefully shod feet. A pinch of rouge saved her pale complexion from pallor.

"Sorry Eja, but I just couldn't wait." Anika perched on the bed and poured herself an espresso. "I thought we'd firm up our plans before breakfast. Bolin might get suspicious otherwise." She waved something glittery in front of me. "Here, take this."

It was an exceptionally lovely pin, fashioned from diamonds and gemstones.

"Oh, Anika. I can't accept something this valuable."

Her laughter was magic, the joyous warbling of a songbird. "It's not jewelry, Eja. Not really. It's a transmitter and recorder. Bolin's people brought it by." Her expression showed me how serious Anika was. "Wear it when you see Wesley. Then we'll have proof."

"What time's our appointment?" I felt groggy and disoriented, despite the pampering.

"Ten thirty, dear. Remember, you're the patient. I'm just there for moral support." Anika fidgeted, as if she were working up to something big. "Eja . . . about last night."

I summoned a suitably blank expression. Frankly, it wasn't hard to do. "Yes?"

Anika squeezed my hand with surprising strength. "You won't mention anything to Dem, will you?" She seemed close to tears. "The thought of what he'd do terrifies me."

"It's women's work," I said with a wink. "We'll save the rough stuff for the guys."

I SAT IN WESLEY Townsend's waiting room like the poster child for composure: perfect posture, legs crossed demurely at the ankles, and one of CeCe's Chanel bags on my lap. Unfortunately, the inner Eja was a tangled, jittery mass of frayed nerves. All doctors unnerved me, but shrinks topped the list. My fragile ego wouldn't survive much pinching and probing even for a good cause. Despite her pledge of moral support, Anika accompanied me into the office, exchanged pleasantries with Brenda, the receptionist, and vanished like yesterday's wind.

"Never expected to see you here, Ms. Kane." Brenda raised her eyebrows. "Great brooch, by the way."

I clamped my hands together to avoid fingering the pin. Duplicity was scarcely my strong suit. "It's hard to believe." I lowered my eyes. "Marriage is more stressful than I ever imagined. I need something to steady me."

"Hmm," she said in her soothing voice, handing me a questionnaire. "Don't worry. Lots of people get wedding jitters. Just relax and confide in the doctor. He's very nice." Brenda flipped through her calendar as if it were a prop instead of an office tool. "His schedule's a mess! Way too many patients for one person. Well, it's not my problem. Not anymore."

I kept my tone light and teasing. "Oh? Leaving for greener pastures, are you?"

Brenda shrugged and dialed the doctor's number. "Everything runs its course."

Just then, Wesley Townsend, beaming a kindly shrink smile, opened the door. "Ms. Kane. So nice to see you again." He waved me into an inoffensive office, scrubbed clean of any personality.

My panic escalated as I bit back the urge to spill my guts. What was it, some substitute for the confessional of my youth? Townsend's first question was a showstopper that sucked me into a vortex from the past.

"Why don't you deserve Deming Swann?" he asked. "That's your question, isn't it?"

I stuttered, trying desperately to field a glib reply. The man had a point. I wasn't wealthy, but I had something to offer, didn't I?

I recited the litany of ailments I'd memorized from the American

Psychological Association's page on anxiety. Some of them were even true. While I emoted, Townsend stared at me with a ventriloquist's fixed smile.

"My future in-laws sing your praises, Dr. Townsend. I've tried to relax, but I can't. Now my sleep is disturbed too. Is there anything—anything at all—you can do to help me?" My eyes are my best feature, and despite my rusty seduction skills, I used them to advantage. Maybe childlike passivity would ring his bells.

Fifty minutes later, we finished our session without ever mentioning CeCe, Anika, or hypnosis. Against all odds, he'd actually helped me or at least given me something to consider. I'd revealed more than I ever intended to despite the recording device affixed to my breast.

When we concluded, Dr. Wesley patted my shoulder and looked me in the eye. "You don't need me," he said. "You've got the answers inside you."

I stumbled into the waiting room, feeling a curious mixture of relief and revulsion. I'd failed miserably as a detective and a prospective spouse. Wesley Townsend hadn't bought my act for a second. Still, I felt terrific, as if a weight had been taken from my chest.

"He's good, isn't he?" Brenda asked. "Quite a healer when he wants to be."

Her calm chestnut eyes flashed intelligence and a first-class bullshit detector. I decided to go for broke.

"Look, tell me just one thing. Where was he that Sunday, the day Ms. Swann died?"

Brenda sighed. "I shouldn't tell you this, but what the hell. He's free on weekends, you know, unless a patient calls him or goes berserk." She flipped through the calendar. "One thing I can tell you. Dr. Townsend left that Saturday for Hawaii. Medical convention." A sly smile covered her face. "Plenty of golf, of course, but for tax purposes, it was all work and no play."

I leaned over her desk. "How come you're so sure?"

"That's easy." Brenda twirled a paper clip on the blotter. "I was with him."

AT THE BRISTOL Lounge we snagged a window table, complete with full view of the Common. That didn't matter one bit to Anika. She picked at her lobster salad as if it were made of clay. I should have followed suit, but stripping my soul for Wesley Townsend had left me ravenous. I ingested an obscene number of carbs and calories without feeling even a pinch of guilt.

"You're sure? You believed her?" Anika asked. "Maybe Brenda was covering for him. Maybe he hired someone."

"I don't think so. She had no reason to lie if she's quitting." I crunched a carrot and eyed the pastry tray. "I'm sorry, Anika. He's still a sleaze, but I don't think he did it."

Anika looked close to tears. "So that's it. Where do we go from here? Maybe we should let the police handle things."

I'd given that serious thought. Jem Russell was mean enough but lacked the wit to tie his own shoe. With Raven and the shrink out of the suspect pool, there was only one other potential source. CeCe's office. After all, she'd spent most of her waking hours in a snake pit that even Pamela Schwartz called tense. Time to resurrect my cover story as CeCe's biographer. Time to act.

"Don't give up yet," I told Anika. "Let's convene a council of war with the guys. We all need to be on the same page."

Her smile eclipsed the noon sun. "You have a theory. I can tell." She scrolled down the screen of her iPhone. "I'll text Bolin and ask him to arrange things."

Of course Bolin Swann would make the arrangements. He'd do anything his beloved Leda asked of him. Even murder.

Later that day as I dashed into my condo to freshen up I recalled the envelope Deming had given me. Probably another meeting of the Condo association, or God forbid, another escalation in fees. I tore it open and scanned the page while rummaging in my closet. It was terse. One line of simple, unambiguous prose that left my knees weak.

Back off, bitch, or you're next.

Eighteen

I STEADIED MYSELF against the bedpost, trying desperately to quiet my skyrocketing pulse. Brave words flow glibly in a novel but dry up fast in the face of real danger. Someone had actually threatened me, Eja Kane, writer of a dozen edgy thrillers. Someone daring and evil enough to murder my best friend and toss her off a building.

I shivered despite my sturdy wool robe and fleece-lined slippers. Where was Cato when I needed sharp teeth and swagger? For that matter, where was Deming? When the phone rang, I leapt for it like a hungry trout. It was cowardly and unseemly, but even feminists are permitted the occasional rescue fantasy.

"Deming?" My voice quivered with hope.

"It's Jem." His normally hardy voice held an unaccustomed note of desperation.

"You have some nerve. I have nothing to say to you."

"Wait! Don't hang up."

His prodigal son act had gotten old. "Watch me."

He made a noise that sounded like a sob. "Help me, Eja. I've been arrested."

That stumped me for a moment. A panoply of offenses spun through my mind: extortion, drunk driving, and statutory rape . . . the possibilities were endless. The big galoot deserved his fate no matter what it was. Still, CeCe had been fond of him. My guilt meter twanged.

"What'd you do this time?"

Jem's baritone edged toward soprano territory. "Nothing! I swear. That woman hates me. She won't listen to anything I say."

"What woman?"

"Euphemia Bates." He gulped as if he were oxygen deprived. "She thinks I murdered CeCe."

After a moment of stunned silence I told Jem to hold tight and keep his mouth shut.

I disconnected, plopped down on the bed, and dialed Bolin Swann.

ONE HOUR LATER, Po transported me to Swannland in the big Mercedes. Despite streaming sunlight and vivid colors, the big house felt grim and forbidding today. It had a funereal air as if CeCe's loss had sucked the joy from every room. I walked on tiptoe toward the study where I heard the rumbling of deep voices. Po nodded, and I entered, unsure of what I might find. They were a disparate trio—Bolin and Jake bracketing either side of the sofa like bookends, sipping something dark and rich while Euphemia Bates sat in the wing chair opposite them, her spine straight enough to shame a Victorian.

"I did some checking after you called, Eja," Bolin said. "Lieutenant Bates feels confident that Jem Russell killed my daughter. Proving it is another matter."

Jake's handsome features were etched in stone. As a physician, he was trained to repress emotion; as CeCe's lover he seemed numbed by grief.

"Why would Jem Russell call you?" Jake asked. "I thought you two weren't friends."

I shuddered at the idea of being linked to Jem Russell. "He swears he's innocent, and he thinks I have influence with Lieutenant Bates." I curled my lip and nodded at Mia. "Shows how delusional he is."

Bolin took a deep breath and slowly exhaled. "It seems his alibi fell apart. He was at his condo when Cecilia died. Lieutenant Bates got him to admit that."

Jem Russell was the ultimate screw-up who couldn't even fabricate a decent alibi. Despite the odds I wasn't convinced of his guilt. Naturally, he'd lied to the cops. Lies were mother's milk to con men like Jem. He wouldn't think twice about lying. Jem was many things, but he wasn't naïve. He could smell a setup a mile away.

I glanced at the notes I'd scribbled on my pad. The murderer was someone with an intimate knowledge of CeCe's life and habits. Someone smart enough to lure her to the roof garden against every instinct she possessed. That profile of an aggressive, intelligent killer excluded Jem Russell, a sad sack whose few working brain cells fell south of his belt buckle.

Euphemia Bates seemed untroubled by those inconsistencies. If she had doubts, she cloaked them in the confident smile of a huntress who'd trapped and bagged her prey.

Bolin came right to the point. "I understand that Jem Russell has no alibi for that Sunday, Lieutenant. Is there other evidence?"

"We're working on it," Mia said without losing that smile.

Jake stayed silent, but I fought the urge to speak up. There were many reasons to loathe Jem, none of which made him a murderer. That didn't make him innocent either. If anyone waved enough money in his face, Jem would cheerfully cooperate. I'd felt all along that he was hiding something.

"He called me," I said. "He might tell me something."

Mia rolled her eyes. "Not going to happen, Ms. Kane. Sorry."

"What could it hurt?" Bolin asked. "Once he gets an attorney, he'll keep quiet."

"He already has one." Deming burst through the door like an uncaged beast, a wild, particularly sexy beast.

"Dem?" Bolin gave his son a quizzical look.

"I called Pam. She's down there now. It's a Band-Aid. Just temporary."

Mia smoothed her jacket and flashed that killer smile at us. "I'm not at liberty to say more. You understand. If he has good legal representation, that's fine with me."

"Who told you?" I pasted a hopeful smile on my face. "About the alibi, I mean."

"Confidential informant. Anonymous." Mia rustled papers on her lap in a gesture that was pure theater. "Sorry I can't tell you more. At such a preliminary stage nothing's certain. I should have just phoned."

Ever the gentleman, Bolin rose and shook her hand. "Is there anything . . . anything at all that we can do?"

Mia's eyes softened for a moment. "We're still constructing our case, but his motive seems fuzzy. There's no evidence of violence in his past."

Deming snorted like an angry bull. "Motive? Money. It always came down to money with that guy. My sister turned him down, and he lost it. Murdered her."

"I don't think so, Dem."

I'd forgotten that Jake Harris was in the room. Now all eyes turned to him.

"CeCe planned to invest with him, Lieutenant, and she was very shrewd when parting with her money. She discussed his proposition with me. You know, it actually sounded pretty good."

More snorting from Brother Bjorn. "That guy only knows one kind of proposition. Sex. His currency of choice." Deming's rage was palpable, a thing of awe and beauty.

Mia stayed statue-still as she processed information. "You'll need to amend your statement, Dr. Harris. At your convenience. Mr. Russell swears that he's innocent, and this might bolster his claim. Of course, impetuous people like him are hard to predict." She drew up to her impressive height. "Good evening, all. I'll keep in touch."

The silence in the room was oppressive. Bolin sipped his scotch without saying a word, Jake looked lost and vulnerable, and Deming—he was another thing entirely.

When I mentioned the threatening note his reaction was volcanic. He shot out of his chair, splattering scotch all over the floor. "The cops were just here, Eja. Why the hell didn't you mention it then?"

I felt heat rise in my cheeks, proof positive of an unbecoming flush. Deming was a bully, plain and simple, and I was sick of his antics.

"Leave her alone, son. There's more." Anika slipped into the room wearing a filmy peach gown. "Tell them, Eja. About our experiment."

It took moxy to discuss Wesley Townsend with them. Moxy, a good old-fashioned word my grandma often used. I angled my body to avoid Deming and weasel-worded my way into the narrative. Anika snuggled against her husband, encouraging me all the way with smiles and thumbs-up gestures.

"You went to his office without telling me." Deming's eyes lasered in on me.

"Let's not waste time quarreling. Here's the bottom line: Wesley Townsend is innocent, or at least not guilty of CeCe's murder."

Deming's expression was positively saturnine. "What the hell!"

"Listen, darling," Anika said. "We're narrowing down our list of suspects."

I quickly explained the Hawaiian odyssey. "There. Wesley couldn't have murdered CeCe."

"You've heard of murder for hire, I presume." Deming's voice dripped icicles.

Once again, Jake intervened. "I'm no expert on shrinks, Dem, but Wesley strikes me as the cautious type. Risk adverse. He wouldn't get his hands dirty or risk exposure by hiring someone."

"Even someone like Jem Russell?" Bolin spoke quietly. "The location bothers me. It's too coincidental, using his building. I think Jem's involved somehow."

I nodded. "When Deming and I questioned him, I got this feeling, you know, that he was hiding something."

"Stay out of this, Eja. If you blunder into something . . ." Deming wagged his finger.

"You're not my father, Deming Swann, or my boss! I'll do as I please."

Bolin shook his head. "Do I have to referee again? Déjà vu time."

"They've been sparring for years," Anika said, winking at me. "Come with me, Eja. We'll get some tea."

When we reached the kitchen, she took me aside. "It's up to us. Jem has a soft spot for me. If he knows anything, I'll get it out of him."

"Jem has plenty of soft spots—in his head! Deming . . ."

She laughed. "Let me handle my son. Just go with me to the police station tomorrow."

"But Lieutenant Bates said . . ." Sputtering had become routine around Anika.

A fetching set of dimples appeared in her cheeks. "Bolin and Deming are lawyers. Let them handle dull legal things. We'll tackle the rest."

WE NEVER MADE that trip. Anika phoned me early the next morning with startling news: Jem Russell had been released from police custody. He'd never really been arrested, merely detained for questioning. Mia Bates had released Jem without charging him.

"What happened?" I asked.

"Pam Schwartz found a witness. Someone who saw Jem that morning." Her voice trailed off. "He was arguing with someone about noise—loud music apparently. They almost got into a brawl. The neighbor was very certain."

I tiptoed around the critical issue. "What time was it?"

Anika made a sound somewhere between a sob and a gasp. "Between eight thirty and nine. Both men called building security to complain. Pam said it was solid."

Jem Russell was a lucky man. Too lucky. He was involved somehow in CeCe's murder, and I planned to wring it out of him one way or another.

"Are you up for a social call?" I asked.

Anika paused. "You mean . . .?"

"Exactly. Meet me at Jem's building around ten."

ANIKA EMBODIED elegance, but I barely registered on the style scale. The concierge, a gum-snapper just past puberty, took one look at Mrs. Bolin Swann and waved her toward the elevator. He gave me the fish-eye.

"You do the talking. I'm only here for moral support." I guided Anika around the corridor to apartment 2810. "We can't let him off the hook this time. He knows something."

Anika blinked and straightened her shoulders. "I'm ready, don't worry."

I pressed the buzzer and rapped firmly on the door. The big lug was probably cowering, terrified that the cops had changed their minds. More likely he was sound asleep. No matter. I was the instrument of justice, and he wouldn't escape.

Anika twisted the knob, gasping as the door swung open. I hung back, but she charged into the condo like Jeanne d'Arc herself. Amidst the clutter of pizza boxes and beer bottles, we saw Jem sprawled on the couch with a newspaper covering his face. That surprised me: I'd never known him to read anything, even the comics.

"Jem. Jem, dear, its Anika." She glided up to the couch and gently shook his shoulder.

He rolled onto the floor with a resounding thud. We both shrieked, freezing in place as Jem's motionless body lay there. I closed my eyes and prayed for a miracle.

The Lord has a strange sense of humor. Jem Russell belched, shook himself, and dazzled us with his smile.

"What's wrong, ladies? Think I was dead or just hoping?"

Anika recovered first. She grasped his hand and showing the practical benefits of a personal trainer, pulled him to his feet. "Don't be silly, dear. We came for your help."

Sincerity was never one of his virtues. The bastard hugged her, puffed out his cheeks, and lied. "I'd like to help but I can't."

"Can't or won't?" I asked.

"I've already made another arrangement. A lucrative business arrangement."

Anika was cucumber cool. "Whatever you're making, I'll double it. Please, Jem."

"Sorry, ladies. No can do. You see, I need a business partner to fund my new venture. CeCe was my first choice, but of course that's impossible now."

"Sounds like extortion," I said. "What would Lieutenant Bates say?"

He didn't even flinch. "Let her check with my attorney. Now if you'll excuse me . . ."

"Stop." Anika wedged her slight frame between Jem and me. "What do you know about my daughter's murder? Please."

He gave a sly smile, the look of cocksure guys without a clue. "I'll tell you this much. Ask yourself how CeCe accessed that roof garden."

Every nerve in my body emitted distress signals. That very question had plagued me since CeCe's murder. Possibilities from dumb luck to planned meeting rattled around my brain. All were inadequate, far too chancy for my persnickety pal. Her time was too valuable to waste on anything other than a sure bet.

"Go on, Jem. Tell her." Deming Swann, dressed head to toe in black, stood in the doorway with his arms crossed.

I expected fists to fly, but Jem's face actually brightened as he looked up. He gestured toward Deming with an exaggerated flourish.

"Here he is, ladies. My new business partner."

"Son?"

Despite his genial air, Deming was furious. His hands were balled into tight fists, a tell established early in childhood. He kissed Anika's forehead, but I was not so lucky. He gave me the narrowed eyes and tight lips of the Brother Bjorn stare.

I returned that glare with interest and then focused my wrath on Jem. "Okay, cut the crap. How did CeCe get on that roof? Don't lie either. I can tell."

Deming nodded, and Jem spilled his guts. "The simplest way possible. She used my key."

Nineteen

GAPING IS UNREFINED, but I couldn't help it. The simplest possibility was the one I'd never considered. CeCe used a key. Jem's key.

"I gave it to her that morning," Jem said, smacking his lips. "She'd earned it the night before."

Deming flexed his fingers as if he might pummel his new business partner.

"Why did CeCe want it?" I asked. "You said she was terrified of that roof."

He shrugged. "I didn't ask, and she didn't say. But I'll tell you one thing. She had that look on her face. The one she got right before putting the screws to someone."

"Did she say something—anything—about who she was meeting?"

He furrowed his brow, a sign of deep thought in bozo land. "Oh yeah. 'Checkmate.' She said she'd reached the endgame, whatever that meant. You know how she loved chess. Never got the hang of it myself."

My eyes met Deming's as if we were visualizing the same scene: CeCe the chess master locked in mortal combat with Bolin. Sunday afternoons were their special time, chess matches in which father and daughter gave no quarter. No wonder CeCe had been jubilant when boarding the elevator that morning. Winning was everything to her. Always had been. She'd gone to that rooftop to vanquish an opponent. The question was which one?

"Why was she with you that night? After all, she was in love, engaged to be married." I was prepared to slap that sneer off his face, but Deming beat me to it.

He strode up to his new partner and grabbed him by his collar. "Enough. Tell her the truth if you want to see that money."

"Jeez. No sense of humor." Jem sighed. "Okay. I got drunk at her place and passed out on the couch. Nothing happened. All she could talk about was that Raven guy."

"You mean she was meeting Raven on the roof?" My heart ricocheted back and forth.

"Nah. At least I don't think so. She didn't name names. Said she was playing 'head games,' whatever that means." Jem's eyes lit up. "She kept looking at some message on her iPad. Whatever it was, she got all excited. That's when she asked for my key."

CeCe would have synced everything with her phone and computer. Unfortunately, someone had grabbed her iPad, stolen her computer, and trashed her phone. She'd been lured to that rooftop and betrayed by someone she trusted.

"I've got our tech guys researching her service provider. They'll track that message down one way or the other." Deming's eyes were glacial shards, dead ice, impossible to read. He looked rootless, dangerous. His tenderness toward Anika stood in sharp contrast to his coolness toward me.

"Can they do that, son, even with her computer gone?" Anika's emotions were on a short tether. She'd funneled her grief into our investigation, but it was a palliative. The wound had reopened and was exposed to sunlight, raw and throbbing.

"Don't worry, Mother. If the authorities don't subpoena Comcast, we'll find an alternative." He ignored me, reverting to the brusque behavior of our youth. My stomach clenched, and I steeled myself for rejection. I was strong enough to endure the pain, human enough to mourn the loss.

"Come with us, Eja." Anika held out her hand.

"No problem. I'll catch a cab. I really need to get home, or Cato will be furious."

I SPENT THAT evening plotting literary mayhem. Writing soothed my soul and comforted my mind. To hell with Deming Swann and his petulance! I'd vowed to avenge CeCe, and that's one pledge that I would meet. If I spent my days alone, so be it. Alone didn't mean lonely. After all, I still had Cato.

The day's activities took their toll. Despite my pledge to write all night, I awakened at midnight, draped over my keyboard with a raging migraine for company. Cato immediately gave me the canine equivalent of an eye roll.

"Okay, I'm a bad doggy mom, but give me a break. This stuff is new." I found his paraphernalia, grabbed the keys, and dragged myself to the elevator. The lobby was deserted, and the cacophony of street noise wafted through the door. I cautiously picked my way down the sidewalk while Cato moseyed along the curb, truculent as ever. That anonymous note and its menacing content kept swirling through my brain in an endless spiral of doom. I was exhausted, desperate for sleep but terrified of revisiting CeCe's horrific plunge. It happened every time I shut my eyes, unless *he* was by my side. Deming was a better soporific than Ambien!

Deep in thought, I followed Cato as he strained toward a fire hydrant. When a dark figure approached, passing me from behind, I shrieked in terror.

"Jesus, lady, what's your problem?" A jogger in coordinated running gear sprinted ahead, giving me the finger.

Bad manners aside, his question was worth considering. I examined my conscience, cleaned up after Cato, and tugged him toward my building. Suddenly he stopped, guard hairs straight up, growling softly as strong arms encircled my waist, and a familiar scent enveloped me.

"Are you crazy?" Deming asked. "Wandering around a deserted street at midnight when a murderer's loose?"

I touched his sleeve, feeling the soft, luxurious cashmere of his jacket. Lust seeped through my pores like a noxious gas. I banished the superlatives flooding my mind and played it cool.

"What a surprise. Not stalking me, are you?"

He nuzzled my hair and whispered. "I was worried. Couldn't stay away with everything so crazy." His lips feathered kisses up and down my neck. "I thought if I kept watch, at least you'd be safe."

I forgot my pact with spinsterhood and fury. I forgot everything but the gentle touch of his lips and the strength of his arms.

"If you came upstairs I'd feel much safer. No strings."

Deming grunted as he towed me and Cato toward the lobby. "You don't get it. I'm sick of fighting you. I want strings, damn it. Chains even."

I bit my lip to keep from babbling. He was the most mercurial man I'd ever met! Gruff yet tender, controlling but distant. My mind and lower body parts roiled with fear and expectation.

Deming frowned as my front door swung open. "Good thing you've got CeCe's place now instead of this thing."

"It's adequate. Cato and I are comfortable."

"Don't get touchy. CeCe's building has more security. That's all I meant."

"If you say so." I stifled a yawn. "Look, I'm really tired, and tomorrow's a big day."

"I'll hold you 'til you fall asleep. Then I'll leave."

Fat chance. We both knew exactly what would happen, and that was fine with me.

I LEAPT UP AT six a.m., energized and action-ready from a good night's sleep. After some wrangling, we'd agreed on a plan, one final move in this deadly chess game. At first Deming refused, but eventually he'd succumbed to a potent blend of sex-laced logic. We'd be a team again just like in the old days, two musketeers fighting to avenge the third.

He was still dozing, snoring with that steady masculine hum I'd missed so much. Our union last night had been passionate, filled with unspoken words and fiery promise. I tried to dampen my hopes, even as my feelings for him grew. I couldn't say the word even to myself. *Love.* How could one word—four letters—have such power? Deming was kryptonite, capable of destroying me with one misstep. All those years we'd danced around each other, sniping and trading barbs instead of acknowledging the truth. My whole being would implode if he discarded me even though we were wildly mismatched. Deming was a practiced lover; I was a rank amateur, leading with my heart, unable to dissemble.

"You're the early bird," he said, gliding into the kitchen. "Any chance for espresso, or is this Maxwell House?"

"Funny. You missed your calling." I handed him a cup of the precious brew. "I think we should show up together. At the firm. You know, united front."

He grinned as he sipped his drink. "Still posing as my fiancée, are you?"

I felt the blush flaming up my face. "Don't worry. Not much longer. I'm positive the murderer is linked to that law firm. The same person who threatened me."

Deming made a noise somewhere between a growl and a hiss. "I don't like you meddling. It's dangerous."

"Breathing is dangerous these days. Besides, you'll have my back."

My plan was simple but elegant. I'd amble back to Sevier, Miles and Swann to capture their fond memories of CeCe. In the process, I hoped to capture something more: damaging admissions. Someone who knew CeCe well, someone whom she trusted, had betrayed her and lured her to the rooftop. Following the clues we'd gathered so far, I surmised that my pal had sprinted out to that roof to confront an adversary. "Head games" sounded like CeCe's code for her shrink. She probably thought he'd turn over those tapes and free Anika from blackmail and torment. Either Wesley Townsend had a confederate at the law firm, or someone knew about the sleazy shrink and traded on CeCe's devotion to her mother. Someone with ambition, a rook bent on capturing the queen. Motive was another thing entirely. The stakes had to be incredibly high to dispatch a prominent player like Cecilia Swann in broad daylight. My money and hopes rested with Pamela Schwartz, a barracuda with the strength and will to subdue an army. I had absolutely no proof, except a mile-wide streak of jealousy. I could live with that.

"You look different today," Deming said, holding me at arm's length.

"Better or worse?"

He lowered his eyes and sighed. "Different. You fixed your hair and put on makeup."

"I have my moments. Remember, I'm playing a role here." I patted his cheek. "Wouldn't want a frumpy fiancée, would you?"

I'd done my best to master Harpo's hair and makeup regimen, but it was an uphill battle. Still, my curly mop had been subdued, and my face had a certain glow to it. I'd never win any prizes, but at least I could compete.

"Come on. Cato's sleeping." We tiptoed past the spaniel, found the Porsche, and took off.

"Stay with Malcolm," Deming said. "While you beguile the staff, I'll see Lieutenant Bates."

"The cops! They'll screw up our plan."

His piercing scowl was a bad dream from childhood. "Have sense, Eja. I'm an officer of the court. Bates has to know about that key."

He was right, but I still didn't like it. "What about Jem's lawyer? Can't Pamela handle that?"

Deming snapped his fingers. "Good idea. I'll take Pam with me. Makes it more official."

I sagged back into the soft leather seat, cursing my big mouth.

Jealousy was foreign to me, but without CeCe's soothing presence it had become a habit.

"Dad made all the arrangements," Deming said. "They still jump to his tune at the firm. Do I have to tell you to be careful? You take some wild chances."

"I'm not a child, you know. Stop lecturing."

He gave me a look that hiked my thermostat skyward. I'd always fought my own battles, but self-reliance paled in comparison to this. I glimpsed another life where Deming cosseted and protected me like Bolin did Anika. It was an intoxicating fantasy, a sweet, seductive respite from reality. I pinched myself and broke the spell.

"Let me handle this," I said. "Downplay your involvement."

His eyelids flickered. For a moment I saw pain, until the snarky Deming Swann came roaring right back.

"Suit yourself. I'll check on you later." Deming wrenched the Porsche to the curb and hopped out. "You have my number if you need anything. I'll find Pam and liaise with the cops. It may take us all day."

MALCOLM WAS WAITING for me, wearing his Brooks Brothers suit like armor. His expression was set on neutral, impossible to read or decipher. I'd given that some thought. To keep my cover, I'd need to focus on CeCe's reaction to adversity and her dealings with the other principals. My objective was to narrow the possibilities and find out who had access to her cases. That might entail a serious charm offensive and girl talk over drinks with her paralegal.

"Jem Russell told me the strangest thing today." I lowered my voice to whisper level. "On the morning she died, CeCe got a text setting up the meeting. That's why she went on the roof. She used that dimwit's key."

Malcolm raised his eyebrows. "Dimwit?"

"Jem! For heaven's sake man, keep up. Anyway, they're tracing her phone log right now. Hopefully we'll find something."

He folded his arms and stared at me with a puzzled look on his face. "There's no mystery there. I sent CeCe that text myself."

"You!" I choked out the word despite my shock. "Why didn't you say something?"

Malcolm shrugged. "No one asked. Everyone, especially the police, seemed confident that it was suicide. I never thought . . ."

I gave him my insect larvae stare. "Tell me everything."

"There's not that much to tell. I texted Ms. Swann that morning around seven to remind her about an appointment." Malcolm held out his hand like a traffic cop. "And before you ask, the meeting popped up suddenly after Ms. Swann left Friday evening. I was worried that she might not check her calendar on the weekend."

"Sunday. Unusual time for a business meeting, no?"

He shook his head. "It was personal, not business. I kept both calendars for her, but the off-duty one was secret. She obsessed about privacy. Couldn't bear the idea of anyone scrutinizing her life, especially Ms. Schwartz."

"Who was she meeting?" I spoke with a stranger's voice, flat and unemotional.

He spit out the words like a robot. "I don't know. She used code names. Byron. He'd called her before. On her private line."

"Are you sure this Byron is a man? CeCe was unconventional, after all." I racked my brain, dredging up every esoteric scrap about Lord Byron. His poetry was electric, but his sex life jolted eighteenth century Brits from their prudish perch. Was that why CeCe dubbed her friend *Byron*?

Malcolm blanched. "I never actually spoke with Byron. I just assumed . . ."

"Where did you keep her private calendar? I want to see it." Maybe I'd find something, some clue that would have meaning to me alone.

"Lieutenant Bates already got everything. I printed out the whole year for her."

Malcolm slipped behind his desk and tapped the calendar icon. "See for yourself. She didn't list everything. Just after-hours meetings. Mostly social. You know how lawyers are about billable hours."

I scanned CeCe's social calendar for the past six months. It was cryptic, just as Malcolm predicted. The names Eja and Raven figured prominently on the pages, but Byron only appeared once: the morning she was murdered.

"What did she say when you spoke with her?"

He winced as if I'd inflicted a wound. "Remember, Ms. Kane. I texted her. That's what she preferred on her free time. Believe me, Ms. Swann got enough calls during the workweek. She needed a break from talking."

The man was maddening! One more evasion, and I'd shake him

like a rag doll. "Okay, did Ms. Swann respond to your text?"

Malcolm shook his head. "I never heard from her again. If only I'd known . . ."

I prayed he wouldn't get maudlin. Who needed a hysterical male shedding tears all over a Brooks suit? I patted his well-tailored shoulder. "That's okay. Tell me once more what it said."

"Meet Byron on Sunday at forty-five Province Street to consummate deal. Rooftop garden, 8:30 a.m." His voice was listless, devoid of inflection. "That was it. I was the murderer's accomplice." His voice broke, and he grasped the edge of the desk for balance.

"Unwitting accomplice. Remember that, Malcolm. You couldn't have known."

"That address! I should have recognized it as Jem Russell's." A light went on in his eyes. "I wondered about that meeting place. Her acrophobia was no secret. Kind of an office joke, actually."

"This *deal* must have been something special," I said. "Sounds more business than personal. Are you sure you can't connect Byron to any clients?"

He shook his head. "I'll try again. Meanwhile, I'll call Meribeth over. She really has more inside scoop than I do when it comes to court cases."

"Hold on," I said. "What was CeCe's reaction? After losing the cases, I mean."

"I couldn't say. Ask Meribeth."

I clenched my fist to keep from giving Malcolm the universal hand sign. "I'm asking *you*. You saw her every day, and I know for a fact that CeCe told you everything. Now cut the crap and tell me—unless you have something to hide."

His face grew even more pale than usual. "Me? I loved Ms. Swann. I'd never hurt her."

"What then? You're shielding someone."

Malcolm sank into his desk chair, his legs trembling. He closed his eyes and took a deep breath. "At first she was devastated. You know how she hated to lose anything."

"And then . . .?"

"When it happened again, she grew calm, analytical. She traced every step in the process, who had information, who knew what when." Malcolm hesitated, as if the memory was too painful to recount.

"Go on. She probably figured there was a mole in this office. Who were her suspects?"

Beads of perspiration bracketed Malcolm's forehead. "You understand, Ms. Swann was under enormous pressure. Mr. Michaels blew a gasket. I heard him shouting at her one afternoon. That never happened before."

"Answer my question. Who were her suspects?" I gripped my pencil so hard it snapped in half.

More hesitation from Malcolm. The bustling, confident man of yore had vanished, leaving a quivering stranger in his place. He reached for his water and took measured sips.

"She'd narrowed it down to three people. That last Friday, she planned to confront them. Then she got the news about her nomination and kind of lost focus."

My eyes pinned him like a laser beam. "For God's sake man, who were they?"

Malcolm's lips parted as angst gave way to acceptance. "She told me herself who they were: Pamela Schwartz, Meribeth . . . and me."

Twenty

I'VE NEVER HAD a poker face. When Malcolm spilled the beans, all I could do was gape and pray. *Please make it Pam.* It was unworthy of me, but I prayed anyhow. Pamela Schwartz, that sexy vixen, envied everything about CeCe. She was perfect for the quisling role. Making a few bucks on the side was just gravy.

"Did CeCe have any proof? She was a firm believer in proof. She'd never blatantly accuse anyone."

Malcolm shrugged. "I never asked, and she never said. Anyway, she didn't have to."

"How come?"

"I was sick of deceiving her. I confessed right away."

"You?" I gasped, thinking I'd imagined it. "But why? She trusted you."

He grinned, and for a moment I recalled the old Malcolm, CeCe's devoted scribe.

"It didn't seem so bad at first. Corporate espionage. Kind of dashing when you think of it. My finances tanked, and I needed money. The other side made overtures, and I leapt at the chance. I told myself they wouldn't blame Ms. Swann. Not with her connections." Malcolm blinked back moisture. "A convenient fiction, of course. Most criminals delude themselves like that, I guess."

"But she would have helped. Loaned you the money if you'd asked. Hell, CeCe would have given it to you." I shook my head. "I can't believe it."

The confession diminished him both physically and emotionally. Malcolm's raspy breathing and clenched fists proved that. "Don't you see? I wanted her to admire me. To see me as a man for once, not just some needy employee."

I got one of those rare aha moments. "Oh my Lord! You were in love with her! But you're married . . ." The role reversal stunned me. Men often fell in love with their secretaries. Why should women be immune? It was possible if not probable.

He swallowed hard. "That would have changed in a flash if she'd wanted me. But she didn't. Cecilia Swann let every loser in New England break her heart, but she never even saw me. Not that way. Maybe this Raven was worthy of her."

I thought of Dr. Jake Harris, her best and final choice. "He was. Now what did CeCe decide to do? About your activities, I mean. She was too ethical to let it slide."

His eyes hardened into bright shards of Kilkenny coal. "I've already submitted my resignation. Management thinks I'm grieving, and maybe they're right. Ms. Swann gave me an excellent reference. Told me to start fresh." We faced each other over the battlefield of his desk. "You can scuttle that if you choose to, but either way, after next week I'm history."

Who was I to thwart CeCe's plans? She'd dealt with Malcolm as she saw fit, and I'd honor that. "I have to tell the Swanns, Malcolm. They'll probably abide by CeCe's wishes. You'd better tell Lieutenant Bates yourself. Don't worry about me as long as you're telling the truth."

"I am. I suppose the cops will ultimately trace Byron's call. Meribeth took it. Maybe she remembers something about the voice." He dialed a number. "I'll buzz her."

"One more thing. Who was your in-house contact?"

He gave me a quizzical look. "What do you mean? No one. I was contacted directly by the other litigants, or more precisely, someone on their team. Word got around I guess. The same firm handled all three cases."

"Hmm. Listen, tell Meribeth to meet me at Miel. CeCe told me you guys all love that place. I'll treat her to lunch."

Perhaps the combination of French fare and atmosphere might make her nostalgic. After all, Meribeth claimed to be CeCe's close friend. I prayed that Amex was a forgiving institution that would stretch my credit line one more time. As I fumbled for a handkerchief, I felt an envelope in my purse. It was heavy ecru vellum with the unmistakable Swann emblem emblazoned on the flap. I recognized the handwriting immediately and shamed myself by flushing head to toe. *Deming Swann strikes again!*

Since Malcolm had retreated to his desk to make luncheon reservations, that allowed me to turn away and discreetly pry open the envelope. The contents fluttered to the floor, giving me five peeks at Benjamin Franklin's face. Five hundred dollars! The engraved note card said it all. *For incidental expenses. Go, Nancy Drew!*

MIEL GRACES THE lobby level of the luxurious InterContinental Boston hotel. It's stunning and way out of my normal price range. CeCe loved it, and I'd accompanied her there several times to celebrate minor social and professional triumphs. Come to think of it, we'd lunched there the day my divorce was finalized.

Miel won the restaurant trifecta—French comfort food, attentive service, and stylish décor. Meribeth Foye must have agreed. She was waiting for me at the entrance, shifting giddily from foot to foot like a nervous filly in the breeding shed. We took our seats and exchanged wan smiles.

"It's so kind of you, Ms. Kane. This is such a special place." She adjusted her headband, sweeping nonexistent crumbs off the table. Headband! Even I knew that style had gone the way of scrunchies and frosting caps.

"I need your help," I said as Meribeth buttered a breadstick. "What does the name Byron mean to you?"

She furrowed her brow. "Byron. Like the poet?"

I shrugged. "Close your eyes and say anything that comes to mind."

Meribeth was a trooper. She closed her eyes, pursed her lips, and crunched. "Just one other thing. That man who called Ms. Swann."

My heart lurched. "What about him? You're sure it was a man?"

"I guess so. The voice was deep, but I didn't pay much attention. Just took the message and gave it to Malcolm." Meribeth snorted. "I'm not a secretary, you know. That's *his* job."

I clucked sympathetically and probed a bit more. "Did you catch the caller ID?"

"Maybe. Let me think." Meribeth ran a hand through her scraggly locks. "Nope. Sorry, I just don't remember. It rang on *his* desk, but of course Malcolm was gallivanting somewhere. Thinks he's too good to be a secretary, you know."

Her diatribe stopped when our waiter arrived. He patiently recited the entrées du jour as Meribeth debated the merits of half the menu. Whatever shortcomings she had, the woman certainly appreciated French food—all five courses of it.

"I just remembered," Meribeth said over scrumptious Pistou soup. "Ms. Swann had several calls that day that really upset her."

"Oh? Any idea why?" I spooned soup into my mouth, acting normal.

She wrinkled her brow. "Oh, I know! Something about her mother. That's it."

"Anika?" A glacial chill descended, causing me to shiver.

Meribeth shrugged as she swallowed an asparagus spear. "I didn't catch the whole thing, but it had something to do with that doctor. You know, her therapist."

I forced myself to remain calm. CeCe had been negotiating with someone, probably Wesley Townsend, about those discs. Part of the negotiation had involved a handgun, but she'd gone to that rooftop armed only with a smile. Something allayed her suspicions. When CeCe scented victory, nothing deterred her, even a phobia she'd wrestled with for years. She'd sublimate her fears if it meant saving her mother.

"Is something wrong, Ms. Kane?" Meribeth's lips puckered. "I thought of something else. Of course, it probably doesn't mean anything."

Who was the patron saint of forbearance? I needed heavenly help to keep from pinching her chipmunk cheeks. "I value your insights, Meribeth. Anything will help."

"Ms. Schwartz stayed late that Friday night. I mean, she always stays late but not usually on Fridays." Meribeth smirked. "Date night, you know."

My mental wheels starting clicking. Pamela Schwartz had a deep gravelly voice that might easily be mistaken for a man's. Could she be the elusive Byron? I was positive that her boudoir exploits eclipsed anything George Gordon ever tried. The stumbling block was motive. What arrangements would she possibly consummate with CeCe on that rooftop? More importantly, why would Pamela kill my friend?

"Did you hear me, Ms. Kane?" Meribeth's chestnut eyes gleamed with malice. "We all thought Ms. Schwartz might get married. She hinted around about it."

"No kidding. Who's the lucky man?"

She lowered her voice to a near whisper. "Why, Mr. Swann of course. Your fiancé."

"Deming?"

Meribeth nodded sagely. "Ms. Swann went berserk when she heard that. They really had it out. I happened to be outside her office getting a file."

I forced myself to button my lips. She'd blab if I just stayed silent.

Guaranteed. It was a rare opportunity in an otherwise humdrum life for her to claim the spotlight.

Meribeth averted her eyes in girlish demurral. "I abhor gossip," she said. "It's un- Christian. But you of all people understand why Ms. Swann was upset. Her very own brother. Her twin. She said, 'The only way you'll marry Deming is over my dead body!'"

Every muscle in my body went on red alert. I leaned forward, oblivious to the crème brûlée congealing on my plate. "How did Ms. Schwartz take that?"

"She moved in real close and hissed. I mean it. She actually hissed."

Chills swept through my body despite the restaurant's perfect temperature control. "Too bad you couldn't hear what she said."

Meribeth gave me a superior smirk. "Are you kidding? I heard her loud and clear. She said, 'Over your dead body? That can be arranged, Cecilia.'"

I gulped down an enormous swig of Perrier, anything to calm my nerves and keep the conversation flowing. "She must have been kidding. Pam Schwartz doesn't look like an assassin to me."

Meribeth Foye pursed her lips. "You're right, I'm sure. Ms. Swann was livid. She stormed out of that office, grabbed her briefcase, and slammed the main door. That wasn't like her at all."

"High stress jobs! I'm sure everything was forgotten the next week."

She closed her eyes while inhaling a spoonful of chocolate mousse and dabbed the corners of her mouth with a delicacy that surprised me. "They never got the chance to patch up their quarrel," she said. "Ms. Swann died that Sunday."

I PAID THE CHECK and drifted out to the curb in search of a cab. My head spun with a dozen different theories, none of them good. Blaring horns shocked me back to reality as I narrowly missed death by cement mixer. I staggered back to the curb, dazed.

"For Christ's sake, Eja. Have you no sense?" Deming flung open the passenger side door of his Porsche, oblivious to the murderous looks and hand gestures of fellow drivers. "Hop in, unless you're planning ritual suicide."

I tried to act civilized. His love life was no business of mine, and I did need a ride. Instead of shrieking, I burrowed into my purse, found the envelope, and thrust it at him. "I spent some for lunch, but the rest is here. Thanks for the gesture."

Deming surprised me. I expected a harangue, not the reaction I got.

"I wasn't patronizing you," he said softly. He clutched my hand, gently kissing each finger. "Sometimes I'm insensitive. I know that. You've spent most of your time helping us with Cecilia instead of working, and I just thought . . ."

I was prepared for anything but kindness. I closed my eyes to suppress any emotion. Revisiting Meribeth's gossip helped to stiffen my spine. My response was terse, fueled by anger and uncertainty. "I had no idea you and Pam Schwartz were so close. That she expected to marry you."

"What? Who fed you that garbage?" Deming's face lost all color, and his lips formed a cold, hard line. "I thought you knew better than that, Eja. You disappoint me."

A cab pulled in behind us, blaring its horn. Deming ignored it as I gave him a quick but thorough account of my lunch date.

"The woman's bonkers," Deming said. "Meribeth, not Pam. I can assure you that marriage was one issue Pamela and I never discussed. She's already had two husbands and wants no part of a family."

That floored me. "Family? You don't seem like the family type."

His lips twisted in a sly grin. "I could be, with the right woman. Every man wants a son."

Tread softly, Eja. Dangerous territory. As a childless woman who had never been pregnant I was ill equipped for this discussion. For all I knew, I might be as barren as the Gobi.

"Pam admitted she had a blowout with CeCe right before she died." I shrugged. "Could be she had designs on you after all."

Deming skillfully maneuvered the Porsche into the flow of traffic. "No sense asking. She'd only deny it. Besides, are you seriously suggesting that Pamela Schwartz lured my sister to that rooftop and murdered her over me? Sounds like one of your novels."

Déjà vu time. He'd managed to erase all my warm, fuzzy feelings with one caustic comment. I was proud of my books despite Deming's snide remarks. I'd worked hard to succeed, but a man who measured success by dollar signs would never understand that.

"We'll see." I flashed a Mona Lisa smile and said no more. CeCe might well have charged out onto that roof if she were meeting Pam. Even as a kid she'd never backed away or turned down a dare. It wasn't in her nature. "There's more," I said.

After hearing Malcolm's confession, Deming uttered a vivid scatological term. "We don't know that he's telling the truth. He may have engineered the whole thing. Probably did, the bastard. My sister could have ended his career or gotten him tossed in jail. Now *that's* motive."

He hooked a sharp left turn and sped down a side street.

"Wait a minute," I said. "Where are we headed?"

"My place. I thought you could use a drink. Frankly I need one."

"But . . ."

I'd never been to his home, or what CeCe called Deming's lair. Like everything about him, it was exclusive, elegant, and very private. The building's official name was the Carleton House, but insiders called it the Old Ritz. As Boston locations go it was primo: on the park where Commonwealth Ave kissed the nape of Newbury Street.

He valeted the Porsche and shepherded me through the cloistered lobby to the elevators. Everything was smooth and effortless as one might expect in a property that claimed to be the most coveted residential real estate in Boston. After inserting the elevator key, we sped silently up to the tenth floor. Deming had commissioned a total renovation by a Manhattan firm that was a regular in *Architectural Digest.* I steeled myself for grandeur, but the joke was on me. The room was a monument to Asian minimalism, a spare, yet oddly sensuous aesthetic rather like Deming himself. Even the colors reflected restrained passion: muted grey, black, and cream with crimson splashes.

"It's lovely," I said, glancing around. "The perfect bachelor pad."

He grunted something unintelligible and headed straight for the bar. "Pumpkin martini? Hope I got it right."

I was touched by the gesture. "You said the mere thought sickened you. What changed?"

Deming shrugged. "I tried one, just for fun. They're not half bad." He turned away as he wielded the silver cocktail shaker like a pro. Suddenly classical music flooded the room from some unseen source. Mozart I think, although it might have been Beethoven.

Deming led the way to the sunken living room and gestured toward the couch. My body parts tingled as I nestled into the sofa's downy cushions awaiting the unknown. Deming sat across from me in a charcoal wing chair, staring with such intensity that I quivered.

"You like this place?" he asked. "Most women do."

That subtle statement reminded me I was one in a pack of females who had graced the premises. Perhaps Deming got a volume discount. No problem. Romance aside, we shared only one goal. Anything else was unimportant.

"What happened at the police station?" I asked. "Did Mia Bates freak out?"

"Not hardly. That woman was colder than snow. Told Pam that Jem Russell was still a person of interest. Oh yeah, she mentioned you."

"Me?"

"Said you should butt out of her investigation, and I agree with her." He folded his arms as if he were the Lord High Executioner and that settled the issue. Words like arrogant and pigheaded immediately sprang to mind.

"Thanks for the advice," I said, taking a healthy swallow of my martini. "Did you, Lieutenant Bates, or Pamela happen to solve CeCe's murder? That's what we're here for, after all."

Deming's passion hiked my thermostat to the ceiling. I took a deep breath, ignored my carnal urges, and focused on the case. "We've narrowed down the suspects. That's half the battle. If we just . . ."

He slammed his fist down on the black lacquer side table. "Stop! You're delusional. We're no closer to finding my sister's murderer than we were a week ago. This isn't a game, Eja. You're playing with fire." His voice softened. "If something happened to you, I couldn't bear it."

I crossed the room and perched on the arm of his chair, ignoring the urge to touch and comfort him. Suddenly Deming whirled around, taking me by surprise. He folded me into his arms, blanketing me with a wall of rock-hard muscle. "I'd rather have you with me than risk your life," he whispered.

"Even if means that we never find her murderer?"

"Don't you get it? I care about you." Deming laid his cheek next to mine. "Damn it, I love you."

I opened my mouth to say something—anything—but words eluded me. Everything I'd dreamed of and yearned for welled up inside me with volcanic force. My throat closed, forcing me to swallow convulsively.

The ringing of his cell phone shattered the mood. Deming answered it, listening without comment to the caller. When he hung up, everything had changed. His manner was grave, his eyes unfocused.

"There's been a development," he said. "Jem Russell's gone."

Twenty-One

MY SENSES WENT on overload. The point/counterpoint of love and death was beyond my ken. I blinked furiously, trying to process everything.

"Gone as in dead, or missing?"

Deming shrugged as if it were irrelevant.

"Are you sure?" I asked. "About Jem, I mean."

"That was my dad. He just spoke to Lieutenant Bates." Deming stared vacantly into space, as if he'd entered a different cosmos.

"Did Jem leave a note or something?" I tripped over my tongue, trying to elicit information without appearing ghoulish.

"Pam went to his place. She had a key." Deming leapt to his feet and began pacing. "It's an admission of guilt. Has to be. Why else would he vanish?"

Jem Russell was the most self-centered male I'd ever encountered. He was also the least likely candidate for suicide or recriminations. There was no time for delicacy.

"So he's not dead? No signs of mayhem?"

"Not that I know of, but the cops consider his disappearance suspicious. Apparently they found something—my sister's missing laptop and BlackBerry."

"In his condo? Oh, my God!" My pulse quickened as I visualized it. CeCe's personal and professional life was encapsulated on those gadgets. Jem Russell with his pigmy brain and goofy grin could barely spell technology, let alone access it. He'd readily take her things to pawn, but he simply wasn't the type for sentimentality or souvenirs.

"Big deal," I said. "That means nothing. If Jem found that stuff, it probably freaked him out. You know how cowardly he is. He'd bolt."

Jem's disappearing act was a boon for the police and the real murderer. Dead men tell no tales. Neither do ones who vanish. If Euphemia Bates pressured Jem, he would have sung like the celestial choir. Someone or something had spooked him.

"Get your things," Deming said. "I'll drop you at your place."

"Wait a minute. Where are you going?"

He averted his eyes until that legal training kicked in. Then Deming Swann, Esquire, shrugged, summoning that blank, guileless look that spelled treachery. "My dad asked me to do some errands. Business."

In a departure from his lovey-dovey mood, he flicked a wing of coal black hair over his ear and grimaced.

"Poor Pam," I said, watching him closely. "She must be devastated."

His elaborate shrug was a dead giveaway. "I suppose."

"Drop me at your parents' house. Maybe Anika and I can comfort Pam. Female solidarity. You know the drill." I forced myself to call his bluff and damn the consequences. Deming's errand had nothing to do with business: He was going to Pam. I saw that with astounding clarity even as I slipped out of his arms, pretending to believe him.

I focused instead on the convenient loss of Jem Russell, a sad sack with the moral compass of a felon. CeCe compared him to anti-freeze, sweet tasting and lethal as hell.

He loved playing angles, thinking he was smarter than God or nature ever intended. This time his luck may have finally run out. Jem had a highly developed fight-or-flight instinct with emphasis on flight. Ten to one, he was either dead or holed up somewhere licking his wounds and seeking consolation.

The alleged evidence didn't faze me. Anyone can fabricate evidence. Television shows schooled us all in the basics of police procedures. Planting things in Jem's apartment was someone's quick, tidy solution to a thorny case. Jem had no motive to kill CeCe, and I wasn't buying his absence as an admission of anything other than panic.

"Eja, listen to me." Deming wore his serious, Perry Mason face. "You need to go home. Mother's not up for visitors right now."

"Maybe Bolin wants company," I said. "After all, I'm used to dealing with the press."

I saw the signs of seismic eruption. Deming Swann, emperor of all he surveyed, was seriously pissed. His reaction reinforced what I'd always suspected. Deming needed a different kind of woman, someone credulous who'd swallow his line of nonsense with a sweet smile. Not a caustic scold like me.

"For Christ's sake, let it go. He murdered my sister. Why can't you accept that?" Deming grabbed my shoulders as if he might shake them.

Acting on pure reflex, I speared his shin with my high heel. "Don't threaten me, Deming Swann. Ever."

He yelped like a schoolgirl. "What the fuck! You're insane! Always have been. I remember when you clobbered me in the head with your book bag."

We locked eyes in a searing battle of wills, neither one of us yielding an inch. Finally, he came to his senses and backed away. "Let's get moving. If you must know, I'm dropping in on Pam. As friends. Nothing more."

"Of course," I said. "You're right. Maybe I should go home. Cato, you know."

We maintained a stony silence for the next half hour as Deming retrieved his car and drove me home. The moment he reached my building, I hopped out, forestalling any chivalrous gestures.

"Hey listen," Deming said. "About this afternoon . . . what I said . . ."

"Already forgotten." I painted a faux smile on my lips and strolled away.

SLEEP ELUDED ME that night. I awakened the next morning to a horrific headache and swollen eyelids that were nobody's fault but mine. The sell-by date for fantasy had passed me by long ago, especially ones involving my best friend's brother. Dumb, dumb, dumb. I'd allowed a known lothario to invade my mind and capture my heart without firing a shot. Who could blame Deming for fleeing to Pamela Schwartz at the first opportunity? They shared primal passion without guilt or commitment, no I-love-yous or studied lies required, given, or expected. In short, the perfect relationship for the consummate bachelor.

For some unfathomable reason, I dialed Wesley Townsend's office. He was a loathsome sleaze, but he'd made me feel good about myself. Maybe a return engagement would rekindle the spark. It might also shed some light on CeCe's murder.

Brenda answered right away, using that impersonal voice endorsed by robots everywhere.

"I thought you'd left," I stammered. "Didn't you say you were quitting?"

Her sigh wafted right through the phone line. "Easier said than done. My job offer fell through, and in this economy . . ."

"Say no more. Look Brenda, I'd really like a session with the doctor. Today if possible."

She made sympathetic clucking noises before responding. "Sorry. No can do. He's out of the office all week. Another of those damn conferences. He's got someone to handle emergencies though."

I suddenly felt foolish, ashamed of my weakness. After all, I'd made it through a divorce without imploding. A nagging little voice inside me wouldn't let it go: *You had CeCe to console you. Now you have no one.*

"That's okay, Brenda. Thanks anyway."

"Hold on. I'm a really good listener. Occupational hazard. Why don't we get together after work?"

I hesitated, summoning my skills at diplomacy. Brenda was nice enough, but I needed a trained professional, not a sympathetic clerk.

"Ah, come on. What can it hurt? Besides, it'll be fun."

I told myself that it was only an hour out of my day. Besides, my only female confidant was Anika, mother of the man I was trying to forget.

"Okay. Where and when?"

I could feel her smile across the phone line. "Great! Cactus Club at six. Their margaritas are to die for."

I'M NO EXPERT on Boston's bar scene. Running the gauntlet of appraising male eyes is among my least favorite things. CeCe . . . well, she was a superstar who sailed into any room with confidence born of wealth and beauty. I summoned my courage and slipped into the bustling Cactus Club wearing a Plasticine smile and oversized shades. No need to scout out a table. Brenda waved merrily from a discreet corner spot, perfect for a tête-à-tête.

"Sit down," she chirped. "I've already ordered your drink."

"I'm not much of a drinker . . ." My bout with cognac had proven that. On the other hand, boozy confidences flow much more freely.

"So . . . what's troubling you?" She twirled her swizzle stick. "The doctor is in."

"It's nothing. Hardly worth mentioning."

Brenda reached across the table and squeezed my hand. "Deming Swann, isn't it? I took a peek at your file this afternoon."

A blast of heat made my cheeks burn. "They're confidential!"

"Big deal. Wesley trusts me with all his passwords. Has to. The man is brilliant, but when it comes to computers, he's back in the Stone Age." She gave me another squeeze. "Don't worry. I'd never tell."

Something told me to loosen up. "I've known the Swann family since I was five. We were schoolmates, the twins and I."

Brenda nodded. "No wonder Ms. Swann and you were so close. I know all about twins. I'm one myself."

"No kidding? How cool. I'd love to have a twin."

"Fortunately my sister and I aren't identical. Fewer problems, you know." She sipped her margarita and eyed me speculatively. "There's something else, isn't there?"

Discretion was the first casualty of my well-lubricated state. Two margaritas loosened my tongue. "Do you know anything about Dr. Townsend's habits? With women patients, I mean. Any complaints?"

Brenda squirmed in her seat. "None that I know of. Why?"

I leaned forward. "Does he video his sessions? Especially the hypnosis ones."

Her eyes widened in either fear or recognition. "He records all his sessions. For his protection and theirs. It's standard industry practice. You signed a disclaimer last week."

"Even when he assaults his patients?" I thought of Anika, elegant Anika, stripping before that shrink. How many other women had been victimized?

Brenda pushed back her chair and leapt up. "You're wrong! He'd never do that." She foraged in her purse, found some bills, and threw them on the table. "I can't be part of this. I won't." She grabbed my wrist with surprising strength.

"Prove it," I said. "If he's innocent, no harm, no foul. If not, we may have the motive for my friend's murder."

Her mouth opened in a perfect *o*. "Murder? Dr. Townsend was in Hawaii then. I told you that."

"Maybe he paid someone. Someone CeCe trusted."

Brenda clamped her hands over her ears. "No! I won't listen to this."

"You said he'd be gone all week. We could check his files and find out."

Her face had a ghastly pallor. "We? You're not touching those records. No sir!"

I sensed an opening. "Does that mean that *you* will? Please, Brenda. It's important. I know Mrs. Swann would be very grateful."

Brenda needed a job, and times were tough. If I dangled money and a position at Swann Industries in front of her, she might succumb. It was bribery, pure and simple, but it worked for me.

"How much does he pay you?" I asked.

Her eyes widened. "Why?"

"Swann Industries will double it, guaranteed, if you come through with those discs."

Brenda's chestnut eyes had dollar signs in them now. "They'd do that?"

I summoned my earnest scholar look. "They're always hunting for talent, and you're a most capable woman. Deliver those discs, and the job is yours."

She staggered to her feet. "Let me think about it. I've got your number."

Funny thing: I had her number too.

I COULDN'T COUNT on Brenda. Her discomfort reeked like cheap cologne. This crusade depended on me with a little help from my friends. The next morning I did a Google search for the American Psychiatric Association. Just as I thought, the 164th annual convention was ongoing in the city of brotherly love. I mentally thumbed through the list of registrants until I saw a familiar name. Dr. Wesley Townsend, seminar leader and major honcho, would be thoroughly occupied in Philadelphia for at least three more days. Time enough to formulate a plan that would free Anika from fear and avenge CeCe. I couldn't prove that he murdered her. Maybe he didn't. Either way, by destroying those awful tapes I'd fulfill part of my friend's agenda and give Dr. Pervert his comeuppance.

According to Anika, he kept the damn things in his office, hiding in plain sight. All I needed was ten minutes of access to Wesley Townsend's inner sanctum. There were elements of risk to be sure. Penal servitude has never appealed to me, and if my plan tanked even Bolin Swann might be powerless to help. I'd written this scene—intrepid heroine risks all to find justice—a hundred times, watched it on television even more. A partner would really come in handy. Lord Peter and Harriet, Nick and Nora, Tommy and Tuppence—the literary woods were full of them! My first thought was Deming, but that wouldn't work. Anika had sworn me to secrecy, and besides, he'd never agree to something illegal. Suddenly Malcolm Cates popped into my mind. He owed CeCe big time, would be cool in a crisis, and had muscles to boot. I grabbed my directory, found his number, and dialed.

Malcolm didn't answer. Instead, the nasal twang of Meribeth Foye assaulted my ears. I asked for Malcolm, praying fervently that she wouldn't recognize my voice. No such luck.

"Ms. Kane, is that you?"

What choice did I have? Caller ID complicated life for us all. "Hi, Meribeth. I'm looking for Malcolm. Is he around?"

I could hear her sneer through the phone line. "He's quite independent now. Seems he's got another job lined up and doesn't really care."

"Is he at work today?" I fought the panic that seeped into my voice. The window of opportunity was pitifully short. To beat Townsend at his own game I had to act fast.

"Wait a minute, Ms. Kane, he just came in." I heard some mumbled conversation and a sharp click.

"This is Malcolm."

After a brief greeting I went for broke. "I need your help. If you ever cared about CeCe, meet me at her place tonight. Eight p.m. Tell no one."

"Tonight? What's this about, Ms. Kane?"

"I already know that you're a risk taker. We have a chance to finish something that was important to her. Are you game?"

He paused longer than he needed to and gave an enormous sigh. "I guess so."

"Good. See you at eight."

Just one more call to make. I scrolled down my directory and rang up Anika Swann.

Twenty-Two

ANIKA ARRIVED early that evening bearing a picnic basket stuffed with goodies. The thought of food repulsed me until the scent of Po's cooking wafted my way. His kung pao shrimp was food of the gods. No mere mortal could resist, and I didn't even try.

"I told Bolin we were having a girls' night out." Anika arranged our feast on CeCe's Herend platter and set the dining table.

"Oh! Maybe we shouldn't use her good stuff," I said.

Anika shook her head. "Darling Eja. All her things are exquisite. Besides, this belongs to you now."

I forked some shellfish into my mouth. "He didn't question you? Mr. Swann, I mean."

"Relax. Bolin only asked if I was spending the night. He likes me to be home by bedtime. You understand."

Not really, but I was more than ready to learn. If I cuddled up to Deming each night, I'd never leave the house! Between bites of kung pao heaven I described my plan. Anika said little, but her eyes never left my face. I noticed a slight tremor to her right hand.

"You're serious, aren't you? You intend to do this." She brushed aside an imaginary hair and shivered. "If we succeed . . . it won't make up for her loss, but I know she'd be pleased. Cecilia loved winning."

Anika was unafraid, fearless in the face of a potentially dangerous scheme. That pampered and cosseted beauty balked at only one thing. She insisted on playing a direct role. It made sense on several levels, although the thought of Deming's reaction chilled my blood. Finding his mama in the hoosegow wouldn't help our love connection one bit.

By the time Malcolm arrived we'd reached a compromise. Anika would play the distraught patient while I slipped into the restroom to hide. The space was cavernous; she assured me of that. I have my own fears, and claustrophobia is one of them. The closet was deep enough to conceal me, and it adjoined a storeroom, so I'd be able to stretch without any problem. Malcolm would serve as lookout.

"Lookout? Sounds like some old movie. Cinema noir. What next, a getaway car and Tommy Gun?" The affable Malcolm of old vanished, replaced by a sneering stranger who made me shiver. CeCe had trusted him, but I could not.

"Thankfully, we won't need any weapons other than courage. You're a risk taker, aren't you?" My smile was laced with a hint of menace. After all, Anika and I knew all about his misdeeds. One word from Bolin Swann would sever Malcolm's professional lifeline.

Anika played supplicant, stretching her arms out to him. "Cecilia relied upon you, Malcolm. She was always there for you, and she knew you'd reciprocate. Thank you."

He flushed, chastened by her words. "I know what I owe Ms. Swann, and I won't forget it. Count me in."

My nerves grew more frazzled as our timeline shortened. Tomorrow afternoon was D-day. Right before five o'clock, Anika would appear at Townsend's office playing the distraught mother. She knew the stakes and was fully prepared to do whatever was necessary. In the confusion, I'd slip in and hide in the restroom. After Brenda closed up the place, Malcolm would text me if anyone came prowling around. It was a simple plan that just might work. It had to.

"Suppose you can't find those discs?" Malcolm asked. "Maybe they're in a safe or something."

Anika turned away, speaking in a surprisingly strong voice. "He keeps them right on his desk in an antique lacquered box. Taunting his victims, I suppose. It's a lovely piece. Surely you noticed it, Eja."

"Maybe. I was too traumatized to register anything that day. I'll bet he left everything right there. Hubris! Anyhow, it's a chance we'll have to take. At least we're doing something."

We discussed our exit strategy and decided that Malcolm would park his car out of reach of surveillance cameras, just across the street from Townsend's office. If I couldn't find anything in ten minutes, I'd give up and make tracks. Luckily the building was low-tech, with only an hourly sweep by a rent-a-cop.

"His name is Joe," Anika said. "Lovely man. Very friendly. He showed me pictures of his grandchildren one time when I left my keys in the office. His knee acts up, so he's unlikely to be too inquisitive."

"What if Townsend's office is locked? I can't break down the door."

Anika chuckled. "Leave it to me. I'll make sure that door is open."

Malcolm's face never lost its scowl. "What about the secretary? She might work late that night and get suspicious."

"Not to worry," I said. "Brenda's a big fan of Yo-Yo Ma."

"So?" He folded his arms in a contemptuous gesture.

Anika and I exchanged amused glances. "It just so happens that Mr. Ma is performing tomorrow night at eight p.m. Sold-out concert. Tickets impossible to get," I added sotto voce, "unless your name is Swann." The Swanns were personal friends of the famous cellist, and it took only one call from Anika to score the two box seats she'd given to Brenda.

"Trust me, Brenda will be out the door promptly at five. Guaranteed." I checked the time, surprised to find how late it was. Anika rang for Po, Malcolm made a hasty exit, and I grabbed Cato for our postprandial walk.

Although the streets were barren, I didn't feel alone. My boon companion CeCe Swann was there, face alight, cheering us on. From whatever heavenly perch she owned, my friend would watch over us and keep us safe. If we were lucky.

DEMING'S CALL THAT night roused me from a troubled half-sleep. "We have to talk," he said. "I'll be right over."

"No way! I need rest." My protest sounded feeble and unconvincing even to me.

"I won't stay unless you ask me." He hung up, leaving me cursing my own weakness. I buzzed the concierge and curled up once again in my bed. Ten minutes later, Deming knocked on my door. Cato opened one eye and sank back on his nest. As a sentry he was hopeless. He wasn't much better as a roommate.

I'd made no attempt to freshen up. Pam Schwartz would have donned something sultry, totally unlike my sturdy cotton nightshirt. Come to think of it, everything she owned was probably a prelude to seduction. Some women have the knack; the rest of us improvise. I answered the door with more growl than grace and waved him in.

"You really were sleeping, weren't you?" Deming's thick black hair was tousled, giving him the look of an errant schoolboy—a sexy, beguiling schoolboy with all the right moves. Before touching him, I put a sharp brake on my libido. Why succumb to sculpted abs and incredible hair? That resolve lasted until Deming pulled me to him and stroked my cheek.

"We left things sort of messed up. My fault, I know. Ever since Cecilia died I've lost control. Forgive me. Please."

"What's to forgive?"

He pulled back and sputtered a response. "Christ, Eja, stop this nonsense! Stop playing detective and leave it to the authorities. Let it go."

I couldn't believe my ears. Deming, twin brother of my best friend, was giving up. Throwing in the proverbial towel. Despite Euphemia Bates' efforts, CeCe's murder would inevitably be shuffled to the bottom of the death pile. Boston was a big city with plenty of other grieving families and open cases. Even Bolin Swann could push only so far.

"Let me get this straight," I said. "You're abandoning her."

The anguish on his face fed my guilty conscience. I waited him out.

"I'll never give up," Deming spat. "But I've got to move forward. *We've* got to move forward."

He kissed my forehead in a chaste brotherly gesture that chilled my soul. Was this how it would end? I thought of CeCe and "The Hollow Men" again. Deming was dumping me with a whimper, not a bang. Double entendre intended.

"Did you hear me? Christ, do you ever listen to me?"

"Right. Moving forward. Onward and upward. Any more clichés that I missed?" I kept my tone teasing and only slightly acerbic. Deming's response was a cracking good curse and a scowl.

"You haven't a romantic bone in your body. Did you hear me? I want to marry you, protect you, the whole kids-and-family bit." He paused. "You owe me the courtesy of a response, or is that too much to ask?"

Despite my skills as wordsmith and public speaker, I said nothing. My vocal chords were paralyzed by shock.

Deming's features hardened into a stranger's mask. He turned aside and stalked toward the door. It was now or never, do-or-die time. I sprinted forward, colliding with him in a tangled heap.

"I . . . are you serious? You're not joking, are you?" If he toyed with me, my heart would break. Plain and simple.

Deming flashed a ghostly grin and took my hand. "You've been around me long enough to know when I'm serious, Ms. Kane."

"But your parents . . . what will your dad think?"

He gave an exasperated sigh. "You are a major wuss! I'm thirty-three years old, missy, and so are you. I don't need my parents' consent to get married. Besides, they adore you. Always have." He tilted my head back and gently kissed me. "Life with you will be challenging, but I'm up to it. We can tell them tomorrow night. Go out to dinner; make an occasion of it. Include Jake."

A wave of guilt assailed me, washing away the joy. Tomorrow evening, I'd be rifling Townsend's office, not snuggling with Deming. It was important. Had to be done. I owed it to CeCe. Could a relationship built on deceit ever survive?

"Make it Friday. I've got plans tomorrow."

Deming's eyes narrowed. "You're not stalling, are you? I mean, if you're not sure about me . . ."

I stood on tiptoe and stroked his cheek. "I've never been more certain of anything."

WHEN HE LEFT the next morning, Deming's manner was sprightly. This was yet another side of a man I thought I knew. The patrician reserve and class arrogance of past years had vanished. Who knows? Maybe they never existed.

He gulped his espresso and planted a kiss on the top of my head. "Don't get too wild tonight. After all, you're spoken for."

My talent for duplicity astonished even me. What is admirable in a writer could prove lethal for a fiancée. I managed a self-effacing grin and a weak wave as he bounded out the door. I thought of CeCe, my kind and generous friend. If only she were here to share this moment. Cato nipped at my heels, reminding me of his needs, so I grabbed his lead, shrugged into a jacket, and did my duty. In six hours it would all be over.

OUR BASE OF operations had all the comforts that Starbucks affords: coffee, restrooms, and proximity to Townsend's office. I swathed myself in spy black, hailed a cab, and met Anika there at four o'clock. When I saw her garbed in lemon yellow I reconsidered my wardrobe choices. Anika was the picture of innocence and womanly charm. I channeled a downscale ninja. Could two such different women breathe the same air, let alone share a family name?

Anika threw her arms around me, beaming her runway smile. If she suspected something about Deming, she was too well bred to mention it. She laced her fingers around her latte as if it alone held the sustenance she needed. I blinked as her flawless skin and translucent pearls melded into the fading sunlight. The entire scene was surreal, as though I'd stumbled into a portrait by Vermeer.

"You spoke with Malcolm? He'll be here?" Anika fingered her pearls like a rosary.

"Absolutely. I confirmed everything with him this morning. Quarter of five on the dot."

She sighed and freshened her lipstick with the false cheer of a windup mannequin.

"Ready? I see you remembered to wear your camera pin. You figure all the angles, Eja—such a great planner. Remember. Give me five minutes to do my part before you come in. I'll leave the door open."

"Anika, listen. You don't have to do this. Stay here. Wait for me. I won't be long."

"My daughter didn't capitulate, and neither will I." Anika squared her shoulders and rose. "Follow me."

THE CROWDED elevator wheezed its way to the twenty-second floor as Anika and I watched from opposite corners. I used my hood to cloak my identity. She stood perfectly poised like the runway model she once was. When we alighted, Anika strode toward Townsend's door, heels clicking on the marble floor. I hovered near the water fountain, studying my watch. When five minutes elapsed, I ambled over to the office door and opened it a crack. Anika's voice, laced with hysteria, blended with soothing sounds from Brenda. A door slammed and voices raised. That was my cue. I slipped into the office, turned right, and sped down the corridor containing the lavatory and supply room. It wasn't spacious, but it was large enough to stave off claustrophobia. I hunkered down behind cluttered shelves, keeping the door ajar, waiting for the second act to begin.

It didn't take long. Ten minutes later, Brenda opened the restroom door to freshen up. She performed the usual hair and makeup rituals without even glancing my way. From the grumbling I heard, Anika must have played her part to perfection. Brenda extinguished the lights, jangled her keys, and slammed the office door. I waited exactly two minutes before creeping into the hallway. Stealth garb aside, I made a lousy spy. My knees shook, and my pulse throbbed as if I were auditioning for "The Tell-Tale Heart."

Fortunately, I'd brought along a Surefire flashlight courtesy of

Swann Industries. It was fantastic, only six inches long with a beam that could stun a moose. I took slow measured steps toward Townsend's office, giving myself a mental pep talk. The doorknob yielded easily, a testament to Anika's good work. It was kismet. Everything according to plan.

The red lacquered box stared at me from the middle of his desk, emitting a special force field. It was a splendid piece, artfully carved and exquisitely detailed. Beauty aside, if it were locked, I'd smash that thing to bits.

Luck was with me once again. The pin for the hasp was missing, and it gave way easily, leaving the box and its contents unguarded. I raised the lid and flipped through the neatly labeled CDs inside. Each bore a woman's name. As I pocketed Anika's, an outside noise distracted me. An adrenaline surge swept through my body, activating my fight-or-flight response. The jangle of keys meant that someone might be heading my way. Long-forgotten prayers sprang to my lips. Unfortunately, they all focused on St. Agnes, the virgin martyr widely touted by the nuns. I'm neither virgin nor martyr, so I switched to St. Jude. Hopeless causes seemed much more fitting.

I scooped up the contents, trained my flashlight on the room, and sought a quick hiding place. My stomach clenched, protesting too much caffeine and too little food. Out of desperation I made a choice, lunging toward one viable option: the bay window. Thick silk draperies concealed it, and the massive shrink couch lay in front of it. The doorknob rattled as I crouched behind the sofa, enveloped by something stiff and bulky. I fainted as the wide, dead eyes of Wesley Townsend confronted me.

Twenty-Three

I'D NEVER TOUCHED a corpse before. Who could blame me for shrieking the moment I regained consciousness? Instantly a hard slap lashed my cheek, diverting my attention from anything but pain.

"Ow! That hurt!"

"There's more where that came from," Brenda said. "Shut up!"

I was groggy and confused by her reaction. How had I landed on the couch? Where was Wesley Townsend or what remained of him? "He's dead," I sputtered, rising up. "Dr. Townsend."

"Tell me something I don't know." Brenda's chestnut eyes glittered in the lamplight. They weren't attractive anymore. They radiated menace. "You couldn't leave it alone, could you? You and the lovely Anika. How stupid do you think I am, for Christ's sake?" Her hand clasped an Art Deco letter opener with a wicked tip. "Too bad. I really love Yo-Yo Ma." She reached under her coat and found her purse. CeCe's purse, the Hermes Garden Party.

"*You* did it?" I asked. The words sickened me. Had Brenda been Townsend's confederate? Was my friend's purse a spoil of war? "People know I'm here. You won't get away with this."

Her derisive laugh was closer to a cackle. "Let's see. Mrs. Bolin Swann? Nope. Oh, I get it. You're counting on Malcolm to save you." She twirled the letter opener, pointing the tip at my jugular vein. "Sorry. This isn't one of your dopey books. Mr. Cates is unavailable." She checked her watch. "Right about now, he's heading for that concert in my place."

"I don't understand . . . Malcolm hurt CeCe?" I sat upright, feigning confusion, plotting my escape. If I caught her unaware, I had a fighting chance against Brenda and the letter opener she brandished. Her role in CeCe's murder and all that followed was a puzzle best solved when I was free from here. I faked a coughing fit realistic enough to back her away.

"Jesus, stop that! You're too stupid to live," Brenda said. "Creeping around like Sherlock Holmes. You still don't get it. Malcolm

Cates is as clueless as you. He was only too eager to skip out and take the missus to a free concert, especially after that message you sent him."

"Huh?" I played along, acting dull-witted. By feeding her ego, I could buy time and possibly save my life.

Brenda's lips curved in a victory smile. "Oh, yes. You called and left him a message. Told him your plans were canceled, but you'd left Yo-Yo Ma tickets for him at will-call. He was elated. Couldn't believe his good luck." She chuckled. "You know what a wuss he is."

That was bad news. Our plan depended on Malcolm and the getaway car. Anika must be frantic right about now. I had to act quickly while Brenda was still savoring her triumph. My hand curled around a bronze sculpture on the side table. I tensed and hurled it at Brenda's head with all my might. My aim wasn't great, but Brenda's rather large noggin made an excellent target. The sculpture grazed her temple and did the job. She crumpled like well-worn currency as I leapt up, grabbed the contents of the lacquered box, and sped toward the door. My heartbeat scaled the stratosphere as I hit the waiting room. Let Euphemia Bates figure out the details; my only goal was freedom. I fumbled with the deadbolt and twisted the doorknob on the walnut door. A more composed person might have phoned the cops. I thought about survival. Maybe Anika called Deming when Malcolm didn't show. Maybe he was outside. I flung open the door and stared into the doughy features of Meribeth Foye. Anika was at her side.

"Are you okay?" I asked. The pallor of Anika's face and her rigid posture gave the answer. She reached out to me, but her arm was encased in the firm grip of CeCe's paralegal. The triumphant look in Meribeth's eyes proved she was no savior. The glint of metal said she had a gun. I blinked. No wonder those chestnut eyes were so familiar. I'd seen them on Brenda, the fiendish receptionist. She'd mentioned her twin who worked in a law firm. I'd been so focused on the forest that I missed two very sturdy trees! The Janus motive—twins working in tandem to run their blackmail scheme. No wonder Malcolm had never appeared.

Meribeth anticipated my next move. She grasped my shoulders, giving me a hard, backward shove that sent me sprawling into Brenda. Soft moans confirmed that she was unconscious but still alive. In the confusion, breaking free was a possibility. Abandoning Anika was not. They say that murder gets easier after the first kill. Not a theory I planned to test with homicidal siblings.

"You hurt her! You hurt my sister!" Meribeth flung Anika against the couch and ran to Brenda. She cradled her, wiping the thin line of blood that trickled down her face. "Wake up, Sis," she crooned. "You'll be okay."

Brenda stirred and lifted her head. As Meribeth hovered over her twin, Anika and I exchanged glances and cautiously edged toward freedom. My legs were rubbery, weakened by fear, but functional. Unlike the sprightly heroines in my novels, I wasn't brave. I was terrified. Anika Swann was a different story. She slipped off her stilettos, clutched them like weapons, and moved confidently toward the door. My flat-heeled gym shoes offered no such option. Anika turned the doorknob and nudged me out. I plunged toward the illuminated exit sign with her nipping at my heels. With a little bit of luck we'd hit that stairwell before Meribeth remembered us.

Anika's composure never wilted as we reached the exit door and flung it open. She faltered only after we ran head-on into the solid wall of flesh encapsulating Jem Russell.

I was so glad to see the big lug that I hugged him. He seemed unfazed by our sudden appearance, untroubled by my wild eyes and tangled locks. That was my first clue.

"You're alive!" I stammered. "Thank God. Help us get out of here."

Jem flashed his moronic grin as he blocked the stairwell. "Calm down, ladies. Jem's here."

"No time to chat." I was one word short of babbling, but I couldn't help myself. "We'll explain later."

Anika remained poised. She beamed her radiant smile as she drove her stiletto into Jem's meaty neck. Jem gasped, clutched his throat, and sank slowly to the floor. "That's for murdering my daughter," she said.

Murder? It made sense even though I'd lost a step somewhere. I supported the team effort by a vigorous kick to his groin that left him gasping like a gaffed trout.

"Run, Anika," I said. "There's no time."

"You're right about that. Move back, or the rich bitch dies." Meribeth grinned as she leveled her gun at Anika's head.

WE TRUDGED BACK into Townsend's office, prompted by the barrel of Meribeth's gun. Jem stayed splayed across the stairwell, making garbled, guttural sounds. He'd probably survive, unlike Anika and me. I racked my brain for something—anything—to delay the inevitable, but my mind was an arid wasteland. Meribeth waved her gun, motioning toward the leather settee. "Sit. Both of you."

"Tell us why," Anika said. "We have the right to know."

"Awfully big on rights, aren't you," Meribeth snorted. "Think you run the world. Your daughter was the same way."

Hearing her talk about CeCe made Anika stiffen. Her eyes blazed hatred and defiance.

"Why kill Townsend?" I asked. "He was behind all this."

Brenda pulled herself upright on the couch and curled her lip. "Still clueless. Townsend had no idea what was going on. He was a pervert, of course, but too gutless to cash in on clients." She smirked at Anika. "You're photogenic, Mrs. High and Mighty Swann. Where'd you learn to strip?"

Anika's pale skin flushed with either anger or shame. "Forget about me. Why kill Cecilia? She would have paid your price."

I knew the answer right away. CeCe would never have stopped. Not until she found and crushed the blackmailer. Leverage. Good attorneys use it to wring concessions from their opponent. CeCe was a tireless adversary who lived to win.

"We had a good thing going," Meribeth huffed. "We negotiated with five or six clients. Just enough to make ends meet. Nothing greedy. Townsend had plenty more patients. Rich bitches who'd pay anything to save themselves."

Her sense of entitlement floored me, but I faked a look of wide-eyed admiration. "How did you manage it? CeCe knew your voice. You were Byron, weren't you?"

Brenda guffawed as if my comment was comic gold. "That was easy. After all, I knew everything that went on here. Townsend left everything where I could find it. Child's play! I sent dear Ms. Swann messages from the doctor's computer. No direct contact. Sometimes Meribeth pretended I'd called and handed messages to her. It all went like clockwork."

"Yeah. That prick Malcolm loved it when I did his job. No one questioned anything until your daughter got nosey. Too big for her britches." Meribeth beamed a triumphant look our way. "I made up Byron and those threatening letters too. Think about it. You believed everything I fed you. I knew you'd eat up the literary touch. You snobs think you're so smart. What a bunch of saps."

I slipped my hand into my pocket and found the Surefire

flashlight. No match for a gun, but at least it was something. After all, it had special self-defense features. "What happened on that rooftop? Tell us. Please . . ." I banked on their need for recognition. Bet our lives on that slim hope.

"Oh, why not? A last wish for our guests." Brenda patted her bruised head and winked at her twin. "That spoiled bitch broke the rules. Contacted Townsend directly. He panicked, of course. Had no idea what was going on."

"Yeah, do you believe it?" Meribeth's nasal tones were aggrieved. "It was easy to set her up. She thought she'd beaten Townsend. That's all she could think of, getting those discs and saving her dear mama from disgrace."

Anika's tears flowed freely now. I knew she saw her bright, loving daughter springing into action on that sunny day, confident of victory, oblivious to danger. It was no one's fault but a mother wouldn't see it that way. She'd blame herself.

"How in the world did you get her to that rooftop?" I asked.

"That's where I came in." Jem Russell limped through the doorway, clutching his throat. His voice was raspy, barely a whisper. "I told CeCe I'd meet her on that roof. Make her feel safe." Some of his old swagger returned. "It was easy. Her fiancé couldn't make it, and she needed someone. She always trusted me."

A blistering anger surged through me. I'd dismissed Jem as a feckless jerk with zipper problems and a pea brain, but Deming had seen the evil in him. Why hadn't I listened?

"How could you?" Anika sobbed. "She liked you. She was kind to you."

He shrugged. "Yeah. Those are the breaks. You know me, anything for cash. Don't worry. She never knew what hit her. I made sure of that."

"What about your alibi? Lieutenant Bates nailed you to the wall on that one."

Another shrug. "We staged that. Brenda lives in my building. They never even made the connection. I've been staying with her since I 'disappeared.' That's how I ducked out. Bates was hot on my tail." He gave his Huck Finn smirk. "I'm pretty good with most women, but I couldn't fool that cop. No way."

Meribeth shifted her gun and frowned. "Let's end this. Murder/suicide sounds about right. Townsend killed these two when they confronted him, then offed himself."

"Wait a minute," I said. "They'll know that the doctor was murdered. No powder burns or gunshot residue on his hands. Plus they'll compute the trajectory." I folded my arms with a confidence born of desperation. "Guess you're not so smart after all."

Meribeth narrowed her eyes, Brenda glared, and Jem looked puzzled. Every second was an answered prayer.

"Listen, Sis," Brenda said. "She may be right. No big deal. We've got the van. We'll take them through the garage and drive to Maine. They've got miles of woods there. When winter ends, these two will be skeletons." Malice made her face a clown's mask. "Jem can get Townsend later. Roll him up in a rug and dump him somewhere. The cops won't figure it out. I'll play the bereaved clerical grieving for the big boss."

"Yeah, I guess. I'll plant some clues, and you tell the cops some story about Townsend. Threatening letters. They liked the ones I made for Ms. Swann." Meribeth smirked at me and motioned to Jem. "Let's go. Hold on to them this time and take the stairs. I hope you disabled those security cameras."

"Already done, boss lady. You know I follow your command." The eye contact between Jem and Meribeth suggested a double entendre. I shuddered, recalling that twins were his special fantasy.

"The garage!" I squealed. "That's public space. Someone might get hurt."

Jem chuckled. "Didn't know you were so tenderhearted. Too bad." He hoisted me up with one enormous paw and grabbed Anika with the other. "Show time, ladies. Come on."

Meribeth led the procession with Brenda taking up the rear. I considered pushing Jem down the stairs, but the risk was too great. Anika and I might be killed or injured on those concrete steps. I vowed to tough things out. They'd have to murder me before I begged for my life or disgraced myself. Die with dignity, but live if you can. That's my motto. Unlike me, Anika stayed placid. You'd almost believe she was listening to a litany of complaints from the PTA.

I prayed that some casual observer would see us and call the cops. We made an odd quintet, goose-stepping our way across that dank, dark garage. Most of the patrons were long gone, but a few stragglers, a Jeep and the ubiquitous Mercedes sedans, still remained.

Meribeth stopped in front of a Dodge minivan and opened the back door. "Did you switch the plates?" she asked Jem.

He flashed the trademark grin that had won so many hearts. "But of course, fair lady. And don't worry. I lifted this from the long-term lot at Logan. We'll vamoose before the poor sap even knows it's gone."

The garage was surprisingly warm, but I shivered anyway. Once they hauled us out of the city our chances weren't good. Every self-defense manual and grisly crime show made that clear. Somehow, someway, Anika and I must prevail. A parking garage was a poor substitute for the O.K. Corral, but the outcome might be the same. Before I could react, Jem clamped my arm in a vise and flung me into the van. He sandwiched himself between Anika and me, waving an ugly black gun in the air.

"Don't move, ladies. Can't spoil the interior." He chuckled and mugged for his audience.

"Cut the clown act," Brenda hissed. "Someone might notice you." She eased the van out of the space and aimed for the nearest exit. "Shit! We'll have to use the rear exit. This one's closed." She backed up and slowly, methodically, followed the flashing signs.

"Keep cool," Meribeth said. "Couple of cars behind us."

I tried to catch Anika's eye but was blocked by Jem's bulk.

"Relax, Eja. No one's going to save you. They can't even see you." That thought seemed to please him. He rocked back and forth like an antsy toddler.

"Will you *stop* that?" Brenda huffed. She drummed her fingers on the steering wheel as the van crept toward the exit. She reached for her parking pass. "Damn! It won't read this thing! What next?"

"Maybe the doc didn't pay his bill," Jem said, smirking. "I told you not to use a dead man's card. Bad karma."

Brenda swiveled around and faced him. "Shut the fuck up, moron."

I watched Jem change in the blink of an eye. No more mister nice guy. Dr. Jekyll had left the car. Jem lurched forward and squeezed Brenda's shoulder until she shrieked. "Never underestimate me," he growled. "CeCe made that mistake."

Meribeth swung her purse, scoring a direct hit on Jem's nose. "Touch her again, and I'll kill you," she said. "You're not the only one with a gun."

The car behind us honked twice. Brenda lowered her window as the attendant, a tall, gangly redhead, rapped on the door. "Need help, ma'am? Those cards always seem to act up." He took her parking pass and raised the barrier. "There you go. No trouble."

Maybe I was dreaming, fantasizing probably, but he looked familiar. I couldn't quite place him. Redheads with a sprig of freckles aren't that common anymore. I leaned forward and locked eyes with Anika. She was waiting, ready to seize any opportunity.

Brenda maintained a steady, unremarkable pace as we approached the street. No one would suspect that anything was amiss. Our options diminished at warp speed, leading me to mourn the squandered years and mindless drift of my life. If a miracle happened—if I got another chance—I'd change it all.

Suddenly, out of nowhere, everything exploded. The Jeep behind us rammed our bumper—hard. As Brenda swore and veered to the right, I grasped my Surefire flashlight and clobbered Jem on his wounded nose, watching those high-tech aluminum teeth on the tail cap do their job. A satisfying bone crunch, blood spurt, and howl of pain caused him to drop his gun. Anika leapt for it and coolly fired two bullets straight into Meribeth's back. She swiveled toward Jem, leveling the gun at his forehead.

"Don't even breathe," she growled, "or you're next."

Brenda wailed for her twin as she steered the van toward the phalanx of police cars now ringing the street. Her ragged breath and bulging eyes signaled her intent to ram the barrier. Visions of Thelma and Louise, Butch and Sundance flooded my mind. I lurched toward Brenda, hammering her head with my trusty flashlight. That stunned her enough to slow her progress, enough to allow someone to wrench open her door and grab the steering wheel.

"Nobody move." The garage attendant morphed into the familiar freckled face of Patrolman Kyle Jennings, designated driver for Euphemia Bates. He gasped at the sight of Meribeth's lifeless body and Jem's bloody face before regaining his composure. "Drop the gun, Mrs. Swann. Everything's under control."

"Not until you handcuff him," Anika said. "He murdered my daughter."

The passenger door opened, and Mia's voice rang out. "Hand it to me, Mrs. Swann." She pushed aside Meribeth's corpse and trained her weapon on Jem. "Easy now, ladies. Step out of the car. It's all over."

They were waiting, tucked behind the police barrier. We extricated ourselves from the van and staggered toward them too traumatized for tears, too proud to faint. Bolin and Deming rushed forward, offering us comfort and safe passage. I recalled the vow I'd made during that awful siege. No more fear of pain or hurt feelings. Restraint and caution flew to the winds as I found Deming's arms.

Twenty-Four

UNRAVELING THE skein of three deaths can be tricky. After Jake Harris pressured her, Lieutenant Bates agreed to join us at the Swann manse and save the formal proceedings for the next day. "They're in shock," Jake said. "As their physician I insist both ladies remain at home. They really should be sedated."

Deming squeezed my hand to distract me. "You're absolutely right, Dr. Harris. They should go right to bed."

Despite coming within inches of death I still had my wits about me. Deming's eyes twinkled with mischief.

"No way," I protested. "I'll never rest without knowing how you got there." I glanced at Anika and saw her nod. "It won't take long."

That's how we landed in Bolin's study cosseted by cashmere throws and cognac.

Euphemia Bates leaned back in the wing chair and sighed. After trading Kevlar for a stylish pantsuit of palomino-colored wool she sipped daintily from her beverage of choice, a mug of tea.

"Dr. Harris is the hero," she said. "He sounded the alarm."

I did a slow-motion replay of the scene in the garage. Of course! Jake drove the silver Jeep that had rammed our bumper.

"Anika called me when Malcolm didn't show. Before I could get there, she rushed back into that building looking for you." Jake shook his head. "I was just about to pull the fire alarm when the cavalry arrived. I couldn't think of anything else to do."

Anika rested her head on Bolin's shoulder. "I'd already lost one daughter. I couldn't lose another."

"This little fellow came in handy," Deming said, fingering the gold pin on my lapel. "We could hear everything, especially when you screeched about the garage."

"Screeched? I was desperate. Didn't even know if you guys could hear me."

Bolin smiled fondly at Anika. "Guess you didn't know my wife was wired for sound too." He pointed to her diamond watch. "I had that made for her last year after she fainted on Newbury Street. It's got a GPS that beeps Jake and me."

"We'll need that at the trial," Euphemia said, "although Jem Russell is bleating like a lamb. He's willing to testify if we take murder one off the table for him." She sighed. "They both want a deal."

"But he did it," I said. "He murdered CeCe. It's on the recording."

Deming tightened his grip on my hand. "Let it go, Eja. Jem Russell won't escape justice. Trust the system."

Euphemia Bates gave him a strange look that I couldn't decipher. "Well said, Mr. Swann. With Meribeth dead, her sister and Jem both swear she was the mastermind and they were minor players." She shuffled some papers. "One more thing. Both of them say that you shot Ms. Foye without provocation, Mrs. Swann. Be prepared for the media. They'll swarm when they get wind of that tidbit."

Bolin tightened his grip around Anika. "We should consult our attorney, Leda. Just to be safe."

"Of course, Bolin. Whatever you say." Anika dabbed at her eyes with a lace hanky. Her voice shook as she recounted the story. "It's all a blur right now. Guns frighten me, and I panicked. That Foye woman had some kind of weapon. A gun. She threatened us with it in the office, didn't she, Eja?"

An image flashed through my mind like quicksilver. Anika the crack shot had been trained by experts to defend herself and her family. She'd dispatched Meribeth as coolly and professionally as any assassin. This shattered woman cowering in her husband's arms was a total stranger and a charade. *Well played, Anika!*

Deming elbowed me back to reality. "We're waiting, Eja."

"Sorry. It's so painful to even think about. I just knew we were going to die. The three of them were killers. We had no weapons and no hope until Jake rammed the van. I wacked Jem with the flashlight and . . ." My voice broke, and I stifled a sob. "That's all I recall."

Mia tapped her iPad and frowned. "I wouldn't worry about it. You can give your formal statement tomorrow. Funny thing, though. We've got most of the evidence from the blackmail scheme, but nothing involving you, Mrs. Swann. Jem swears it was all there. He gave quite a vivid description." Mia smiled. "Of course, he's a proven liar. Totally unreliable."

I lowered my eyes and shrank back on the couch, comforted by its downy cushions and the sharp edge of the CD in my pocket.

IN THE WEEKS that followed, CeCe's murder faded from the public eye. Not for those who loved her but for the curious masses who sought entertainment in grisly crimes and hapless victims. I joined the Swanns at the preliminary hearing where both Jem and Brenda pled guilty to extortion and manslaughter. Meribeth's death had already been ruled justifiable homicide.

Prison had taken its toll on their bodies if not their spirits. Brenda's puffy face was eloquent testament to carb-laden jail fare. Jem's luxuriant mane had been shaved down to a buzz cut. She stared straight ahead as the bailiff ushered her through the courtroom. He swiveled his head our way and winked at Anika. Deming half-rose from his seat until Bolin squeezed his arm and shook his head. No scenes by the Swann family would feed the tabloids.

The process was a stiff, inglorious end to the life of my vibrant friend. Justice prevailed, but she was gone forever. I ached for CeCe as if a part of my own body had been severed.

Soon afterward, Bolin negotiated the sale of my studio, and Cato and I took possession of CeCe's condo. My vow to avenge her had been honored, and the legacy no longer troubled me.

As summer faded to autumn and another winter passed, Deming slowly slipped away from me. He spent time abroad and ducked my phone calls. We became casual, polite strangers who neither laughed, quarreled, nor made love. Without drama or tears I resigned myself to solitude once more.

Deming was far from lonely. His image accompanied by one svelte beauty after another regularly graced the Metro section of the *Boston Globe*. I wept at first, but eventually the pain subsided as did any hope of sharing his life.

I didn't brood. Wouldn't admit to anyone—even myself—how empty I felt. An occasional dinner with Jake and regular visits to the Swanns kept me occupied if not fulfilled. I even endured a few disastrous blind dates.

With a stipend from the Swann foundation, I wrote a blistering account of CeCe's murder that spared no one, least of all me. It was a catharsis, or it should have been. Jem Russell basked in the spotlight for a time, reciting his version of events to *Sixty Minutes* and *Dateline*. His glory was short-lived however. A well-placed shiv during a prison brawl ended everything. Jem was found alone in the exercise yard with his carotid artery severed. Despite the warden's vigorous inquiry, no one confessed to the crime. There was no evidence.

His story had a macabre ending, but with all the excitement I'm sure Jem never knew what hit him. Just like CeCe.

Critics raved about my book, calling *Swann Dive*, "brilliant" and "riveting." It was nominated for both an Anthony and an Edgar award.

Book signings were different now. Fans lined up to see me, sales exceeded every expectation, and Eja Kane became a media darling. My life was a writer's dream, but it was cold comfort without Deming by my side.

One evening after a particularly hectic event in Back Bay, I gathered up my bookmarks, business cards, and trifles and heaved them into my backpack—CeCe's backpack, actually. I could never bring myself to hand Louis Vuitton that kind of money even though sales had been brisk. Better than good. I was tired but satisfied as I calculated the take.

"Sign one more, lady?"

I whirled around to face him, trying desperately to control the flush that stained my cheeks. Deming Swann, a vision in those tight black jeans and a white knit sweater, gazed down at me with a look that seared my soul.

I fought tears by faking a sneeze. "Deming. What a surprise. Good to see you."

My brittle words didn't faze him at all. He aimed a tender smile at me instead. "We have a date, don't we? Nine sharp, Parker House, pumpkin martinis."

I forced myself to stare straight into those hazel eyes. "Don't do this to me, Deming. Please. I just can't take it."

Pride flew out the window as my body shook with sobs. I fled the store and sped up Arlington Street toward the Common. He caught me at the traffic light, enveloping me in a hug so fierce it took my breath away.

"I missed you," Deming said. "Missed you so much." He gently stroked my hair. "New hair style. Nice. Mom says you're a big hit."

I swallowed my tears and said nothing. I'd seen the women he dated. Svelte, shiny debs with big trust funds and bright futures. No amount of hair gel or designer clothing could transform me into that. I'd never make the grade as Deming's companion.

"I sent you the book. About CeCe, I mean. You probably haven't read it. I know you've been busy." My voice was steady and unemotional. I was proud of that.

He traced the outline of my lips and kissed my forehead. "Read it?

I've practically memorized every word. It's good, Eja. Better than good. Congratulations. You're on your way."

Truth spoke where I could not. "Am I? Everything feels so empty."

Deming took my hand and slowly kissed each finger. "I know all about emptiness. I haven't felt whole since you left me."

I wanted to scream, shout, or shake him senseless. Instead, I kicked him. Hard.

"What the fuck! You're insane. Always have been." He nursed his ankle, wailing like an infant.

"*My* face wasn't spread all over the *Globe*. *I* didn't flee the country. That's your specialty."

Deming's scowl morphed into a dazzling smile. "Seems like old times, doesn't it?" He pulled me to his side. "Truce?"

Courage born of desperation fueled my anger. "I can't be your friend, Deming. It hurts too much."

I stifled the urge to touch his face and run my fingers through those thick curls. I'd come to terms with losing him, admitted only to myself how much I ached for him. I wouldn't survive a return engagement. Couldn't risk it.

"You don't get it, do you? I love you. Always have. I told you that already." He folded his arms as if that settled everything. "I let you down. You and my mom could have died, and I wasn't there to protect you. I had to do something for my sister."

Now I knew for certain what I'd always suspected. Jem Russell's demise was more than a prison brawl. Deming and probably Bolin had seen to that. As Jem the ultimate pragmatist once observed: Those are the breaks.

I could live with that.

Deming caressed my cheek. "I knew I didn't deserve you, couldn't bear to face you. That's why I took off and dated those vapid, rich girls. To torture myself."

Anika had said something like that. "Don't take Dem seriously, dear. He's punishing himself. He'll come to his senses. I know my son."

"Some torture," I said. "You could have dated ugly girls, you know, instead of goddesses. They were all amazing."

He grabbed my backpack and pulled me to him. "They weren't you. Nobody even came close." Deming forced me to meet his eyes.

"Tell me how you feel once and for all. I'll abide by anything you say. Just tell me. Is it possible? Could you still love a man like me?"

It was now or never, do-or-die time again. I'd been granted another chance for happiness. Time to risk everything, go for broke, and damn the consequences.

I swallowed hard and summoned my courage. "CeCe knew us better than we knew ourselves. All those years of fighting each other, resisting the truth. Wasted time."

"You married that creep," Deming spat. "I . . . that day was very painful for me. I didn't understand until later. It sent me into a tailspin. Glenlivet and Mozart. They were my therapists."

"As I recall, you were no hermit. You had a different girlfriend every week. CeCe told me."

Deming hung his head. "I read all your books. More than once." He rubbed my hand against his cheek. "Stop stalling. Tell me now. I can take it."

Our sidewalk drama drew stares from several pedestrians. I motioned to Deming and tried to pull away.

"Tough," he said, thrusting out his chin. "I'll stand here all night until you answer me. I have nowhere special to go."

I pointed toward the lights of Beacon Street where CeCe Swann had lived and loved. "Could I love a man like you? Not any man. Just you. Come home with me, Deming. Never leave again."

His face brightened as if the sun had bathed us both in happiness.

We strolled through the Common, hand in hand, walking toward our future.

Readers' Guide

The Boston Uncommons Mystery Series.

SWANN DIVE

1. Cecilia Swann appeared to lead a charmed life, but despite having brains, beauty and money to spare, she was no stranger to tragedy. Do we often assume that celebrities and prominent people have it all?

2. CeCe and Deming shared a special bond. Are twins particularly attuned to each other? Does this intensify the pain when one of them is lost?

3. The power of loyalty, friendship and family is the major theme of *SWANN DIVE*. Discuss how this influenced the quest for truth in the death of Cecilia Swann?

4. Despite coming from a middle-class background, Eja Kane is not intimidated by the Swanns' enormous wealth. What does that say about her character?

5. Most portrayals of middle-aged mothers-in-law are less than flattering but Anika Swann is gracious, beautiful and brave. How does the relationship between Eja and Anika add another dimension to this novel?

6. Deming Swann is a complex, passionate character whose strengths and weaknesses are not dissimilar to Mr. Darcy's in *Pride and Prejudice.* Discuss this.

7. What unites Eja and Deming and what threatens to tear them apart?

8. Lieutenant Euphemia Bates and Dr. Jake Harris are both strong, smart people of color. What was your reaction to these characters? Does ethnic/racial diversity in a novel heighten the experience for readers and reflect the world as it is?

9. Bolin and Anika Swann have an intense, loving marriage with an erotic edge. What does this portrayal suggest about them and their relationship?

10. Justice is often an ambiguous term. Did you agree with the outcome in *SWANN DIVE?*

Coming Next

MANTRAP
BOOK TWO, THE BOSTON UNCOMMONS MYSTERIES
(Available July 2014)

Does a victim's character predict his murder? MANTRAP, the mystery series explores the nature vs. nurture debate and the enduring power of love amidst violence.

Dario Peters, avid cyclist, ardent environmentalist, and heir to a munitions fortune lives the dream, until a nasty spill on a Cape Cod bike trail ends his life. Everyone calls it a tragic accident—except Persus Cantor, Dario's doting grandma. When psychic Merlot Browne brands it foul play, Aunt Pert begs amateur sleuths Deming Swann and Eja Kane to find Dario's murderer. Despite misgivings, grumbling and elaborate excuses, Deming is pressed into service. After all, Pert is his mother's favorite aunt, and family comes first. Eja embraces the challenge. As a mystery writer all deaths seem suspicious to her and she leaps at the opportunity to spend time on a majestic Cape Cod estate with her sizzling fiancé.

Bayview, a tranquil seaside village, is seventy miles and several decades removed from bustling Boston. Residents treasure tradition and family values, two things that Dario Peters openly renounced. Case in point was his marriage to Paloma, a study in excess with body parts as suspect as her lineage. Dario's scheme to rezone staid Bayview into a cycling paradise was another venture that riled locals and investors alike. In old Cape Cod, low-end tourists are a burden to be endured not encouraged.

About the Author

Arlene Kay is a mystery writer with a dark past. In another life, the author of INTRUSION, and DIE LAUGHING, was a Senior Executive with one of those alphabet agencies that strikes terror into the hearts of all Americans.

Since moving to Cape Cod, she abandoned government work to craft fiendishly clever mysteries with a touch of mayhem and a splash of romance. Her previous works include five novels in the Grace Quinn/Patrick Fong mystery series.

She recently completed SWANN DIVE and MANTRAP; the first two books in her new Boston Uncommons Mystery series featuring two intrepid sleuths who live the good life while vanquishing criminals in the very blue state of Massachusetts.

arlenekay.com

kkay3@comcast.net

49439756R00126

Made in the USA
Lexington, KY
05 February 2016